A TEACHER FIRST

by

Gary Sprague

A TEACHER FIRST

1

The first day back to school after Christmas vacation is always a difficult one for both students and teachers. The kids are excited to show off the new clothes and phones they've gotten for Christmas, but they'd rather be lying around on the couch playing video games. And many of the teachers, still suffering the effects of a New Year's Eve hangover from two nights earlier, would rather be anywhere else than in front of a classroom full of restless teenagers.

Coach Zim stood outside his classroom, herding students into the classroom with the efficiency of a cattle rustler. A junior with a patchy beard kissed his freshman girlfriend goodbye as the bell signaling the start of class rang and continued kissing her after it had stopped. Coach Zim cleared his throat. When that didn't seem to deter the couple, he pulled on the young man's earlobe. The kid whipped around, ready to fight the person who'd dared interrupt true love, and looked up into the face of his history teacher. For an instant, fear flashed over his arrogant face. Then he sneered and walked slowly into the classroom.

"Get to class," Coach Zim snapped at the freshman girl, who hurried off.

The portly figure of Vice Principal Simon approached from down the hall. The vice principal held up his index finger, signaling Coach Zim to wait. Coach Zim stood impatiently, glancing at the ruckus going on inside the classroom while Simple Simon took his sweet time.

"Afternoon, Jim," the vice principal said, slightly out of breath from his thirty-yard walk. "Do you have time to meet with Principal Craggy after class? It'll only take a few minutes."

"Sure, I guess so. What's he want to see me about?"

"I don't know," he lied. Coach Zim knew it was a lie, because Ed Simon was a nosy bastard and a habitual liar. Lying was how Simon had become vice principal, Coach suspected; it certainly wasn't due to his educational or administrative gifts. "But he said it's important."

"Yes, I'm sure it is." Coach sighed. "Okay, tell him I'll be there."

The last class of the day went by quickly, mostly because of the subject matter. The first week of January in Coach Zim's class was always spent studying the historical significance of Elvis Presley, whose birthday fell on January 8. Today, the first day back from break, each class was dedicated to listening to and discussing Elvis's music. The rest of the week they'd discuss his impact on both music and culture. It wasn't a typical history class topic, but it was a fun, easy way to ease back into school after vacation.

The final bell of the day rang. The classroom emptied in approximately five seconds. The sounds of lockers slamming shut and hundreds of footsteps and young voices laughing and yelling filled the hallway outside Coach's classroom. Trying to make his way to the principal's office right now would be like playing a game of Frogger, with him as the ill-fated frog. He sat at his desk, knowing the hallways would clear out in a matter of minutes.

A couple of surly-looking teenagers sat in small chairs outside Principal Craggy's office, pecking away at their iPads. Coach Zim walked past them and smiled at Emma, Principal Craggy's secretary. Emma Dugan had been a student of his, Class of '03, a smart, very pretty girl with a sarcastic streak that she hadn't lost over the years. It was something Coach Zim appreciated in the politically-correct, sterile halls of twenty-first century education.

"Any idea why he wants to see me?" Coach asked.

Emma shook her head. "No, but Simple Simon's in there, too, so it must be something really important." She rolled her eyes.

Principal Craggy's office was designed to intimidate the students of Apple Brook High School. The Man sat in a tall leather chair behind a large solid oak desk that he'd paid for himself. Across the desk was a small wooden chair for the bad boys and girls to sit on, and against a side wall near the door was a small couch. On the side walls of the room were several large photos of the principal with various political figures – both Presidents Bush, Maine's current governor and his predecessor, and several senators. Hanging from the dark wall behind the desk were various educational awards he'd won over the years, and on a large shelf in the center sat several trophies from when Garth Craggy was a slightly above-average athlete at the school he now lorded over.

Coach Zim sat on the couch next to Vice Principal Simon. At six-foot-four and two hundred twenty pounds, he was half a foot taller than the vice principal, although they were almost even in weight. Simple Simon nodded politely, formally, and then slid over as far as possible to his side of the couch.

"Good afternoon, Jim," said Principal Craggy from behind the enormous desk.

"Garth. What can I do for you?"

Garth Craggy leaned forward, resting his elbows on the desk. He steepled his fingers and tapped his forefingers against his lower lip, gazing at Coach Zim intently. He said nothing for a long time. It was a look that Coach Zim imagined had struck fear into the heart of many a disobedient teen, but he was not a teenager nor one to be intimidated. He was impatient, though, and let out a long sigh while meeting Craggy's gaze.

"Jim, you've been here for a long time, as long as I have," Craggy began. "We're peers, you and I, and I have a lot of respect for you. A hell of a lot." He paused to let this sink in, then let out his own sigh. "Which is why I'm going to be honest and straightforward with you. We've decided to make a change."

Coach Zim leaned forward. "What kind of change?" he asked slowly. He felt Simple Simon shift nervously next to him.

"A change in the baseball program. We've decided to hire a different coach."

"I've told you before, Craggy, I don't need another assistant. And if I do, I'll choose him myself."

Craggy shook his head. "Not an assistant coach. We're going with a new head coach for the baseball team."

Coach Zim was confused. He was the head coach. How could they go with another head coach?

Then understanding set in. He was being fired. It felt as though someone had punched him in the gut. Never would he have expected this, not in a million years. He tried to say something, to protest, to argue, but there was nothing but confusion and the overwhelming desire to throttle Garth Craggy.

"I realize this is going to take some time to sink in." Craggy gazed at him solemnly, but Coach swore he saw amusement in Craggy's eyes. "But it can't be completely unexpected, Jim. After all, you haven't made the playoffs in two years, and last year's team had a losing record."

"My two best starting pitchers broke their arms in skiing accidents before the season started," said Coach, trying to keep his voice level. "What are the chances of that? Nobody could win with a team lacking a decent starting pitcher."

"The program has been going down for a long time now, Jim."

"We were in the championship game three years ago."

"And if I remember correctly, you lost." Craggy held his hands up in a placating manner. "Jim, this isn't meant as a personal attack. Like I said, we all appreciate how much you've done for this program. But all things must pass."

Coach Zim, who hadn't expected his high school coaching career to end for another twenty years, stood up. "Who decided this? You said *we*." He turned and glared at Simple Simon, who sank deeper into his seat and looked away. "Were you a part of this decision?"

Ed Simon shook his head vigorously, like a dog shaking off water.

Craggy said, "It was my decision, Jim. And it was a hard one, a damn hard one. But I truly believe that this is the best decision to get our baseball program restarted."

"Uh-huh. And who have you chosen to replace me?"

Craggy hesitated for a moment, then said, "Todd Horne."

In spite of his anger, Coach chuckled. "Todd Horne, the gym teacher?"

"Physical education instructor, yes."

"Todd Horne, your nephew?"

"That has nothing to do with this," Craggy snapped. "He's very qualified."

"Uh-huh. We'll see. I'm the best baseball coach in the state, and you know it. I'm not just walking away from the program."

"And we don't expect you to," said Craggy. "We still want you to be involved with the team during the baseball season. Jim, we'd like you to announce the games."

"Huh?"

"You know, announce the games from the booth, on the radio, for the fans." Craggy smiled insincerely. "Nobody knows the game better than you."

"Fuck you, Craggy," he said. "And fuck you too, Simon," he said to the cowering figure on the couch.

He walked out of the office and slammed the door behind him. Emma looked up from her desk, a look of curiosity on her face, but Coach Zim shook his head and walked past. He walked the empty hallway, thankful nobody was coming his way. He entered his classroom, grabbed his coat and CD player, and turned to walk out. Then he noticed a short boy with glasses and an acne-riddled face seated at a desk near the back of the room. The boy's neck was bent down, his eyes staring at his school-issued iPad, his fingers tapping away. It was standard contemporary teenage posture.

"Ackerson," snapped Coach Zim. "What are you doing in here?"

"Nothing. Just waiting," the boy said, eyes never moving from the screen.

Coach Zim watched him for a few moments. "Are Collins and his gang of idiots giving you problems again?"

Ackerson nodded. "They're waiting for me to come outside. But I think they'll get bored and leave in a few minutes."

"Want me to walk you out?"

"No thanks." Still not looking up. "They'll just pound on me harder next time."

Coach Zim nodded. "I understand. I'm going to have a talk with Mr. Collins on my way out. You'll be safe to leave in a few minutes."

The boy finally looked up. "Coach Zim, I'd be careful with those guys. They're crazy. Crazy enough to take a swing at a teacher."

A wide smile filled Coach's face. "Ackerson, I really hope you're right," he said, leaving the room.

2

The only people who referred to him as Jim were his wife and those who knew him before he became the greatest coach in the history of Maine high school baseball. As a student of Apple Brook High during the 1980's, Jim Zimmerman broke every school and most state batting records while leading the baseball team to state championships his junior and senior seasons. One of his teammates was Garth Craggy, who was a year older than Jim and had the misfortune of playing the same position – center field – as the young star, meaning he had to switch positions if he wanted to play. Young Craggy was a good player, but not great, and was very bitter about having to move to right field to make room for a younger player. It was a bitterness he'd never let go of.

The New York Mets made Jim Zimmerman their first draft choice the year before he graduated high school, but he surprised everyone – especially the Mets – by choosing to go to college instead of accepting a large signing bonus and entering the minor leagues. This decision was made to honor the wishes of his mother, who believed it was more important for her son to graduate college than to play in the major leagues. He'd argued that he could go to college after making it to the majors, but mother and son both realized the chances of that happening were very slim. His mother would not – could not – force him, and it was his decision to make. In the end, he decided to play ball in college and play professionally after he'd graduated.

That dream came to an end midway through his sophomore season, after a bad motorcycle accident tore up his knee and shoulder. The knee recovered but the shoulder didn't, not completely. He could throw with velocity but his aim was inconsistent, at best. He'd lost power in his swing, too. After committing nine throwing errors and getting just one hit – a single – in the first five games of his junior season, Zimmerman was benched for the rest of the year. He tried again his senior year, but decided to shut it down for good before the season started when it became clear the shoulder hadn't improved.

His baseball career was over, but he did have a degree. Jim wanted to be involved with baseball, somehow, so he applied for a job at his old high school. The principal at Apple Brook High, Bill Berry, was thrilled to give his favorite alumni a job teaching history and even happier to insert him as coach of the junior varsity baseball team. It felt strange, at first – he wasn't much older than the kids he was teaching and coaching – but Jim found that he had a knack for it, and while coaching would never replace the thrill of being on the field, he was good at it. Duke Vincent, the varsity coach, proudly stated that he believed Jim Zimmerman would someday be as good a coach as he was a player.

He got the chance to find out three years later, when Duke Vincent decided to retire from teaching and move to Florida. He'd been the varsity baseball coach for thirty-eight years and the Apple Brook Warriors were a perennial playoff team under him. In a blue-collar town where sports mattered, the only person more well-known and well-liked than Duke might have been the football coach. The new coach was going to have a hard time of it, stepping into Coach Vincent's shoes. Who coached the Packers after Vince Lombardi quit? Nobody knows, because he was coaching in the shadow of a legend. It would take someone confident, not to mention good, to follow a local legend. That's why they chose the town's biggest local legend, Jim Zimmerman, as the new head baseball coach.

He was successful right away, but for the first couple of years everyone said it was because he'd taken over Duke Vincent's team. After a few years, though, when the team continued to make the playoffs every year and the championship trophies began accumulating in the school trophy case, Jim Zimmerman became known as Coach Zimmerman, quickly shortened to Coach Zim. Duke Vincent's improbable prediction had come true – Jim Zimmerman had become more well-known for his coaching success than his playing achievements.

"What are they going to call me now?"

He sat at the kitchen table across from his wife, Angela. She'd cooked a large pot of beef stew with dumplings – the way he liked it – and although he hadn't felt like eating, he'd almost finished his second bowl and was thinking about a third.

"They're going to call you Coach Zim, of course. You are always going to be Coach Zim," she replied.

"But I'm not a coach. Not anymore. After a cop retires, nobody calls him Officer Jones. He's just Bill Jones now."

"How about presidents? Bill Clinton is still introduced as President Clinton. George Bush is still introduced as President Bush."

"That idiot," mumbled Coach. He swallowed a large spoonful of stew. "I can think of other names he should be called."

"Yes, well, be that as it may," said Angela, "it shows that some people retain their title, even after they no longer hold the job. It's a sign of respect. And nobody has earned more respect in this town than Coach Zim."

"Neither of those guys was fired. You can start a war with the wrong country and keep your job, but I get fired after winning eleven state championships. Where's the fairness in that?"

Angela stood up and reached across the table for his empty bowl. She filled it from the crockpot on the kitchen counter and set it back on the table in front of her husband. It was hot, perfect for a cold winter's evening, and steam floated up from the bowl. Coach stirred it with his spoon, blowing on it as he did so.

"I just don't know what to do," he said.

Angela, who was a foot shorter and weighed almost a hundred pounds less than her husband, glared across the table. Coach Zim saw the look on her face and immediately cast his eyes downward.

"You do the same thing you do every day," Angela said. "You go to school and teach your students and expand their knowledge and help them inside and outside of the classroom. You stand proud and be the man everyone knows and respects. You dig in and fight back. Isn't that what you'd tell your players after a loss?"

"I don't have any players. I've been fired." He looked at his wife, sighed, and nodded his head. "Yes, that's what I'd tell them. You're right. I'm feeling sorry for myself. But this is all new to me. I've never been fired."

"Well, now you have." Angela sat back down. "It's unexpected, but it happened. Brush yourself off and get back up to the plate."

"You think I should fight to get my job back?"

"Your job is teaching," she said, with a meaningful stare. "Coaching is your secondary job." She paused, and her voice softened. "I know how much this means to you, Jim. But I don't know if fighting for your coaching job is the best way to go about it. Sounds like Craggy has his mind set."

"It's been over forty years since I wasn't either playing or coaching baseball."

"I know." She nodded sympathetically. "But things have a way of working out. There's a reason this happened, I know it."

"Yeah, because Craggy's an asshole who's been waiting for years to do this. We've had two consecutive seasons without making the playoffs for the first time ever, and he saw this as his opportunity. That's the reason."

Angela chuckled. "I can't argue with that." She took a sip of her water. "Go to work, do your job, and things will work out. They always do."

Coach nodded and started eating his stew. She was right, as usual.

It took until the end of the week for stories of Coach Zim's firing to begin spreading. This was highly unusual, because the high school grapevine usually transmitted information faster than the internet. In the case of this news, only four people within the school knew about it – Coach Zim, Principal Craggy, Vice Principal Simon, and physical education instructor Todd Horne. Four people were usually enough to get a rumor going within the high school in two minutes, five if they were sworn to secrecy. Considering that firing Coach Zim had long been an obsession of Principal Craggy's and that Vice Principal Simon was a gossip queen, it was almost a miracle that the story took so long to get out.

Of course, most of the stories buzzing around school that Friday were completely wrong. Coach Zim, who was embarrassed about the firing and had said nothing, first became aware of the rumors during his third period class. A large, assertive junior named Jenny Tarbox raised her hand during a discussion of Elvis Presley's drug addiction and asked if it was true that he and Coach Watson were swapping teams – Coach Zim taking over football, Coach Watson baseball. This made Coach Zim chuckle, and he answered with an honest no. It was the first of many rumors he heard throughout the day, each one as outrageous as the last.

In the cafeteria, he heard that the school was eliminating the baseball program because of budget cuts; in the teacher's room, Harold Iannucci, a nerdy but well-liked biology teacher who wanted nothing more in life than to be named Teacher of the Year, asked nervously if it was true that Coach Zim had quit coaching to focus full-time on winning the Teacher of the Year award; and before the last class of the day, a concerned student darted out from the demolition derby that is a high school hallway to ask Coach Zim if it was true that he'd developed an allergy to sunlight and had to quit coaching.

After school, as he straightened up his desk before leaving for the weekend, the two team captains of the varsity baseball team, elected at the previous year's award banquet, entered his classroom. Kids rarely wore varsity jackets anymore, which Coach Zim found sad; he'd taken a great deal of pride in wearing his when he was a student. More importantly, the varsity jacket with *Captain* written on the sleeve had gotten him laid quite a bit. He wondered if these guys knew what they were missing out on but figured they probably did alright without the jackets.

"Hey Coach," said Devin Krane, shortstop. Great fielder, strong arm, average bat. Big mouth, but in a funny, likeable way. "We've heard a dozen rumors about you today and we'd like to know if any of them are true."

"Yeah," mumbled the shorter boy, Adam Nass. Second base. Good glove, weak arm, patient hitter. Fast as lightning on the base paths, came within two stolen bases of the state record the previous year. Wouldn't say shit if he had a mouthful, but that was okay. His best friend and co-captain talked enough for the both of them.

"Is it true that you won't be coaching us this year?"

Coach sat down at his desk and leaned back. If he was going to get the third degree, he wanted to be comfortable. "Yes, that's true."

The two boys exchanged worried glances.

"We heard it, but we didn't believe it. What happened? Did you quit? Did you get fired? Are you allergic to the sun?"

"Which question would you like me to answer, Krane?"

"All of them."

"No, yes, no."

The boys stared at him for a moment, then looked at each other, confused. "Wait. What? I can't remember the order of my questions. Which question did I ask second?"

Adam Nass shrugged.

Coach Zim gazed at them fondly. Yes, they were dim as twenty-watt bulbs, but they were good-hearted kids and they loved baseball. He'd coached Devin Krane's father in JV years before, during his first year of coaching. His dad wasn't a very good ballplayer but he had been one of the most popular guys on the team. He worked as a television weatherman now, a perfect job for someone who liked to talk a lot, and Coach saw him often at his son's games.

Adam Nass's parents were a different story. His mother was a cocaine addict who'd left for California when

Adam was seven and hadn't been heard from since. Tyler Nass wasn't much better. He'd stayed behind to raise his son, but most people would agree that Adam would have been better off if both parents had left, allowing him to wipe the slate clean. Tyler Nass was a member of The Grim Disciples, a bike club known for such entertaining recreational activities as gang raping women and assaulting with chains and pipes anyone brazen enough to make eye contact for more than three seconds with a Disciple.

Coach Zim knew plenty of bikers, including some who belonged to clubs. Most were good guys. Tyler Nass and his crew were not a club, they were a gang. And like most gangs, they never traveled alone. On the occasions that Tyler Nass showed up at his son's games (to sell drugs, Coach Zim suspected), he was loud, obnoxious, and always with at least one other Disciple. Nobody dared tell him to be quiet, because doing so would earn that person a beating by several bikers. To Coach Zim they were cowards, but saying so would only earn him a stomping. They were cowards, but they usually got their way.

Adam Nass grew up in this atmosphere, yet he was a good kid. Very quiet, and Coach wondered if it was because he'd learned that talking would either get him ridiculed or punched in the face. Coach Zim called most of his players by their last names but often called Adam Nass by his first – he figured carrying that name was enough of a burden without him bringing it up. Adam spent most of his time at the Krane's house – he'd practically moved in – and his father either hadn't noticed or didn't care.

"I'm not allergic to the sun," Coach finally said.

The boys looked at each other, confused again. Adam shrugged.

"Wait. Okay. So you said no twice, and that's one of them. What else did I ask?" Krane looked to Adam for help.

"I asked if he quit or got fired, right?" Adam nodded. "Was that one question, or two?"

"Two, I think."

"Okay," said Krane. He smiled at their fine show of deductive reasoning. "So that means you either quit or got fired. There's no way that you got fired. You're the greatest coach, like, ever." He paused to think, then asked, "So why'd you quit?"

Coach shook his head. "You aren't thinking of going into law enforcement, are you, Krane?"

Krane stared blankly. "No, why?"

"Just wondering."

"Nope, I'm going to college for meteorology, like my dad. I figure it's an easy way to get famous."

Coach considered giving a speech about how fame is fleeting and of little importance, and how the easy way is usually the wrong way, but then realized that becoming famous for reading the weather forecast on television was exactly what Krane's father had done. He liked Harvey Krane, and being a weatherman had worked out well for him professionally, so Coach Zim decided to keep his comment to himself. Instead, he informed the boys that he'd been fired as coach.

The boys wore stunned expressions as he explained to them that the principal wanted to go in a different direction with the baseball program, how he'd been coaching varsity baseball for twenty-two years now and maybe that was enough (he didn't really believe this), and how Mr. Horne was taking over and would do a fine job, maybe even better than he himself had done (he sure as hell didn't believe this).

"Mr. Horne? Nutsack Horne?'

Todd Horne wore shorts – usually white – while teaching his gym classes every day, even in the middle of winter. As if this wasn't enough, the shorts he wore were extremely short and tight. So tight that, as the name implied, the outline of his scrotum could often be seen clearly. So short that, once in a while, when doing certain exercises, unlucky classes had been known to catch a glimpse of that scrotum through the bottom of his shorts, because Todd Horne was also not a fan of underwear.

"Be respectful, guys. Mr. Horne is a teacher at this school and your new baseball coach, whether you like it or not."

"Not," said Krane.

"Yeah, not," agreed Adam.

"So what are you going to do, Coach, if you can't coach? We need you."

Coach Zim sighed and rubbed his face with a big palm. "I don't know, fellas. Principal Craggy mentioned having me help out with announcing the games."

"Sweet!"

"How is that sweet?"

"You can help us out from up there, Coach! Picture it over the PA system: *Now batting for the Warriors, Devin Krane. Krane is hitting over .500 with ten home runs in seven games –* Coach Zim rolled his eyes – *and especially loves the curveball, which Smith will probably throw him after throwing two fastballs like he's been doing all afternoon. Krane should watch for Smith biting his lower lip, which he tends to do before throwing a curveball, or scratching his ass, which he seems to do for no apparent reason."*

Coach laughed, as did the co-captains. He stood up and grabbed his coat. "You boys have a good weekend. Mrs. Zimmerman says that things will work out the way they are supposed to, and it's not often that she's wrong."

He slapped both boys on the shoulder and led them out of his classroom. They turned left, to slip out the side entrance, while he went right, toward the front. He passed the art room and noticed Brandon Ackerson sitting by himself. He was bent over, absorbed in whatever he was drawing. Curious, Coach Zim walked into the room to take a look. Ackerson was so engrossed in his work that he didn't notice someone had entered the room until a shadow crossed his paper. He jumped back, causing his chair to slide backward, and looked up in fright.

"Easy, Ackerson. It's just me." A thought crossed his mind. "You aren't hiding from Collins and his group, are you?"

Ackerson shook his head. "No, they usually leave early on Friday. I just got caught up in my drawing and didn't realize how late it was." He glanced up at the clock. "It happens sometimes."

Coach Zim looked at the paper on the desk. Ackerson had drawn a picture of a log home surrounded by forest, with mountains in the background. In front of the home was a meadow filled with uncut grass and wildflowers and peaceful-looking animals, and on the porch a young man and woman sat, watching them. It was done in colored pencils – Coach Zim saw the pencils on the desk, as well as the one still in Ackerson's hand. He knew nothing about art, but he knew talent when he saw it.

"Ackerson," he said, his eyes still on the drawing. "This is very good. You've got a real gift, you know that?"

Ackerson appeared nervous, like he wanted to snatch the drawing away. "It's alright." He shrugged.

"Alright?" Coach Zim looked at him. "Son, this is better than alright. I'm no art critic but I know good art. And this is beyond good."

The boy's face reddened, and there was a flicker of a smile. "Miss Folger says I'm one of the most gifted students she's ever taught."

"When you consider that she's been teaching for about a hundred years, that's pretty high praise."

He smiled fully now. The change in his features made him appear somewhat handsome. "She says I'll be able to attend any art college I want after I graduate."

Coach Zim gazed at the drawing for a few moments. "I have no doubt that she's right, son."

"I want to go to New York. Maybe London. Far away from here."

The bitterness in the boy's voice came through clearly. Coach Zim had never experienced being picked on, or not being popular. He'd been talented at athletics, one of the elite. Brandon Ackerson was elite, too. Only Ackerson's skill was in art, and high school artists didn't get laid by the prettiest cheerleaders, or admired and envied by grown men and women. That might happen later, but in high school artists are picked on for being different. Throwing a ball through a hoop or hitting a ball with a wooden bat is rewarded over all else in high school and in all of American society. Professional artists don't have a 24-hour cable channel celebrating their daily exploits, nor are they routinely offered eight-figure endorsement deals.

"I've been to London a couple of times," Coach Zim said. "Believe it or not, I've never been to New York."

Brandon had pulled his chair close to the desk and was back at work, his pencil working quickly but delicately to create shadow in the forest. After a few seconds of silence, Coach Zim asked, "You need a ride home, Ackerson?"

The boy shook his head quickly, concentrating on his work.

"Well, okay. Take it easy, then."

Coach Zim left the art room and walked toward the front doors, hoping Ackerson didn't end up getting locked inside the school for the weekend.

3

For the faculty, Valentine's Day at Apple Brook High was a day full of evenly dispersed four-minute blasts, during which they tried to corral a thousand horny students. Every fifty minutes, the bell rang to mark the end of class, and for the next four minutes, until the bell to start the next class, teenagers ran and pushed and shoved each other to get a glimpse of the boy or girl they'd fallen madly, eternally in love with earlier in the week. It was the same as most other days, but worse, because on Valentine's Day students proclaimed their undying love for one another, making them even hornier and more irrepressible than normal.

When Coach Zim had started teaching, separating students kissing and groping in the hallway on Valentine's Day had been an uncomfortable task, and he often dealt with it by looking the other way. He was twenty-three years old when he started teaching, not much older than the kids he was admonishing. As he got older, he became less tolerant of the excuses and the high school puppy love and had no problem physically pulling couples apart and sending them on their separate ways. At this point, after twenty-five years, he had no patience or sympathy for either the lovelorn or the heartbroken teenagers who riddled the hallways.

At least he hadn't experienced what Joel Waterhouse, a fellow history teacher at least ten years past minimum retirement age (the joke around school was that Waterhouse was so old he taught most of history by memory) had seen on Valentine's Day three years earlier. Entering the bathroom near his classroom after school to take a leak for the tenth time that day, Mr. Waterhouse was greeted by the sight of two students going at it in one of the toilet stalls. Luckily, it was a male and a female – at his age, Waterhouse couldn't have handled the thought, let alone the sight, of two young men fornicating. As it was, seeing the young man ramming his paramour from behind and hearing the rhythmic *bink, bink, bink* of her head against the porcelain was enough to send the old man home for a week to contemplate retirement. In the end Mr. Waterhouse came back to teaching, but he only used the toilet in the teacher's room from that day forward.

As a precaution since Waterhouse's experience, Coach Zim avoided the bathroom on Valentine's Day. Outside of his classroom, he avoided students all day long. He stayed in his classroom between classes and spent his free period and lunch in the teacher's room. He was all for young love, but when necking in the hallway graduated to doggy style in the toilet stall, it was time to fight or avoid it. And when the enemy was comprised of a thousand horny teens, he chose to avoid it. Pick your battles, his father used to say.

He sat on a worn but comfortable chair in the teacher's room, drinking coffee and reading the sports section, when a shadow stretched across the page of his newspaper. Coach Zim looked up to see the tight white shorts of Todd Horne, Physical Education Instructor. The students weren't exaggerating – Horne's nut sack bulged like the cheeks of a squirrel with a mouthful of acorns. He closed his eyes and groaned.

"Good morning, Coach Zimmerman." Horne had a loud, boisterous voice, like someone who believed everything he had to say was important. "I was wondering if we could talk for a few minutes."

"Alright," Coach Zim said. He opened his eyes, saw the nut sack, and looked away. "But either sit down or put some pants on. Jesus."

Horne looked down and grinned. "Jealous of the legs, huh?"

Todd Horne had the legs of a bodybuilder – thick, defined, and shaved. It was clear that he loved them like most parents love their children, and the short shorts were his way of showing them off to the world. He wasn't on Facebook, but Coach knew enough about it to hazard a guess that Horne's profile picture was a photo of his bare legs (it was). Though not on a par with his legs, Horne's upper body was thick and muscular, and Coach Zim had no doubt that he was on steroids. Over the years he'd found that gym teachers vain and stupid enough to take steroids were usually lousy athletes, and he assumed the bulging physique was designed to cover up a general lack of athleticism. He wondered if Horne had ever played baseball.

"Yup. Nothing I'd rather have than a pair of smooth, pimply legs."

Horne ignored this. "I'd like to talk about the baseball team. I hope there aren't any hard feelings between us about my taking over."

"I feel the same way about you as I always have," Coach Zim said. "This hasn't changed my opinion of you one bit."

"Good, good. Well, I wanted to ask what you usually begin with. Pitchers and catchers, right?" Coach Zim nodded. "Okay, and what do I have them do? Just pitch and catch? A few calisthenics, maybe?"

Coach folded the newspaper, set it down, and stared at Horne. "Have you ever played or coached baseball?"

"I was on my junior high team but I didn't play much. Politics, you know. As for coaching, I was an assistant coach for my nephew's T-ball team last year. We won the championship," he added proudly.

"Congratulations. T-ball, huh? Well, I can see why you are confused about pitching."

Todd Horne frowned. "No, I understand pitching. I'm just wondering about the practice for pitchers and catchers. I was thinking, maybe you could come down and help me out for the first few days of practice next month. Maybe it would help make the transition easier for the players."

"This is your team now, Horne, not mine. Principal Craggy made that very clear to me. I don't know if you had anything to do with it, but I assume you did." He opened the newspaper back up. "You made your bed, now lie in it."

Todd Horne glanced around. There were five or six other teachers in the room – some clearly watching them, the others pretending not to. Horne was embarrassed and confused, unsure of how to respond to what he was almost certain was an insult. In the end, he responded the way he did to most threats – he tightened and flexed his muscles, blowing up like a pufferfish. Coach Zim glanced up from the paper, rolled his eyes, and kept on reading.

A few seconds later the bell rang. Horne, his face bright red, exhaled and slowly deflated. Coach Zim set down the newspaper, walked slowly past Horne and out of the room. Horne waited until everyone left the room, then looked in a floor-length mirror and quickly flexed. Yup, pretty damn intimidating. Satisfied, he adjusted his shorts and strutted off toward the gym.

A few hours later, Nutsack Horne sat in a small chair across the desk from his uncle, Principal Garth Craggy. Craggy stared in mild disgust at his nephew – on his wife's side, he told everyone who would listen – as the younger man shifted uncomfortably in the wooden chair. Who wouldn't be uncomfortable in those shorts, thought Craggy. They looked almost as bad as the Speedos the old Canadian men wore on Old Orchard Beach during the summer. He'd heard the nickname the kids called him. Craggy didn't smile often, but that nickname made him smile.

"I asked Coach Zimmerman if he'd help me out with the baseball team," Horne was saying. "I don't think he's going to. He didn't seem very cooperative."

Craggy sat forward, steepled fingers under his chin. It was a pose that made him appear thoughtful yet stern, very useful when dealing with teenage hooligans and idiot nephews. "No, I have a feeling Jim Zimmerman isn't going to be very charitable about giving coaching advice to the man we fired him for."

"Yeah, he's kind of a dick."

Craggy nodded. Though not the way he'd have phrased it, his nephew's words perfectly described his feelings for Jim Zimmerman.

"I did offer him a job as an announcer for the games," Craggy said with a smirk. "So far, he hasn't appeared interested."

"I'm starting to have my doubts about the job. I'm not sure I'll be a good baseball coach."

"I thought you told me that you'd like to coach a team if an opening presented itself. Were you lying to me?"

"No, Uncle Garth, of course not. But gee whiz, I thought I might become a coach on the football or basketball team. Those teams are terrible and nobody would care if I screwed up. But head coach of the baseball team!" Horne unconsciously flexed and rubbed his forearm. "Do you know how seriously people in this town take high school baseball?"

"Indeed, I do." Craggy rubbed his knuckles gently over his sharp chin stubble. "Did you know that I was captain of one of the greatest baseball teams ever at Apple Brook

High? My senior year, we went undefeated and won the state championship. First time a Maine Class A baseball team ever went undefeated."

"I did know that. Coach Zimmerman was on that team too, wasn't he? I heard he was the best ballplayer this state's ever seen."

Principal Craggy ignored his nephew. "What a spring that was. I went out for burgers almost every night after practice and didn't pay once. Everything was free – bats, gloves, gas, movies, haircuts, tires for my car. Anything I wanted. Ron Munson let me buy beer every weekend at his market, even though I was only eighteen. Well, I didn't really buy beer, because Munson wouldn't take my money. And the girls, practically throwing themselves at me. Not just high school girls, either. I never had as much sex as I did that spring and summer. I felt like a rock star." He smiled at the memory. "Yes, this town loves high school baseball."

"Sounds perfect," his nephew said. He imagined some of the girls in his gym classes naked, as he did several times each day.

"It would have been, except for Jim Zimmerman. I was the captain. Center field was mine. The scouts started coming to watch me play during my junior year, and you should have seen them pack the stands for the first game of my senior year."

"Sweet."

Craggy scowled at his nephew, then continued, "I did okay – one for three with a double – but Jim Zimmerman hit two home runs that day. He hit one the following afternoon, too. Next thing I know, I'm moved to right field so Zimmerman can play center. The scouts continued to show up, but they weren't there for me anymore." His hands, no longer steepled, were balled into fists. "I thought I was going to play for the Yankees, and instead I ended up playing for the University of Southern Maine."

"Look at you now, though, Uncle Garth. You're the principal of your old high school. You've done pretty well, I'd say."

"Hmmm." His idiot nephew was right. He had done well. Better than Zimmerman. "And now is your chance to do well, Todd. Do you know why you were named head coach of the baseball team?"

"Because I'm wicked fit." He flexed a bicep, then stopped when he saw the look on Craggy's face. "And because you're my uncle?"

"Of course it's because I'm your uncle! You have no coaching experience of any kind. Why else would you have been named head coach?" Craggy paused to take a breath. "So don't blow it. You have a good team this year. A monkey should be able to coach them into the playoffs. I'm hoping you are at least the coaching equal of a monkey."

"I am."

"Don't blow this. If the baseball team stinks this year, not only will Zimmerman get his job back, half the town will be after *my* job. I'm counting on you, Todd." He tried to smile, but it was too difficult. He settled for an encouraging nod.

"I won't let you down, Uncle Garth," Horne said. He stood up, and Craggy noticed with disgust that his shorts had ridden halfway up his ass. "I'll be the talk of the town before this season's through." He started for the door, hooked his thumbs into the bottom of his shorts and pulled, snapping them out of his butt crack.

"Todd." He turned around, and Craggy said, "Do us all a favor, and don't wear those shorts on the baseball field."

Horne grinned, gave his uncle a thumbs-up, and walked out of the office.

4

Johnny Jones sat at the desk in his large office, eating a salad and reading the latest edition of *The Apple Brook Journal.* It had been sixteen years since he'd graduated high school and moved away, and for a long time his attitude toward Apple Brook was goodbye and good riddance.

But now he was older, nearing middle age. His mother had told him recently that nostalgia was a side effect of growing older, and as usual, she was right. Outside of holidays with his family, Johnny hadn't visited the town since leaving for college. Then, the previous year, he'd decided last-minute to attend his fifteen-year class reunion. Talking with old classmates, teammates, girlfriends and teachers, Johnny realized how much of his past and who he had turned out to be was in Apple Brook. Now he drove up from Boston every month or so, and instead of confining his visits to his parent's house, he visited and went out to dinner with friends. He looked into real estate in the area and was considering buying a small cabin on Wishing Lake, about five miles outside of Apple Brook, for his weekend getaways. And, he bought a subscription to the weekly town newspaper.

The Apple Brook Journal was small, between twenty and twenty-five pages, and divided into two sections – sports, and everything else. Johnny turned to the front page of the sports section and almost choked on a piece of lettuce when he read the top headline: *Warriors Baseball Team Set to Start First Practices under New Coach Todd Horne.* Under the headline was a photo of a young, muscular man in very tight shorts.

Johnny continued to chew, very slowly, as he read the article. He wondered if something bad, maybe an illness, had forced Coach Zim to step down. Todd Horne was a gym teacher who realized he'd be trying to fill some big shoes by taking over for Coach Zim but he'd do his very best, according to the article. Near the end was a statement from Principal Craggy that Coach Zim was hopeful to remain a part of the baseball program by providing commentary during the live broadcasts of the game for local radio station WMBL, nicknamed "Mobile Radio".

Johnny Jones read the article again, frowning when he got near the end. Craggy. What a dick. There had been bad blood between him and Coach Zim back when Johnny was on the team, and he wondered if that had something to do with the coaching change. He skimmed through the rest of the newspaper, eating slowly and thinking.

Snow flurries fell from a gray sky and the air was very cold, as late February in Maine tends to be. At just past four o'clock, the streetlights, along with the lights in the house, were on. Coach Zim hung up his heavy LL Bean jacket and leaned against the wall of the foyer. He removed his insulated boots and slid his feet into warm slippers. Picking up his laptop case, he followed the inviting smell of homemade spaghetti and meatballs into the kitchen.

"What a day. I'm glad this week is over." He grabbed a beer from the refrigerator and plopped down on a chair at the kitchen table. "I had to stay after school to help a couple of students. They're having trouble understanding the significance of Henry Ford's assembly line. Then Allison Perkins stopped by."

"How's her mother doing?" Angela asked, standing by the stove in her apron.

"Poorly. It sounds like the chemo is only making her sicker." He paused to sip his beer. "The mother's dying and the teenager is watching it happen. She has no one else – no father, no siblings. I hate hearing these stories. Why do the kids all come to me with their problems? Especially the girls."

"It used to be because you were young and athletic and good-looking. Now it's because you act mean and tough but the kids all know you're just a big teddy bear underneath."

"Well, I wish they'd stop coming to me," he said. Angela smiled because she knew he didn't mean it. "Now I have to worry about Allison Perkins and her mother. Like I didn't have enough to worry about. And that artist kid I was telling you about, Ackerson. I walked out to the parking lot to find that punk Tom Collins and his friends pushing Ackerson around, ripping up some of his artwork."

"Tom Collins?"

"Yeah. He brags that his father named him after his favorite drink. I know his father, and that's the sort of thing he'd do. What a family of assholes."

"Did you stop them from picking on him?"

"For today, I did. Collins tried to give me some lip so I grabbed his ear and dropped him to his knees. He shut up and returned Ackerson's artwork after that."

Angela shook her head and sighed. "You shouldn't have done that, Jimmy. You know you can't touch a student these days. You can get charged with assault, or even sued."

"At least they can't fire me from my coaching position."

"This is serious." She dipped a large wooden spoon into the spaghetti sauce and tasted it. "What if that boy calls the police?"

"Tom Collins wants nothing to do with the police. That kid calling the cops is about as likely to happen as a rabid pit bull licking the dog catcher."

"Think he'll try to get back at you?"

"Probably. I did embarrass him in front of his friends. But I'm more worried about him taking it out on Ackerson. That poor kid is an artistic genius but he's completely helpless." Coach Zim sat back and took another large sip of beer. "I just want to eat dinner, grade a few tests, and relax in front of the TV with a couple of beers."

"Then you aren't going to be happy." He frowned, and Angela continued, "Johnny Jones called a little while ago. He's up from Boston for the weekend and asked if he could stop over. I invited him to dinner tonight."

"Johnny Jones," he mused. "One of the smartest kids I ever coached. That kid knew more about baseball than I did."

"It was nice hearing from him. When I told him I was making spaghetti and meatballs, he said he'd be over as soon as it was ready."

"That kid used to eat here more often than I me, I think. So when will it be ready?"

There was a knock on the front door, and Angela smiled.

"It's ready."

They talked for a while about Johnny's parents, Johnny's life in Boston, and Angela's career as a freelance writer. After finishing his second plate of spaghetti and meatballs, Johnny Jones poured himself a second glass of wine and finally got down to the reason for his visit.

"I don't want to stir things up, Coach, but I saw in the paper that you aren't coaching this year. You and the missus look pretty healthy to me, and since illness and death are the only things I can think of that would keep you away, I'm guessing that it wasn't your choice to leave."

"No, it wasn't my choice. I thought I'd coach for another twenty years. But we've gone two years without making the playoffs and it seems that's too long."

"Too long for who, Craggy? For you, two years is an unheard-of slump. But for most high school teams, making the playoffs every three or four years would be a success."

Coach Zim shrugged. He agreed, knew it was true, but he'd finally realized that there wasn't a whole lot he could do about it.

"What do you plan to do now? I read that you might announce the games for WMBL."

"I read that too. I never agreed to announce the games. Craggy offered it to me as an insult, a way to rub salt in the wound right after he fired me. The only reason I'd agree to it is for the kids and to stay close to the game. I don't know what I'm going to do without baseball this spring." He looked down and played with his food. "Listen to me, I sound like someone died. It's just baseball, right? No big deal." He looked up and smiled. Angela returned the smile. Johnny did not.

"It is a big deal, Coach. This is what you were born to do, like Willy Wonka was born to make chocolate."

"Thanks, Johnny. It's not every day I'm compared to Willy Wonka."

Johnny laughed. "It's true, though. You need to stay in baseball. The game needs you, and you need the game. Which is why I'm here."

Coach Zim was one of the few people from Apple Brook that Johnny had kept in touch with over the years.

When he graduated from college and was hired to work in the Red Sox front office, nobody had been happier for him than Coach Zim. And that meant the world to Johnny – after his parents, the first person he'd called after getting the job was Coach Zim. They'd continued to stay in touch over the years, although sporadically, primarily because of Coach's aversion to email. It wasn't that he was against the idea of it, but he was a two-finger typist. Composing even a short email with his slow, thick fingers sapped both his time and patience.

Johnny Jones was now the Assistant Director of Baseball Operations for the Boston Red Sox. It was a very stressful and time-consuming job, which partially explained why Johnny had never gotten married. It was also a high-profile, well-paying job, and Johnny had been named on a number of Boston's most eligible bachelors lists. That was the other reason he had never married.

"We're looking for a player development assistant. Someone who really knows the game. We've got two kids right in Portland, playing for the Sea Dogs, that we think very highly of. We're hoping that both of them will be with the main club by next year. But they both have some kinks to work out."

"Wait a minute," Coach Zim said. "Are you saying you want someone to work with these two kids?"

Johnny grinned. "I'm saying I want *you* to work with these two kids. With the whole team. Nobody knows players better than you, Coach. I've been around major and minor league coaches for over a decade, and you're still one of the best coaches I've ever seen."

"You want me to work with the Portland Sea Dogs?"

"You'll be working for the Red Sox, with all of our affiliates – Greenville, Salem, Pawtucket. But mostly Portland, so you won't have to travel from home often."

He looked across the table, saw Angela grinning, and grinned himself. He'd always thought, if for some reason high school coaching didn't work out, he might like to go up to the next level, college. Now, he was skipping that level and moving up to professional baseball. It wasn't coaching, exactly, and it wasn't the major leagues, but it sounded like a hell of an opportunity.

"This is a very important job, Coach," Johnny said, as though reading his mind. "You won't be managing, but you'll be developing these players, which is of greater importance." He took a sip of his wine. "I've been looking for someone to fill this position for a few weeks, modeling my perfect candidate after you, to be honest. When I read the article about you no longer coaching, I couldn't believe my luck."

"When would he need to start?" Angela asked. Her smile faded and she went into business mode. "Is the job full time? He can't just up and quit his teaching job."

"It is a full time job, and I'd like you to start yesterday. However, I do recognize why that isn't possible. How about if you work part time until the end of the school year, and then full-time?"

"You'd have to quit teaching," Angela said, with a worried expression.

Coach Zim nodded.

"I'm sure you have a lot of questions and you'll need some time to think about it. Let me just say that the pay will be at least double what you make teaching. Plus, you'll get all the Red Sox tickets you want, travel reimbursement, insurance, etcetera. Take some time, and call or email me with any questions you have. I think this is a great opportunity for you, Coach. For you and the Red Sox."

Coach Zim agreed to think it over and have an answer for Johnny within a week. They finished their wine, and Johnny left soon after. Coach sat down with his laptop to grade some tests, but his mind was racing with thoughts of working for the Red Sox organization, and he stopped before completing even one. Angela opened another bottle of wine and they stayed up late into the night, talking and dreaming about the new road that had opened up for them.

5

Baseball sign-ups took place in early March, followed a week later by the first practice. Because it was usually about thirty degrees with snow on the ground, March practices were always held inside the school gym. These workouts consisted mostly of exercises - stretches, push-ups, sit-ups, sprints – and a lot of catch. Pitchers and catchers benefited most from these early practices, and for that reason they were the only ones for whom the practices were mandatory.

Coach Horne sat on the bleachers wearing a whistle around his neck and an Apple Brook Warriors baseball hat on his head. Next to him sat April Spring, the team manager. April was a blond senior with a killer bod, and Horne hoped to sleep with her by the beginning of the season. She was eighteen – he'd asked – and legal. Right now she held a clipboard and was going over the names of the pitchers and catchers with Horne. She was an energetic, cheerful speaker, and her breasts jiggled delightfully as she pointed out the different players. Horne found himself getting a woody, but luckily his shorts were tight enough to restrain it.

He hadn't spoken much to the players because he had no idea what to say, having never coached before. He had them do calisthenics – push-ups, sit-ups, jumping jacks – because that's what he had students do at the beginning of gym class. Calisthenics were going to be a big part of his coaching strategy, he'd decided. Go with your strengths, he always said. He knew a lot about calisthenics, so that's what they'd do. There'd be a lot of time spent in the weight room, too. All anyone had to do was look at him to see that he knew a lot about lifting weights.

After calisthenics, Horne told them to break up into pairs and start tossing the ball around. Realizing they weren't going to have much guidance, the catchers grabbed mitts and masks while the pitchers measured out sixty feet, six inches (or somewhere thereabouts). Then they began warming up, the way they always had under Coach Zim.

After an hour of basically coaching themselves, the players stopped throwing and stared impatiently at their new coach. Horne didn't notice; he was gently massaging a knot out of April Spring's delicate neck. Brock Cooke, a thick, solid pitcher who fantasized about April at least thirty times a day and was thinking of asking her to the prom, briefly considered delivering a fastball to the side of his new coach's skull. Instead, he stuck his two index fingers in his mouth and whistled. The sharp, piercing sound echoed in the gym, distracting Horne from what he hoped was a sensual, arousing massage. He looked toward the group of players, annoyed.

"What should we do now, *Coach*?" Brock spoke this last word with so much sarcasm, even Nutsack Horne got it.

"Let's hit the weight room. I'll teach you boys how a man works out." Horne stood up and flexed his legs. After a last wink at April, he walked down the bleachers. The pitchers and catchers watched as he headed for the weight room, pulling his short shorts out of his butt while maintaining a full flex in his legs. The players all looked at each other, shook their heads, and slowly followed. It was going to be a long season.

Passing by the gym doors on his way out of school, Coach Zim couldn't resist taking a quick peek inside. He saw what he'd expected – young athletes in need of guidance playing catch while their coach sat on the bleachers, flirting with a cute girl. He knew of Nutsack Horne's reputation as a flirt and had heard the rumors of him sleeping with various students over the past few years. These type of stories often developed around young high school teachers – he suspected he'd been the subject of a few, years ago – but it wouldn't have come as a surprise if the ones about Horne were true.

Resisting the very strong urge to walk in and take over, Coach Zim continued on down the hall. The sun was shining, and though the air was still cold, there were small puddles on the brick walkway leading to the parking lot. He avoided them with satisfaction – puddles, no matter how small, meant the weather was finally warming up. There might still be two feet of snow on the ground, but spring was coming.

He could still hear the sharp pop of fastballs hitting catcher's mitts from inside the gymnasium. It filled him with an adrenaline he could only get from baseball. Spring baseball, the time when everyone was fresh and new and ready to show how much they'd improved over the past year. High school baseball was over for him, but he had newer, bigger mountains to climb.

He was heading to Portland for a four o'clock meeting with the Sea Dog's manager, Sparky Webster, and a few of the players. He'd taken the job. The Boston Red Sox were the only team he'd ever imagined himself playing for – how could he refuse? He was excited and, surprisingly, a little nervous. It had been a long time since he'd been nervous about anything regarding baseball.

Despite the puddles in the walkway, much of the parking lot was covered in a thin layer of slippery packed snow. Coach walked slowly, sort of an old man shuffle that allowed his feet to slide across the snow, a style of winter walking that every Mainer developed early.

He moved toward his Dodge Ram pickup truck in the teacher's area of the parking lot, shuffling along and whistling "Here Comes the Sun" in the cool, still air. Except for a couple dozen cars – teachers and students staying after school for detention, sports and clubs – the lot was empty. A teenager will never move faster than immediately after the final bell of the day has rung. Most reached the parking lot in seemingly impossible time.

As he drew closer, he noticed a dark object lying in an empty space a few feet away from his truck, at the back of the lot. It resembled a pile of clothes, but as he drew near Coach Zim realized it was a person, unmoving. A student, judging by the backpack and papers strewn on the ground nearby. He hoped it wasn't an overdose. Heroin, once unheard of in Apple Brook, was fast becoming a popular drug with both adults and teens in the area. In the past year seven students, including one in junior high, had overdosed. Luckily none had died, but everyone knew it was just a matter of time.

He shuffled faster. When he saw blood on the snow – the color of spilled wine on a white tablecloth – his heart began to pound. How could he have missed it, he wondered; there was so much. He glanced at one of the papers strewn on the ground and saw a drawing – a very good drawing, of a boy and a girl running through a field, smiling, while an unseen tiger crouched nearby, ready to pounce. "Shit," he mumbled, hurrying his pace.

If he hadn't seen the artwork, he wouldn't have recognized Brandon Ackerson. His grandfather had fought in World War Two, his father in Vietnam, and Coach Zim imagined that what he was looking at was similar to what they may have experienced on the battlefield. Blood was matted in the boy's hair, darkening it and the packed snow beneath his head. Both cheeks were grotesquely swollen, his nose twisted toward the left side of his face. A goatee of congealing blood covered Ackerson's face from his top lip to the bottom of his neck. It was difficult to see much else due to his heavy winter jacket, but his hand seemed to be lying at a strange angle, as were a couple of fingers.

"Shit," he mumbled again. He thought to check for a pulse, reached for the twisted wrist, and changed his mind. With fumbling fingers he pulled out his cell phone and dialed 911. As he lifted the phone to his ear, he noticed a small white cloud float from Ackerson's bloody lips, and then another. The kid was still breathing.

Coach Zim told the 911 operator that there had been an assault in the high school parking lot and that a student was unconscious and bleeding badly. He stayed on the line, kneeling in the snow with a hand resting gently on Ackerson's soft jacket, until the flashing, wailing ambulance pulled into the parking lot. Standing to the side, feeling slightly dazed, he watched as the EMTs quickly checked the boy over and loaded him into the ambulance. He got into his truck, then back out to retrieve Ackerson's papers. Using his sleeve, he wiped snow off the papers and stuffed them into the boy's backpack, which he then placed on the passenger seat. Without waiting for his truck to warm up, Coach Zim followed the ambulance to the hospital.

The first thing he did upon arriving at Apple Brook Medical Center was call Angela. He explained briefly what had happened and asked her to find the phone number for Brandon Ackerson's parents. Then he sat down in the emergency room waiting area and picked up a six-month-old Sports Illustrated magazine. He skimmed through it, retaining little, and continued to glance up for a doctor or nurse to come through the ER doors and give him an update on Ackerson's condition.

About an hour later – it seemed much longer – he looked up from a National Geographic article about sharks, suddenly remembering that he was supposed to be in Portland, meeting the manager of the Sea Dogs. He found Sparky Webster's phone number in his contacts list and was about to call when the waiting room's sliding glass entry door opened.

A short, dark-haired woman with a wild look on her face hurried inside. She glanced around frantically, and Coach Zim knew immediately that this was Ackerson's mother. He slipped his phone back inside his coat and walked toward the woman.

"Excuse me, Mrs. Ackerson? I'm Coach Zim. I found Brandon and called the ambulance."

"Yes, your wife called me." She looked up at him with red, teary eyes. "Thank you. Is he okay?"

"They haven't told me anything."

Mrs. Ackerson went to speak with the woman at the reception desk. A minute later she took a seat next to Coach Zim. "They don't have any information for me yet." She gripped her jacket and clenched her hands into little balls. "How bad is he?"

He thought of lying, but opted for the truth. She'd find out soon enough. "He was pretty banged up. Unconscious, bleeding. Broken nose, I think." Tears rose like a tapped well in her eyes, and he quickly added, "The ambulance guys did a great job, though. Got him here quickly. And the doctors here are really good. Brandon's being well taken care of." He patted her hand gently.

"I can't thank you enough for helping him. He'd probably still be lying in the parking lot if it wasn't for you." She stared quietly at the soundless TV on the opposite wall for a couple of minutes, then wiped her eyes. Softly, she said, "Brandon is such a kind, gentle boy. He'd never hurt anyone.

He's a vegetarian because he won't eat anything that can bleed. Or is it breathe? Oh, I can't think." She made a choking sound, and the tears poured again. "Who would do this to my son?"

"I don't know," he said. It wasn't exactly a lie – he didn't have absolute proof – but there was little doubt in his mind about who had beaten up Ackerson.

When the police arrived he told them the same thing. Coach Zim didn't normally lie, or even omit the truth. In his history classes, he made sure the students understood that even great men had secrets, from the orgies that Ben Franklin and Martin Luther King took part in, to the numerous affairs of FDR and many other presidents, to Henry Ford's anti-Semitism. It was important, he told his students, to understand that the high standards to which many of our heroes are held are unrealistic.

But there he was, lying to the police and to Mrs. Ackerson. By this time she had disappeared into a hospital room with her son. Brandon Ackerson had a broken nose – they'd done the best they could but it would never be straight without plastic surgery – a broken wrist, three broken fingers, and bruised ribs. He also had a concussion and a few cuts and bruises. Pretty banged up, the doctor said, but teenage boys heal well and he'd be up and about in no time. Mrs. Ackerson hugged Coach Zim tightly before following the doctor, and he promised to visit the following day.

He gave the police a statement – both officers were former students and very respectful to him – and left the hospital. Even with the recent turning ahead of the clocks for daylight savings it was dark by six o'clock, and it wasn't until his headlights swept across the front of his house that Coach Zim remembered his Sea Dogs meeting. He was a no-call, no-show. Pulling that on your first day would get you fired from any job.

But he was too tired and strained to worry about that right now. Angela had been too worried to cook anything and was working under a deadline, so they sat at the table and ate take-out Chinese food. They didn't talk much – Angela preoccupied with the article she was trying to finish, Coach Zim playing over the previous three hours in his head. By the time he'd finished eating, he'd decided not to call Sparky Webster until the morning.

Instead, he sat on the couch and drank four beers while watching episodes of *Cheers* on Netflix. It helped his mood a little. And when Angela, wearing a short silk teddy, told him it was time for bed, his mood improved significantly. He'd doubted he'd be able to sleep that night, but an hour later he was snoring with a smile.

6

Word about what had happened quickly got around the school the following morning. Of course, the stories going around rarely approached the truth and ranged from mild stretches of the facts – Brandon Ackerson had been rushed to the hospital by Coach Zim after slipping on the ice and hitting his head – to outrageous fabrications – Coach Zim had punched Ackerson in the parking lot and spent the night in county jail. The number of suspicious looks he received from students in the hallways told him that this story had somehow gained traction, and nothing he said could have changed their oblivious teenage minds.

To his annoyance, Coach Zim was called to the principal's office during his free period. Dorito bag in one hand and Pepsi can in the other, he gave Emma a wink, walked into Craggy's office without knocking and plopped down on the couch. He scooped a handful of chips into his mouth – spilling several crumbs on the couch – and smiled at Craggy without saying a word.

"Most people knock before entering my office," Craggy said.

Coach Zim tried to reply but his mouth was too full and all that came out was a muffled "Mmphh." Half-chewed Dorito bits flew from his mouth, landing on the couch and floor. He took a swig of Pepsi to help wash it down, then smiled again.

Craggy glared, but his voice remained calm. "I heard about the Ackerson kid. Chief Walsh called me up last night to tell me about it. Lucky you were there to find him."

"Would have been luckier if I'd gotten there earlier."

"Chief Walsh told me you didn't see who committed the assault."

"No, by the time I got there he was lying unconscious on the ground. Nobody around. Probably happened just a few minutes before I got there."

Craggy leaned forward. "Any ideas who might have done it? Anyone that had it in for Ackerson?"

Scooping more chips into his mouth, Coach Zim shook his head. For the third time, he was not exactly telling the truth about the assault. Not a lie, not technically, but not exactly the truth, either. Although, it occurred to him as the chips crunched loudly in his mouth, he hadn't said anything this time so it couldn't be a lie.

"I asked around. Kate Folger, his art teacher, said she'd seen Tom Collins giving him a hard time in the hallway a couple of times. None of the kids will say anything because they're scared shitless of the punk. I'm going to talk to Collins in a little while and see what I can get out of him."

Coach swigged Pepsi and shrugged. "I doubt you'll get anything out of him. He's not the kind that intimidates easily, I don't think. You know the type."

"Indeed I do," said Craggy, looking thoughtful. Then he smiled – or as close as he could come to one – and said, "Baseball practice started yesterday. Coach Horne informed me that the team looks pretty good already."

Stories were going around school about this, too. Coach Zim had heard about it early that morning, when several of the players stopped by before first period. After an hour of nothing but jumping jacks and playing catch, Nutsack Horne had stood up from his seat next to the beautiful April

Spring and led the team into the weight room. There he tried to intimidate the players with the amount of weight he could lift and the size of his muscles. At one point, he loaded several large plates onto a bar, each with a load clang, until he had three hundred pounds. Then he slid onto the bench, dropped the bar to his chest and pushed it up, face red and veiny with strain. He let out a yell of triumph, causing several of the teenagers to roll their eyes. Then he smirked and asked, "Would any of you ladies like to give it a try?"

All eyes turned to Brock Cooke. Brock was strong. Not weightlifter strong, but natural, farm boy strong. His dad was strong, too, with the sort of strength that people still told stories about with awe. A gentle man, until he got angry. Brock shrugged, lay down under the bar, dropped it to his chest, and pushed it up. It didn't go up as smoothly as Nutsack's lift, but he wasn't used to lifting weights.

Horne stared in disbelief. He added twenty pounds, benched it with a roar, and gestured for Brock to try. He did, successfully. Horne shook his head like a boxer who can't believe his opponent keeps getting up off the canvas. Twenty more pounds, then another ten, and still Brock Cooke matched him.

When the weight on the bar reached three hundred and eighty pounds, Horne paced the room like a caged silverback, grunting and slapping his chest, psyching himself up. He finally lay on the bench and lowered the bar to his chest. With a mighty roar, he pushed up. The bar lifted about four inches and halted. His arms shaking violently, the bar slowly dropped to Horne's chest. The two spotters helped lift the bar and set it back on the bench.

When Horne sat back up, the players gasped. A few stepped back. He'd burst several blood vessels in his eyes. He stood up, gave Brock Cooke a bloody glare, and pointed to the bench.

"Aw, no Mr. Horne. I don't need to. I doubt I can lift that."

"Do it, you pussy."

Brock tried to let Nutsack off easy, but he wasn't going to be called a pussy in front of his friends. He got on the bench, lowered the bar and struggled to push it up. Slowly but steadily it rose, until he locked his arms and thrust the bar back onto the bench. His teammates cheered as he sat up and rubbed his shoulder.

Horne was furious. "You're lucky I did chest yesterday! My muscles are still healing." He pulled his shirt off, threw it on the floor and hit a most muscular pose. The site of a fully shaved man wearing nothing but shorts the size of speedos caused most of the players to wince and turn away. "Look at this! You think you're stronger than me?" He slapped his chest. "Look at this power!"

The players took this as a sign that practice was over. They picked up their gloves and filed out of the gym, shaking their heads and laughing while Coach Nutsack stayed behind and stared at his fully flexed body in the weight room mirrors.

"You know what I heard?" Coach Zim said to Craggy. "I heard he had the players lifting so much weight that Brock Cooke couldn't raise his arm more than halfway this morning. That's Brock Cooke, the team's best pitcher. His father's furious, from what I hear."

Craggy knew of Carl Cooke's reputation. He frowned but said nothing.

The bell rang. Coach Zim stood up, lifted the Doritos bag and dumped the rest of it into his mouth. About three-quarters of the chips reached their target; the rest tumbled like orange flakes of snow to the floor. Chewing loudly, he crumpled the bag and banked it off the wall, into Craggy's metal trash can.

"I've still got it," he said, washing down his chips with a swig of Pepsi. "Gotta go, Garth." He headed for the door,

"Jim. Are you going to talk to the Ackerson boy?"

"I'm going to see him at the hospital later. I promised his mom."

"You'll tell me if he says anything about who did this, won't you?"

Coach Zim nodded and closed the door behind him. He was halfway to class before he realized he'd lied again.

After school, just as he put his coat on, the co-captains, Devin Krane and Adam Nass, stopped by his classroom. They banged on the wall in lieu of knocking and marched up to his desk, serious expressions on their young faces.

"Sorry guys, I don't have time today," Coach said, digging through his pockets for his keys. "Stop by in the morning."

"You don't even know what we want to talk about."

"The players don't like Coach Horne and you want me to talk to Principal Craggy about reinstating me as coach of the baseball team."

Krane and Nass glanced at each other, mouths open. "How did you know that?"

"It wasn't very difficult to figure out. What I *am* having trouble figuring out," Coach Zim said, opening the top drawer of his desk and peering inside, "is where I put my truck keys."

"Got a hot date, Coach?"

"I'm going see Ackerson in the hospital. I promised his mom I'd be there."

"Yeah, everyone's been talking about you saving him. Good job with that," Krane said, adding, "even though he's kind of a loser."

Coach Zim slowly straightened up and glared at Krane. "He's a human being, Krane, and a good kid. He might not be gifted athletically like you guys, but the kid has talent." He walked around the desk to stand before them. They stepped back. "Part of the reason I named you guys co-captains is because I thought you had integrity and compassion. Was I wrong?"

"No, sir," Krane said, and Nass shook his head. "Sorry. I actually like Ackerson. He's just not popular, is what I meant. Not that there's anything wrong with that," he added quickly.

"People in this school follow your lead." He jabbed a thick finger at the two of them. "Remember that next time you think about opening your mouth."

Coach Zim went back to searching inside his desk. Why was it that he couldn't leave the school without something happening?

"Want us to go see Ackerson with you, Coach?"

"No thanks. What I'd like you to do is help me find my keys."

Krane and Nass hurriedly began searching, eager to win back Coach Zim's respect. Nass got on his stomach to look under the desk while Krane peered into the trash can, poking around with a pen.

Coach Zim bent over to open the desk's bottom drawer, and his keys jingled as they fell from his coat pocket and onto the floor. From beneath the desk, Nass's arm reached out to snag them. He slid out from under the desk, rolled onto his back and held the keys up. Coach Zim snatched them from his hand and help him up.

"Thanks, Nass. I guess they were in my pocket all along."

While Nass dusted himself off, Krane asked, "So how about coming back to coaching?"

"We went over this, guys. I didn't quit, I was fired. Or let go, if you want to make it sound nicer. It all means the same thing. Mr. Horne is your coach now and there's nothing I can do. Sorry, guys."

They followed him to the door.

"Well, you're going to go to the games, right? Maybe announce them?"

"I'm not sure, boys. I've got a lot going on. I'll be at some of the games, for sure, but I can't say any more right now." He turned off the lights in his classroom, closed the door, and strode quickly down the hall. "Gotta run, guys. We'll talk soon, I promise."

He walked to the end of the hall and turned the corner, not looking back. Krane and Nass stood outside his classroom, not sure of what to do, and watched him disappear.

Riding the elevator to the hospital's third floor, Coach Zim thought about what he'd told Krane and Nass about integrity and compassion. Often, he gave talks and speeches to young baseball players, inspirational talks, without knowing exactly what he was talking about. What he said often wasn't as important as how he said it. Coach Zim knew what sounded good and what would motivate young athletes and students – that's what made him a good teacher and successful coach. Ninety percent of the game is half mental, as Yogi Berra famously said, and many times Coach Zim lifted an average team over a superior group of kids simply by making them believe they could do it. He was of the belief that in sports, emotions and desire matter more than talent.

But he knew about decency and compassion, because in high school he'd been a real shit. Not always, but enough to help ruin a young girl's teenage years. He'd done it for no other reason than she was unattractive and because Jim Zimmerman could do anything he wanted.

The girl's name was Norma Henner, and she was in his French class senior year. She sat in the front row in the corner, by the door, while Jim Zimmerman sat in the back row, king of the cool kids. Every day before class and on the many days that Mr. Jones left the room to smoke a cigarette – bathroom break, he'd say, but they all knew better – Jim would slide into the empty seat behind Norma.

As the rest of the class giggled, he'd ask her in a whisper loud enough for all to hear what she was doing that weekend and if she'd like to go on a date. And if the class was finding the act particularly funny that day, he'd ask her if she'd ever given a blow job and if she'd like to practice on him. Sometimes he'd run a finger up and down her back, play with her hair. All the while she stared straight ahead at the blackboard, never uttering a sound.

Thirty years later, he thought about Norma Henner a lot. More every year, it seemed. The idea of his younger, arrogant self, with his lack of empathy, filled him with shame. He'd picked on someone because they were not as good-looking and athletically gifted as his group of friends. Looking back, he realized that the shy kids, the ones that dressed differently or were overweight or just didn't fit in – the Ackersons – had it harder than everyone else. But no, not just looking back; he'd known it then, too. That's why he did it – because he could. Harassing one of the popular kids, an athlete or a cheerleader, wouldn't have been fun or easy. But picking on the helpless - that was fun and easy. That was what entertained Jim Zimmerman, star athlete and big man on campus. Being a bully.

Saying that one had no regrets had become very trendy in recent years. Pop stars, porn stars, nobody had any regrets because the bad things, the drug busts and the STD's, had helped make them what they are today. Coach Zim knew that was a bunch of bullshit. Everyone has regrets. There are those who believe that not acknowledging regrets will make them go away. Usually, though, regret and remorse find a way to surface.

Coach had regrets. He regretted getting on that motorcycle in college and busting his shoulder up, costing him a major league career. He regretted some of the coaching decisions he'd made. But most of all, he regretted the way he'd treated poor Norma Henner when she was a chubby, bespectacled, insecure teen. It ate at him like river water flowing over a flat rock – too slow to notice at first, maybe, but over time wearing the surface raw with grooves that deepened every year.

He wanted to apologize to Norma Henner. Not that it would take away any of the pain he'd caused her – that old children's rhyme about sticks and stones was one of the biggest crocks ever. Maybe, though, a heartfelt apology would make her feel better. And maybe her forgiveness would take away some of his pain, sort of like going to confession to atone for his sins.

It was too late for that, though. Norma Henner had died in a car accident almost twenty years ago, driven into a tree at sixty miles an hour. Her life hadn't gone well, from what Coach had heard; overweight and unemployed, on welfare, three kids with three fathers and a love of coffee brandy. Whether or not he'd contributed to any of that he'd never know. But when Krane called Ackerson a loser, Norma Henner was all Coach Zim thought of. Even now, two decades after she'd passed away. He never wanted anyone to live with the sort of regrets he had. And so he made sure every one of his players knew how important it was to have integrity and compassion, because his lack of it at their age continued to haunt him all these years later.

He turned into Ackerson's room, expecting the worse. What he found was Ackerson propped up in bed, sketching in pencil on a pad with the arm that wasn't in a cast. His nose was swollen (but moved back to the middle of his face), his eyes purplish slits. Even his zits looked like they'd been smeared. He looked up when Coach Zim entered, nodded, and focused on his sketch. Coach Zim sat heavily in a chair near the bed.

"Where's your mom?"

"She went home to take a shower," he said, without looking up. "She hadn't left since yesterday."

Coach Zim looked up at the television on the far wall. *Family Feud.* It seemed that every family in America must have been on the show by now, and he wondered how it was that he didn't know any of them. He glanced at the other bed in the room, where a thin old man in a baggy johnny sipped from a cup of juice and stared at the screen. He seemed oblivious to anyone else in the room.

"So how're you doing, Ackerson?" he asked.

Ackerson shrugged, wincing a little at the effort. "Okay, I guess. They're giving me some good drugs for the pain. The worst is the headache. And my ribs. Those'll take a while to heal, I'm told."

"How long before you get out of here?"

"I can go home tomorrow. They want to keep an eye on me for another night because of the concussion."

Coach Zim sat quietly for a while, observing as Ackerson's hand quickly created lines and shaded areas of the paper flawlessly, as though the sketch was already there and he was just tracing over it. Within minutes, what started as a couple of curved lines became a boy's face, an attractive boy with long hair, a small nose and a crooked grin. Coach Zim had never seen an artist at work, except the guys at the fair who did the caricatures for ten dollars. He stared, fascinated, as the picture grew until the boy clutched books to his chest, leaving a classroom. Baseball was the canvas he was most familiar with, and watching Ackerson sketch was like watching Sandy Koufax paint the strike zone in his prime.

It suddenly occurred to Coach Zim that Ackerson might be gay, the boy in the sketch someone he was interested in. Open homosexuality among teenagers had increased greatly over the past few years, much as marijuana use had flooded high schools in the 1960's and 70's. He understood marijuana a lot better than he understood gay teenagers, but he did his best to be open-minded.

"Anyone I know?" Coach Zim asked, nodding to the sketch.

"No."

He almost said something about the boy being cute, then decided not to. He watched for another minute, then asked, "You want to tell me who did this to you?" Ackerson stopped drawing and looked over at him for the first time since he'd entered the room. "Don't worry, I won't tell the police or your mom. It'll just be between us."

Ackerson stared at him through purple slits. Behind them, Coach knew, were soft brown intelligent eyes. For a long time he said nothing, as though considering how much to tell Coach Zim. Finally, he spoke.

"Like I told the police, I didn't see who did it. I don't remember it happening. They must have hit me in the head first, knocked me out and then kicked me for a while."

"That could be it," Coach said. He knew Ackerson was lying. The kid had seen who'd assaulted him. What was with everyone lying lately? "At least they didn't break your drawing wrist, right?"

The boy smiled, softening the damage to his young face. "You've got that right. This sucks, but at least I can still draw."

He resumed sketching. Coach watched a bit of
Family Feud. He'd liked watching the show when he was a
kid, when Richard Dawson from *Hogan's Heroes* hosted it.
Dawson had seemed so old to the young Jim Zimmerman, but
he was probably no older than Coach was now. He
remembered how Richard Dawson had kissed many of the
women on the show back then, the older ones on the hand or
cheek, the young ones on the lips. Considering it now through
the lens of age and experience, Coach Zim thought Richard
Dawson had himself a pretty good gig.

Still looking at the TV, Coach Zim asked, "You think
it could have been Tom Collins?"

Ackerson's pencil slipped on the paper. Coach saw it
from the corner of his eye but pretended to continue watching
TV. The teen recovered quickly, though, and replied, "Like I
said, I didn't see who did it."

"I was just asking your opinion, that's all." He stood
up from the chair. "You're looking good, Ackerson. A hell of
a lot better than you did yesterday, that's for sure. We'll
probably see you back in school in a week or two."

"Probably." Ackerson glanced up. "Thanks, Coach
Zim."

"No problem, kid. Glad to do it. I'll see you later.
Tell your mom I said hi, alright?"

Ackerson nodded and Coach Zim left the room. He'd
almost reached the elevator when out stepped Mrs. Ackerson,
still looking nervous and frazzled but not quite as out of sorts
as the previous afternoon. When she saw Coach Zim she
smiled - as with her son, it had the effect of softening her
features – and wrapped her arms around him. Or as far
around him as they would go.

They stepped to the side and spoke for a few minutes.
She thanked him for saving her son and said the doctors
expected a full and rapid recovery. Coach Zim promised to

have a week's worth of assignments from all of Brandon's teachers ready by the following afternoon. He offered to drop it off at their home but Mrs. Ackerson said that he'd already done enough, and she would pick the work up in the school office.

As he walked across the parking lot, trying to remember where he'd parked his truck, Coach Zim wondered if there was a Mr. Ackerson. Brandon hadn't mentioned him, but the kid didn't talk much. Mrs. Ackerson had said nothing about a husband. Best not to ask, he decided. Besides, from what he saw from most fathers nowadays, Ackerson was probably better off without one.

7

The last couple weeks of March were warmer than normal – every day above forty degrees, with several well into the fifties. The spring warmth melted nearly all of the snow by the beginning of April and brought a wave of happiness after the long winter. Teenage boys strutted around the school in t-shirts, hoping the girls would notice they'd been working out all winter, while a few of the girls wore shorter, thinner clothing, making it difficult for young men to concentrate on history or math or anything not directly related to sex.

The warm weather was also good news for Apple Brook Warrior baseball, as it allowed the first team practice to be held outdoors. And the wave of cheerfulness brought by the warm weather was not confined to the student body. While he'd never been referred to as cheerful, there was still enough of the baseball-loving boy inside Garth Craggy to induce him to attend practice.

It was the first time in many years that Principal Craggy was seen at a practice. Standing alone by the chain-link fence, arms crossed, Craggy soon wished he'd gone straight home. The team warmed up with some jumping jacks, the co-captains Krane and Nass at the front, counting off. After that they dropped to the ground for push-ups. When one of the players struggled, Coach Horne leaned over the kid and insulted his sexuality. Craggy frowned. His nephew Todd snapped an order to the team like a drill sergeant, if drill sergeants wore white short-shorts and a tight warm-up jacket. Krane and Nass hustled over, obviously questioning what they'd been ordered to do, but Horne just shook his head and gestured for them to return to their areas at the head of the team. Craggy didn't know Krane and Nass well, but he knew they were basically respectful kids and wouldn't argue without reason.

At the front of the group, Krane and Nass looked at each other. They dropped onto their backs, and the rest of the team followed. In their first practice of the season the baseball team did twenty-five sit-ups on the cold, wet field. Craggy watched in disbelief. The kids would now be wet for the rest of practice, and those who didn't come down with pneumonia would almost certainly lose their enthusiasm. It was obvious from the looks on the players' faces as they brushed grass and mud from their wet clothes that Horne had lost the team before he even had them.

He next sent them around the field to run a lap. They moved too slowly – they were wet and cold and discouraged five minutes into practice – so their new coach sent them around again. And again. Craggy's shoulders hurt because his arms were folded so tightly. He considered walking over to his nephew and smacking him in the side of the head, or at least asking him what the hell he was doing.

Instead he turned and walked away, up the trail to the high school and into his office. From the bottom drawer of his desk he pulled a pint of Jim Beam and took a long swig. He winced, breathed deeply, and took another sip. This was his doing. After they lynched Todd, they'd be demanding *his* head. This was more ammunition for the many people who were on his back every day about firing Zimmerman. He sat back, propped his feet up on his desk, and considered how he could fire his nephew without admitting that hiring him had been a mistake. Nothing good comes from nepotism, he thought.

A few minutes later, Principal Craggy left his office and walked out of the building. Through the bare trees separating the school from the practice field the muffled *plink* of an aluminum bat hitting a ball could be heard. Craggy tried to ignore it as he walked to the parking lot, establishing in his head a good defense for the argument that would take place over dinner when he told his wife that he was firing her nephew.

Coach Zim looked up from his tattered paperback copy of *Cujo* and glanced around the classroom. There would be a test the following day, and after quickly going over the material – practically giving them the answers – he gave the students the rest of the class to study. Most students didn't study, and that was fine with him as long as they were quiet. They were allowed to use their school issued iPads in his classroom, but Coach Zim didn't allow phones or iPods. Which is exactly what he noticed in Michael Barrow's hand beneath his desk.

Normally, on a day like this Coach Zim wouldn't say anything. As long as the other students were quiet for the ones who actually wanted to study, he generally let them do what they wanted. This had been more difficult to enforce before Apple took over the world, back when kids used to have conversations and joke around with each other. Passing notes, whispering to each other, random bursts of laughter, all used to be part of high school classroom behavior. Now the students communicated with the person next to them impersonally, by text. They all looked like a herd of feeding animals, heads bent over, grouped together but ignoring one another.

Michael Barrow was a different case, though. A rich kid. A good-looking, rich, pompous kid who sometimes used his money to insult and degrade others, like the kids who had to shop at Walmart for clothes or had to take the bus to school because their fathers couldn't afford to buy them Camaro convertibles and Harley Davidson motorcycles. Being confident was one thing, being an asshole was another.

He grabbed a scrap piece of paper from his desk and slowly crumpled it into a ball. Squeezing and rotating the paper in his fist, he heard shoes squeaking on the hallway floor outside the classroom. Tom Collins walked slowly past, slamming the soles of his boots against the shiny buffed floor. Coach followed his gaze to Brandon Ackerson, who'd returned to school the day before. Ackerson was staring down at his iPad, studying, while the pencil in his right hand drew something on a notepad.

Coach Zim watched until Collins disappeared, all the while squeezing the paper tightly into a ball. When it was nice and tight, he cocked his arm back and whipped the paper ball at Michael Barrow's head. It hit him in the center of the forehead – Coach still had a pretty accurate arm, even with the stiffness and pain – and bounced all the way back to the front of the class, as though asking to be thrown again.

"Ow! What the f—"

Michael Barrow stood up, fists clenched, and noticed Coach Zim smiling and twiddling his fingers in a little wave.

"That was from me, Mister Barrow. An old-school text, you might say. Do you know what that text was telling you?"

"Uh-uh."

"That text was a reminder that I don't allow phones or iPods in my classroom."

"Oh. Well you didn't have to throw something at me."

"But I did, Mister Barrow." Coach Zim shrugged helplessly. "As you know, I do not text. And there seems to be no other way for someone as old and backwards as myself to communicate with someone as young and sophisticated as you. And so, you have now seen my version of a text. Now please sit down, put your phone away, and pray that I don't need to send you another one."

The rest of the class giggled. Barrow sat down. Embarrassed, he needed to have the last word. "It's an iPod, not a phone."

Coach Zim leaned over and picked the paper ball up from the floor. He held it up and raised his eyebrows. Michael Barrow lifted one hand defensively while stuffing the iPod into his backpack with the other. Coach nodded and set the paper ball down on the desk. A minute later, just as he found the place he'd left off in his book, the squeak of rubber soles on glossy smooth flooring again carried in from the hall.

Once more, Tom Collins stopped outside the classroom and, like a lion locking in on a weak gazelle from the herd, stared in at Brandon Ackerson. Coach Zim knew what Collins was trying to do. Bullies like him lived on intimidation. He was skinny, average height, but he picked on those weaker than himself. The worst part wasn't the actual physical violence – although in Ackerson's case, that had been pretty bad – but the intimidation. Driving by the prey's house, squealing tires and throwing things, making comments in the hallway, pushing and shoving – all designed to frighten the prey. And fear was what a punk like Collins thrived on.

Coach Zim had seen many bullies over the years. Every generation had at least one Tom Collins. But Collins was different from most. After dishing out a physical beating, most bullies left the victim alone, or at least limited the harassment to an occasional rude comment. They'd proved their point. But Collins, for some reason, wouldn't leave it alone. He'd handed out the worst beating Coach Zim had ever seen a high school kid receive, yet was right back at it. Maybe it was because Ackerson dared return to school.

Coach glanced at Ackerson. He was in the same position, reading the iPad and sketching, seemingly without looking. If he knew Tom Collins was in the hallway licking his chops, he did a good job of ignoring it. Coach Zim slowly got up from his desk.

Collins was so focused on Ackerson that he didn't notice Coach Zim until his huge frame filled the doorway.

"Something I can help you with, Collins?"

"Nope. Just thought I saw someone I knew."

"Well, you didn't. I've seen you walk past twice now. You lost?"

Tom Collins gave a cocky grin. "Good one. I just went to the bathroom."

"Got a pass?" Collins handed his pass to Coach Zim, who glanced at it and handed it back. "That still doesn't explain why you've walked past my classroom twice. This pass says you left Mrs. Delp's class in the Science wing. This is the English wing. You need a GPS to get around the school, Collins? Maybe we could ask the custodians to put up signs with pictures, in case you're having trouble with the written ones."

Collins's face clouded over. "You callin me stupid?"

"I'd never call a student stupid, even if he was. I'll just say something from a great movie – stupid is as stupid does."

"Great movie, Coach Zim," someone called from behind him. "Forest Gump."

"What the hell does that even mean?" Collins said.

"Exactly."

A few of the students in the classroom chuckled. Collins's face slowly turned red. He glared up at Coach Zim.

"You *are* calling me stupid. You don't want to do that."

"I don't think I need to, Collins. And that sounds like a threat."

Collins lowered his voice so that only Coach Zim could hear. "You don't want to get on my bad side."

Coach Zim stepped out of the doorway until he was inches away from Collins. The top of the scrawny punk's head only came up to his chin. He, too, spoke quietly. "Yes, Collins, I do. Now run along, back to class. Before you get on *my* bad side."

With the obligatory bad-ass stare, Collins took a step backward. He turned and slowly walked away, scuffing his boots extra hard on the floor.

"You want me to tell Luther who's been scuffing up his floor?"

Luther was the second shift custodian, the one who had to pick up after hundreds of teenagers, many of whom thought nothing of spitting on classroom floors and rubbing gum into carpets and blowing snot on the tile bathroom walls and smearing shit in the toilet stalls. Luther spent several hours a week running the huge floor buffing machine through the hallways. Luther had a very bad attitude, especially when it came to teenagers. Luther was a very large man – well over six feet tall, thick shoulders and neck, arms stacked with muscle. He was also black, uncommon in rural Maine. And unfamiliarity breeds fear.

"I don't care what you do," Collins replied, shrugging his bony shoulders. But, Coach noticed, he stopped scuffing his feet.

The bell rang as Coach Zim entered the classroom. A flurry of chairs scraping against the floor as students rushed to leave the room.

"Study hard, people. The Bill of Rights – if you don't know it, learn it. Barrow, put away the phone. You are still in my classroom. And if you tell me it's an iPod I'll take ten points off your grade tomorrow. Binette, leave Miss Grant alone, she's far too classy for the likes of you. Ackerson, stop by after school please. Goodbye, farewell, get out."

The afternoon passed quickly, with lots of engaged students asking questions. He found that the Bill of Rights, if taught correctly, could be interesting, even motivating, to high school students. Several of his students seemed destined for either law school or prison; at this point, it was difficult to tell. Either way, they seemed to understand that the Bill of Rights could be of use to them in the future.

After the final bell, Coach Zim sat at his desk and waited the ten seconds it took for his classroom to empty. He picked up his tattered copy of *Cujo* and read about a page and a half before Brandon Ackerson walked in. The boy's eyes were no longer swollen but the skin beneath them was a sickly yellow, magnified by his thick glasses.

Coach Zim lowered the book. "You ready for tomorrow's test, Ackerson?"

"I think so. I always have a problem with the right to arm bears."

Coach's eyes widened. "A joke, Ackerson? I'll be damned."

"Joking is okay, but laughing hurts. Like the old saying goes, it only hurts when I laugh. And yes, I think I'm ready for the test."

"Because you can wait a few more days, if you think you need more time to prepare. You missed a lot of school. And if there's anything you're having trouble with, you can just ask or, you know, email."

Ackerson smiled. "Email? You don't seem the type, Coach Zim."

"Yeah, you'd be better off to just ask. I only check my email every week or two."

"I'm fine, thanks."

"You feeling okay? You look a lot better."

"Feeling much better. My ribs are still sore, and the itching under my cast is driving me crazy." Holding up his left arm and tapping the cast, he said, "But it comes off in a couple weeks. I can't wait."

Coach asked Ackerson if he was walking home. When Ackerson nodded, Coach said he'd give him a ride. He kept thinking of Tom Collins stopping outside the classroom to watch Ackerson like an obsessed boy stalking a pretty girl.

"I don't need a ride. Thanks, though."

"That wasn't an offer, Ackerson. That was me telling you I'll give you a ride home. Have a seat for five minutes and then we can go."

Ackerson didn't look happy, but he sat at his desk and pulled out his iPad. Meanwhile, Coach Zim lifted his feet back onto his desk and began reading *Cujo* again, wanting to finish the chapter before leaving school. Ackerson looked up, appeared ready to say something, but hunched back over his iPad and began swiping away.

He'd read exactly two sentences when a thin boy walked into the room. A thin boy with long hair, a small nose and crooked grin. He looked familiar. Then he noticed Ackerson gazing eagerly, the look of a puppy hoping to be played with. This was the boy he'd been sketching in the hospital, Coach realized. The boy walked past Ackerson without a glance.

"Coach Zim, I have a message from Principal Craggy. He was hoping you might still be here. He'd like to see you in his office before you leave."

Coach Zim nodded. "Tell him I'll be there in about half an hour."

The boy left. Ackerson continued to stare at the doorway after he'd gone.

"You know him?" Coach asked.

"No. Well, I know who he is. Avery Palmer. He's in my English class." Then his longing expression turned to a frown. "I think I should walk home. I don't want to wait half an hour."

"Oh, ignore that. I have no plans to see Principal Craggy this afternoon."

"Then why did you say you would?"

Coach Zim picked up his book. "For fun."

Less than a page later, Krane and Nass entered the classroom. They nodded to Ackerson as they walked past. Behind them was the entire baseball team.

Coach Zim sighed and put the book down. He folded his hands behind his head and looked up at the boys gathered on the other side of his desk. Twenty of them, at least. Several of the young faces were spotted with acne and a few of the boys were trying to grow moustaches, although the wispy, silly-looking hair above their lips more closely resembled a caterpillar who'd found a place to nap. On each head was a baseball hat, and each player carried a baseball glove.

Krane and Nass looked at each other, then at Coach. As usual, Krane did the talking. "Coach Zim, we need to talk to you."

"Yes, Krane, I assumed that when I looked up to see the entire baseball team standing before my desk."

"We're having problems with Nutsack. I mean Mr. Horne. He's a horrible coach."

"Yeah, Coach," said Dallas Thompson. Best hitter on the team, but played right field like an old lady with cataracts. "He ain't got no idea of how to coach a baseball team."

"Thomas, you speak about as well as you field. Have you ever been to an English class?"

"It's true, though," said Robert Williams, the only black kid on the team. Fast runner, good bat, no power. "He's had us running and doing sit-ups and push-ups and squat thrusts and sprinting like we was going out for the damn track team. I haven't even swung a bat yet!"

"He sucks," said Nass.

Coach Zim looked over in surprise. Nass rarely spoke.

"My dad wants to beat him up," said Brock Cooke, who could finally throw a ball again after out-bench pressing Horne.

Holding his hands before him in a placating manner, Coach Zim said, "I'll admit, what I've heard about him isn't very good, but maybe his coaching style is unconventional. And unconventional can often be good."

"I agree with Nass. He sucks," said Williams.

"He really does, Coach Zim," said Krane. "You aren't the only coach we've ever had, you know. Little League, junior high, all those years we had different coaches. We know what a coach is supposed to do. Nutsack has no idea what to do."

"Okay, guys, you have to stop calling him that. Whatever you think of him, Mr. Horne is a teacher at this school and you can't go around calling him Nutsack. At least not in front of me," he added.

Williams opened his mouth, about to say something, but thought better of it when Coach Zim looked his way.

"I'd like to help, I really would. Hell, if it were up to me I'd still be coaching you guys. But the decision has been made, and this is Mr. Horne's team now. Sorry, boys, but I won't interfere with another coach's team."

"We won't play for him," Krane said. The rest of the team nodded their heads. "We're prepared to sit out the season."

"Krane, don't be an idiot. You guys don't want to do this. Some of you have college scholarships riding on this season. Including you, Thompson, if you can ever learn to field."

"I won't learn to field with that guy coaching me," said Thompson.

Coach stared at him for a moment, because that was the quickest comeback he'd ever heard from Dallas Thompson. The quickest one anyone had ever heard, he'd be willing to wager. Thompson was the epitome of a big, dumb jock, with heavy emphasis on dumb.

"Okay, guys. Hold on. You still have Mr. Rivard, right? I know you guys like him. And he's a helluva coach."

Paul Rivard was a sixty-year-old history teacher who'd been Coach Zim's assistant coach for the past ten years. A short, stocky fireplug, he had threatened to punch Principal Craggy in the balls when he heard about Coach Zim's firing. The players all loved Coach Rivard, partly because of his enthusiasm for the game, but mostly because of his colorful language. Players were often referred to as Dipshit, as in, "Keep your eyes on the ball next time, Dipshit!"

"We do like Coach Rivard," agreed Krane. "Problem is, he won't be back for a couple more weeks because of his granddaughter, remember?"

Coach Zim nodded. Paul Rivard had taken three weeks off because his three-year-old granddaughter needed heart surgery in Boston and he was going to help his daughter and son-in-law while the little one recovered. Coach Zim had called Rivard the day after the surgery and was glad to hear that all had gone well.

"Well, men, this is a challenge," Coach Zim began, feeling a motivational speech coming on. "Perseverance and overcoming adversity, the sign of a winner. We've discussed this. Together, working as a team, you can overcome any obstacle. You can be a bunch of quitters, or you can work past your problems with Coach Horne until Coach Rivard returns. I was proud of each and every one of you when I was coaching, and I'd hate to think that you'd turned into quitters just because things aren't going your way. Are you quitters, or are you winners?"

"Winners!" yelled Dallas Thompson, raising a fist into the air. His deep voice resonated in the small classroom like a fart in church, and his teammates burst into laughter.

"So you won't come back as coach?" Krane asked.

Coach Zim shook his head. "I'm sorry, guys, I can't."

"How about the announcing job? Will you at least announce the games?"

Looking at their youthful faces patched with zits and hair tucked under their baseball caps, Coach Zim couldn't say no. He and Angela had no children of their own. They'd tried, years ago, as most young couples do. He always got a kick out of couples saying, with great eagerness, they were trying to get pregnant, which was just a polite way of saying they were fucking like rabbits. It was even better when the couple was older and had been together for a long time, because the eagerness was replaced with a resigned look, often a sigh, as though they had many things they'd rather be doing and both hoped she got pregnant quickly so they could get this sex thing out of the way.

They'd never gotten tested to see if the pitcher or catcher (his term) was at fault. Judging by the number of young ladies he'd slept with as a star athlete in high school and college without getting anyone pregnant, he suspected his swimmers might not be up to the task. After a while, they just moved on with their lives. Angela went from writing obituaries for the local paper to having a weekly column syndicated in a dozen New England newspapers, as well as writing freelance articles for several magazines. Coach Zim became, well, Coach Zim, the man who had won the most games and championships in the history of Maine high school baseball. Angela was successful, but Coach Zim was a legend.

They rarely discussed it, but neither of them regretted not having children. Angela loved her work and probably wouldn't have been as successful had it been necessary to care for a child (or two, or three). And to Coach Zim, these boys and girls were his kids - the players on his teams and certain students, like Ackerson, who somehow took hold of him. Everything that he may have taught to a son or daughter, the advice he'd have given, the protection he'd have provided, was instead given to these kids. He couldn't imagine having a child of his own could be any more fulfilling than what he gave to, and gained from, these young people.

He looked at them – Krane, the spokesman, with a line of bullshit that would carry him far in either politics or television and, just as importantly, help him get laid; Adam Nass, quiet and mysterious, Brian Jones to Krane's Mick Jagger; Brock Cooke, young and strong like a puppy who doesn't know his own strength, a hard, wild hurler; Robert Williams, five-foot-ten but over six feet tall with his old-school afro, whose quick tongue tended to get him in trouble; Dallas Thompson, a big goofy kid without a mean bone in his body who was only a junior and already had professional scouts looking at him because of his big bat. He loved them and all the others and felt for them what he imagined he'd feel for his own biological children.

So when they asked him to announce the games, he said, "I don't even know if that offer is still on the table. But I'll check with Principal Craggy and if it is, I'll announce the home games. Is that enough to get you guys out of my classroom and onto the practice field, where you belong?"

Krane smiled and leaned toward Coach Zim, his arm extended for a fist bump. Then the rest of the team crowded the desk, fists extended. He reluctantly touched knuckles with each of them. He hated fist bumps and worried that one of the players would end up busting a knuckle or finger or spraining a wrist. High-fives were bad enough, in his opinion.

"Now get your butts out of here. You're already late for practice."

The players said goodbye and left the room, pushing and shoving each other. Coach Zim smiled as he watched them, wishing he was still their coach. This was a group of young men that could go somewhere, he felt. Maybe even the state championship. Of course, he'd felt that way about every team he'd coached.

Still grinning, he leaned back and opened his book. About half a page later, he realized something was wrong. He lowered the book and realized what it was.

Ackerson was gone.

The hallways were almost empty. School had let out half an hour earlier, and the only students left in the building were those in detention or getting extra help or belonging to a club. He walked slowly, glancing down every hallway and stairway he passed, knowing that he wouldn't find Ackerson. The image of Tom Collins staring in at Ackerson once again flashed in Coach Zim's mind. Hopefully he'd find the kid walking home and not unconscious in the parking lot again. Stupid kid.

As he approached a stairway, Luther backed out of a nearby maintenance closet with a mop and a bucket on wheels. His dark bald head gleamed in the overhead lights as he straightened up and closed the closet door. He turned and pushed the bucket in Coach Zim's direction, foamy water slopping over the edge as he did so.

"Afnoon, Coach Zim."

"How's it going, Luther?" he asked.

If he was a janitor and someone asked him this question, he'd probably punch that person in the nose. Surprisingly, though, most janitors he'd met seemed quite content with their lot in life. A few actually seemed to enjoy their job. Most of the happy janitors worked in the elementary schools, where dancing with a broom made the kids laugh and being the janitor's helper for a day was seen as an exciting reward for having done something well. By the time they reached high school, these same kids would be pissing on walls and smearing gum on the floors for no other reason than to make the janitor's life hell.

"It's a livin."

Luther passed by, then stopped and turned around. There weren't many men who made Coach feel small, but Luther came close.

"How you think the team'll do this year without you coachin em?"

"Well, they're a good bunch of kids. Lots of talent. If they stay focused and work as a team, I think they'll do pretty well."

"Tell you what I think," Luther said. "I think Nutsack Horne is an idiot and the New York Yankees couldn't win a game with him coachin em."

Coach Zim felt the same way, and he had to smile. Luther was a big fan of baseball. He'd played high school ball in Peabody and had played in the local twilight league until a few years ago, when an ankle injury that wouldn't heal made running difficult. He attended every one of Apple Brook High School's home games, cutting out of work for a couple of hours and sitting at the back of the bleachers where he wouldn't be seen. Of course, even in the back of the bleachers, a large black man in Apple Brook was hard to miss. Nobody said anything, though; even Craggy wasn't stupid enough to confront Luther. As long as he did his job, nobody seemed to care that he skipped out for a while to watch a ballgame.

"You aren't the only one who feels that way, I'm afraid."

Down the stairway came several crashes, the sound of banging lockers.

"Time to go kick some ass," Luther said. He dropped the mop and headed for the stairway.

"Hold on, Luther." He thought of Ackerson and Collins and started up the stairs. "I'll take care of this."

"You need some help you just yell, Coach. I wouldn't mind an excuse with some of these kids."

Following the sounds of laughter and slamming lockers, he took a right at the top of the stairway. On the right side of the hallway stood a group of Collin's friends, laughing as they watched Collins trying to slam Ackerson's head with a locker door. Ackerson was bent over, struggling to back away, while Collins's hand gripped the back of his neck. Collins's other hand held the open locker door. Every time Ackerson's head neared the open locker, Collins slammed the door shut. Coach Zim watched as the door winged past the top of Ackerson's head, close enough to clip his hair.

"The more you struggle, pussy, the worse it's gonna be for you. If you'd just let me stuff you inside in the first place, we wouldn't be going through this."

Collins's friends noticed Coach Zim first. Their eyes widened with surprise and fear. When he held a finger to his lips, they obeyed. Then he pointed to the end of the hall. The teenagers backed away quietly – Coach Zim continued to hold his finger to his lips – and disappeared around the corner.

Collins didn't notice that his audience had gone until the locker door was suddenly forced open all the way, crunching his fingers between it and the lockers beside it.

"Hey, what the fuck!" He turned around and glared into Coach Zim's chest, then stepped back.

"Ackerson. You okay, son?"

The boy's red cheeks were streaked with tears, his eyes wide and frightened as a fawn's. He stood up straight, wiped his cheeks and nodded.

"Go wait in my classroom. I'll just be a minute."

After Ackerson had turned the corner and his footsteps echoed from the stairwell, Coach Zim turned back to Collins.

"I think you broke my fingers, man!"

"Why?"

"Why do I think you broke my fingers? Cause they hurt like hell!"

"No, numbnuts. Why do you pick on Brandon Ackerson?"

"Cause he's a whiny little faggot."

"I'll tell you why I think you do it." Coach Zim stepped very close. Collins backed into the lockers. "I think you're jealous."

"Jealous?" Collins looked at him in disbelief. "Of that little fag?"

"Ackerson is smart and talented. Really talented. He's going places, and he's going to be a success. Money and fame. You, on the other hand, will most likely spend the rest of your life working in your dad's garage, tuning up motors all day long and going home to a fat wife and punk kids who will continue the cycle. If you don't wind up in prison, that is."

"Ain't nothin wrong with working on cars. It's man's work."

"And you're a man, huh, Collins? You think a man picks on someone just because their smaller and weaker?"

Collins said nothing.

"How do you think it would feel to be stuffed inside a locker? What if I decided to stuff you inside a locker?"

Collins glared at him. He balled his hands into fists, even the sore one. "Try it. I'll kick your old ass."

The question had been hypothetical; he'd never even considered laying a hand on a student before. But being challenged by Collins changed everything. Within seconds he'd bent and twisted and shoved Collins into the locker and slammed the door shut. The lockers were old, installed when the school was built in 1960, back when students carried books. They were built wider back then, designed to hold books and jackets and everything else a student accumulated over a year's time. Still, getting Collins in there was a tight squeeze.

"Let me out of here, you asshole! I can't breathe!"

Coach Zim moved his face close to the metal door. "Of course you can breathe. There are air slots in the top of the door. Three air slots. I'm looking at them right now."

"Get me out of here!" Tom Collins screamed. There was real panic in his voice. "I can't move! I can't breathe!"

"Stop whining. I know you can move because you're banging on the door. Now, while you have some alone time, I'd like you to concentrate on how it feels to be inside a closed locker. This is what you were going to do to Ackerson. I hope you learn something from this experience."

"I'm gonna get you fired for this! You can't do this to a student!"

He walked away, whistling. Considering what he'd just done, how many rules he'd broken, Coach Zim felt surprisingly upbeat. Collins continued to scream, but the steel locker door muffled the sound enough that it disappeared by the time Coach Zim was halfway down the stairs.

Ackerson sat in the classroom, staring down at his iPad and swiping away. Coach Zim called to him from the doorway and they started down the hall, in the opposite direction of the front doors. Ackerson looked confused but said nothing.

In a classroom at the end of the hall they found Luther, pushing a broom between rows of desks. He wore earbuds, moving his head and shuffling his feet to the private beat. Luther didn't see them at first and Coach Zim stayed in the doorway, not wanting to startle him. He turned down another row and finally noticed them. Removing an earbud, he leaned against the broom and said, "Somethin I can do for you, Coach?"

"When you get to the second floor, you're going to find something in locker two twenty one. Something that was trying to hurt my friend Ackerson here. Let it out. You never saw anything in that locker, and you and I never had this conversation. Okay?"

Luther grinned. "What conversation, Coach?" He put the earbud back in and returned to sweeping and grooving.

Coach Zim and Ackerson finally headed for the front of the school. Vice Principal Simon was in the main office as they passed but he was on the phone, facing the other way, and didn't see them. Coach Zim didn't see Principal Craggy but walked faster than usual anyway, and Ackerson had to jog a couple of times to keep up.

A minute later, as they pulled out of the parking lot in Coach Zim's pickup truck, Tom Collins was still banging on the locker door, trying to get out.

That evening, during dinner, Coach Zim mentioned to his wife that he had stuffed a student into a locker after school and left him there. Had he thought it out beforehand, he'd have found something else to talk about.

"You did *what?*" Angela said loudly. Which was unnecessary, since it was just the two of them in their small kitchen.

"Honey, it sounds a lot worse than it actually is," he said.

"Oh, good. Because it sounds like you stuffed a young boy into a school locker and left him there. Why don't you tell me how it actually is, so I'll feel better?"

She glared as though he was a dishonest child. And he reacted accordingly – eyes cast down, glum expression, silently picking at his food. He didn't actually feel that bad about what he'd done – surprising, considering he'd assaulted a student – but pretending to feel contrite was usually the quickest way to quell the storm.

No such luck this time. "Would you like to tell me why you did something so stupid?" When no answer was forthcoming, she continued, "I assume you are aware of what the consequences might be. Suspension if you are lucky, but most likely you'll be fired. Then what will you do?"

"I won't be suspended, because nobody will ever know about it."

"What about the poor boy you assaulted? You don't think he'll say anything?"

"That poor boy is Tom Collins, the asshole who sent Brandon Ackerson to the hospital," said Coach Zim. "And he was trying to do to Ackerson what I did to him. He just won't leave the kid alone."

"Maybe Brandon needs to stick up for himself."

He shook his head. "You don't understand teenage boys."

"I'll admit that's true."

"And as for getting suspended or fired, it won't happen. But if it did – and it won't – I'm working for the Red Sox now. I'm going to be giving my resignation at the school soon."

Angela smirked. Coach stared across the table, confused. What was she smirking about? Did she not believe he was really working for the Red Sox? He had to admit that it really hadn't sunk in yet and there were times even he didn't believe it. But he was working for them. He'd be working for the Red Sox after dinner, in fact.

"When are you planning to give your resignation, Jim?"

He took a sip of milk. "I don't know. June, I suppose. After school lets out. I don't want it to be a distraction for anyone, especially the students."

"You honestly think you'll be able to do it?"

"Yeah, of course. Now that I'm no longer coaching there's nothing holding me to the school. Baseball was the main reason I stayed so long."

He cut himself another piece of chicken. He took a bite and looked up to see Angela smiling broadly.

"For a teacher, you sure can be stupid sometimes."

"What does that mean?" he asked.

"Baseball has always been the most important thing in your life, right?"

"Except for my marriage, of course," he replied dutifully.

"Of course. But you don't seem to have noticed that baseball is no longer the most important thing, and it hasn't been for a long time. The most important thing in your life now is the students. You used to be a coach who was also a teacher. But now, first and foremost, you are a teacher."

"Oh, I don't think—"

"When Brandon Ackerson was hurt, you missed your first day of work with the Red Sox to take him to the hospital. Yes, you don't have to say it – any decent person would have done the same. But then you missed another day to visit him in the hospital. And the fact that you would stick a student in a locker to protect another student shows how important these kids are to you. You may like the idea of a job working for the Red Sox and helping the Sea Dogs players, but you aren't one hundred percent involved. You're having doubts."

"Am not!" he said, like an eight-year-old child.

"We'll see," Angela said. Her triumphant smile was irritating as hell, but he said nothing and finished his meal.

Later that evening he sat at the desk in the small home office, watching video of Anthony Slater, one of the Sea Dogs players, on his laptop. Slater was a player the Red Sox organization had big hopes for because of his speed. He'd stolen thirty bases in Portland the year before at nineteen years old. Problem was, he'd been thrown out on a third of his attempts during the last month of the season, a terrible percentage for someone so fast. Several times the catcher was already on his feet before the pitch was thrown, which meant Slater was tipping them off somehow. Before moving him up to Pawtucket, they needed to find out what the kid was doing wrong.

The kid seemed to do everything right – he took a big enough lead, didn't lean one way or the other. But then Coach Zim saw it – just a quick flick, but as in poker, a slight twitch can be as clear as a flashing neon sign. When Slater was going to steal, he scratched his balls. Or, rather, he flicked them, with one finger. It was fast, but not fast enough, as some catchers and coaches had caught on. Why the Sea Dogs hadn't noticed he wasn't sure, but it didn't matter. He'd found it.

He was excited and couldn't wait to call Sparky Webster in the morning. This was big, made him believe he was earning his money. So when he stood up to stretch after closing his laptop, he was surprised to find himself thinking about the test he'd be giving tomorrow and the students he might have to nudge toward the correct answers. His thoughts drifted to Brandon Ackerson, and he remembered that he wanted to speak with Miss Folger soon about art colleges for the kid to look into. And then his team – his former team – asking for him to return to coaching, and how he'd promised to announce the games. Remembering the happy looks on their youthful faces made him smile.

Then he remembered Angela and her opinion that those kids meant more to him than his dream job, working for the Boston Red Sox. Sometimes, he thought, she wasn't very smart.

8

Around mid-morning, Vice Principal Simon stuck his head into Coach Zim's classroom and hissed that he needed to have a word. Sighing, Coach Zim stood up and walked toward the door. The students were silent, focused on their tests. Most of them, anyway. A couple of students, Coach noted, appeared to be focused on their neighbor's test.

"What do you want, Simon?" Coach whispered in the doorway. He didn't turn his back to the students, lest they take that as an invitation to cheat.

"Principal Craggy wants to see you in his office. Says it's of the utmost importance."

"Fine. I'll be there after class."

"He'd like to see you now."

Coach Zim stepped closer. "Simon, we are in the middle of a test. I'll see him after class."

Simple Simon nodded and scurried away. Coach Zim returned to his desk, moving as quietly as a man his size could. He grabbed a piece of paper, slid it under the desk and crumpled it up slowly and quietly. Then he took aim and fired. The ball of paper hit the cheating student in the side of the head. It would have hit him in the face, had he been facing forward like he should have. A few students looked up and chuckled, while the cheater looked down sheepishly at his test paper. Coach Zim's rule was, first infraction during a test earned a paper fastball to the head. Cheating a second time during the same test earned the student a trip to the office. It was a rare student who didn't heed the warning fastball.

When the bell rang, Coach Zim grabbed a bag of chips from his bag and followed the students into the hallway. Zig zagging like a car in rush hour traffic, he slowly made his way to Principal Craggy's office. Emma sat at her desk in the small outer office. Her face grew worried when he walked in.

"I think you're in trouble," she whispered.

"As usual."

"No, it's bad this time. Tom Collins came in this morning with his father. What a piece of work that guy is. Drunk at eight o'clock, I think. I heard a lot of yelling and swearing in there, and they didn't come out for almost an hour. Then our fearless leader got on the phone with someone from the police department."

"Hmmm." He opened the bag of chips and held it toward Emma, but she declined. He scooped a handful into his mouth. "Well, I'd better get it over with."

"Good luck," she whispered.

He entered Craggy's office without knocking and closed the door behind him. Principal Craggy sat behind his monstrous desk and Vice Principal Simon was on the couch. Craggy gestured for Coach Zim to take a seat in one of the wooden chairs in front of the desk. Instead, Coach Zim took a seat on the couch next to Simple Simon. He held the bag of chips toward the vice principal, who shook his head and leaned away.

"I've had a very interesting morning," Craggy began.

"The old lady finally give you some lovin?"

Craggy ignored this. "I had a visit from Tom Collins and his father. Apparently Tom was stuffed inside a locker yesterday afternoon and left there for a few hours." He paused and stared meaningfully at Coach Zim, who ate chips and stared back. "You don't seem surprised."

"I was waiting for you to continue, Garth. You didn't invite me into your office to gossip about Tom Collins, did you? Because I have a class full of unsupervised kids taking a test right now."

Vice Principal Simon spoke up. "You have a classroom full of unsupervised kids taking a test?"

"That's right." Coach Zim looked at Principal Craggy and jerked his thumb toward Simple Simon. "Craggy, your parrot does a really good job of repeating things. How long did it take you to train him?"

"Why did you leave the children unattended?"

"Because this guy –"he nodded toward Simon – "said that you needed to speak with me as soon as the period ended. I thought it was an emergency. Had I known we were just going to shoot the shit I'd have first found someone to supervise." He stood up. The couch released a sound like a long, deep sigh. "Well, nice talking to you guys. I'm heading back to my class now."

"Sit down, Jim. Ed, go take over Jim's class."

The vice principal's face filled with panic. "Me? A classroom? Garth, you know I'm not trained for that sort of thing. I don't know anything about education."

"That's why you make such a great vice principal," said Coach Zim.

"Sit at the head of the class and make sure the children don't cheat," said Craggy. He looked toward Coach Zim. "That about cover it?"

Coach Zim nodded. The vice principal left the room, head down, as dejected as a child sent to clean his room.

"Tom Collins says that you put him inside a locker. Apparently he was stuck there for a couple of hours until the janitor let him out."

Coach chewed thoughtfully for a few moments, then said, "That's a load of bullshit, Craggy. That's my official statement on the matter."

"He seemed quite believable this morning. Even brought his father in to discuss it."

"Yes, Lester Collins. He's well known for his scruples and honesty." Coach Zim lifted a leg onto the couch and straightened it out. "Did anyone see me do this?"

"No. But according to Tom Collins his friends saw you approaching, as did Brandon Ackerson."

"Uh huh. And have you questioned these young men?"

Craggy had questioned them immediately after Collins and his father left the office. He'd brought in each boy individually, and with frustration written on his face he related to Coach Zim that Collins's friends all said the same thing – they'd seen Coach Zim approach but had not witnessed the alleged locker stuffing. Ackerson had stated to the principal that he'd been with Coach Zim after school and hadn't seen Tom Collins.

"And what about the janitor? Did he have anything to say about this?"

"I called Luther this morning. He said that he didn't let any kid out of a locker. Then he told me to never call him before noon again or I'd be sorry." Craggy frowned at the memory. "Only he didn't put it that kindly."

"OK, case closed. Tom Collins is trying to get me into trouble because I told him to move along in the hallway yesterday. He made up a story which has been proven to be a lie. Give him detention. Suspend him. I don't give a shit, really." He finished his chips and tossed the bag into Craggy's trash can. Then he stood up. "I'll see you later, Garth. I've got to make sure the kids haven't tied up Simon and shaved his head."

"Something about this story doesn't ring true," Craggy said thoughtfully. "Collins and his friends say they saw Ackerson, but he denies seeing them. Somebody's lying."

"They're all lying, Garth. They're high school kids." Then Coach Zim remembered something. "Hey, do you still want me to announce the baseball games?"

Garth Craggy did not want to think about the baseball team. He'd gently broached the subject of firing Todd Horne as coach with his wife a couple of nights earlier. Her reaction was about what he expected. She said no. Just like that. Never looked up from the book she was reading at the dinner table. Shook her head, said no, and took another bite of her haddock sandwich. He'd tried explaining to her that he'd made a mistake and that Todd, although a wonderful nephew, was even more useless as a baseball coach than as a gym teacher.

At this she looked up and glared at her husband, signaling that unless he was no longer fond of his testicles the conversation was over. Craggy found consolation in the knowledge that men more powerful than himself – senators, prime ministers, presidents – made world-shaping decisions every day, yet were not the highest authorities in their own homes. He imagined they took it out on their subordinates, much as he took out his frustration on the misbehaving youths sent to his office.

And so Todd Horne was still coaching. There was nothing he could do about that, for now. His only hope was for the musclebound idiot to do something so stupid that even the missus couldn't overrule him. But in the meantime, to see the great Jim Zimmerman relegated to sitting in a booth announcing the games – it didn't exactly make up for his nephew, but it helped. Craggy smiled and said yes, it would be wonderful to have him in the booth, announcing the games.

Something about Craggy's grin made Coach Zim pause. It may have been the fact that there was any grin at all. Watching that stern face attempt to smile was like trying to open a crooked door with rusty hinges. Coach Zim wouldn't have been surprised to hear Craggy's jaw creak with the attempt.

"See ya later, Garth," he finally said. He left the office without closing the door behind him, just to piss Craggy off. He winked at Emma on his way past, then headed back to his classroom to rescue Simple Simon.

After school, he found the rear tires of his pickup truck slashed. He walked around the truck, looking for any other damage, but the flat tires seemed to be it. He stood back and scratched his chin. Without air in the tires the truck sat low in the rear, like a puppy sitting at attention. Whoever did it must have been in a hurry – jab a knife into each tire and drive away, or disappear into the woods behind the school parking lot.

His first thought was Tom Collins. He hadn't been in school that day except when he and his father came in to complain to Craggy, so he'd had all day to do it. Coach Zim wouldn't have been surprised if his old man was in on it, too. It was easy to picture them pulling over to slash his tires while leaving the parking lot. No doubt they were still wound up after talking to Craggy, the elder Collins probably pulling on a bottle of whiskey. It might also have been Collins's friends, but this was a rush job. Those idiots would have wanted to cause some real damage, broken some windows and put some dents in the fenders.

He called Willie's Tire Shop and asked if they'd make a road call. He didn't want to have it towed unless absolutely necessary – too expensive. Willie Marshall, Class of 2002, had taken Coach Zim's history class and counted it among the very few classes he'd enjoyed in four years of high school. He promised to send a guy right over to mount the new tires. In the meantime Coach wandered through the short wooded trail to the practice field to watch the baseball team.

He stayed near the trail entrance, up on the hill overlooking the field. He didn't want to distract the players or draw any attention to himself. The weather was sunny but with a cool breeze. Coach Zim jammed his hands into his coat pockets and stood next to a large oak tree to block the wind. The boys practiced on the right hand side of the field while the girls softball team and the junior varsity baseball team shared the left side. A hundred yards past the field was another field where the field hockey and track teams held their spring practices.

Coach Zim watched his boys – he still thought of them as his boys – for twenty minutes before anyone picked up a ball or glove. It was all calisthenics – pushups, sit-ups, jumping jacks, running in place, more pushups - each one preceded by a sharp burst from Coach Horne's ever-present whistle. It was like watching military boot camp. He didn't have to see the players' faces to know they weren't enjoying themselves. And if they weren't enjoying themselves, they weren't going to play well. It was enough to make him want to grab Horne and kick him in the old nutsack.

While watching, fists clenched tightly inside his pockets in frustration, he noticed the sun gleaming off the chrome of a couple of motorcycles. In the bleachers sat two men in black leather jackets. Coach Zim didn't need to see the Grim Disciples patch on the back to know that one of the men was Tyler Nass, Adam Nass's father. The other biker was no doubt another member of the Disciples. They rarely traveled alone.

He watched the bikers for a couple of minutes but they appeared to be well-behaved. That wouldn't last long, he knew. The previous spring Coach Zim had told them to leave a practice because they were harassing other parents, mostly women, who were there to watch their kids. After overhearing Tyler Nass crudely proposition a particularly attractive and scared-looking parent, he'd approached them.

"Time for you guys to hit the road," he said. "Go find someone else to harass."

Tyler Nass, legs stretched out on the bleachers before him, sneered. "My son's a member of your team, asshole. He's just about the best player you have and I'm making sure you don't fuck up everything I've taught him."

It was doubtful that Tyler Nass had ever played catch with his son Adam. He wasn't the playing catch type. He was more the 'fetch me a beer before I beat your ass' type. Everything that Adam learned came from his friends and the men and women who'd coached him over the years.

"Yes, you've done a fine job with Adam," Coach Zim agreed. "But I'm still going to need to you leave. Now."

"Or what, *Coach*?" said the other Disciple. "What the fuck are you going to do about it?"

Both men were long-haired and bearded. Tyler Nass was average height and thin and had a mean look about him. The other biker was taller and thicker, with a soft beer belly showing from his open leather jacket. The soft bellied one would be no problem. Tyler Nass, while much shorter and smaller, might be a handful. He was small and fierce as a badger, the type that didn't want to just win a fight, but to seriously hurt his opponent. And both men were undoubtedly carrying knives or other small weapons, possibly guns.

Coach Zim wouldn't fight them unless he had to – not out of fear, but because of all the students on the practice field. Besides, he was too old to fight. He could usually charm his way out of any trouble, but these guys weren't the sort to be charmed. He pulled out his cellphone, about to threaten to call the police, when Paul Rivard appeared at his side. His assistant coach stepped in front of him like a protective bulldog and glared at the bikers.

"Hey, dipshits. I'd advise you to leave." When they laughed, he pointed to a large Ford diesel pickup truck, then to their Harley Davidsons. "I'm walking to my truck. If your motorcycles are still parked there when I get in, I'm running them over."

He stomped off toward the parking lot. The taller biker laughed dismissively, but Nass looked worried. Watching the older man stride toward the parking lot, he said, "He ain't kiddin."

"Who, that old guy? You're worried about him?"

"I am." Tyler Nass stood up. "That's Paul Rivard." When the tall biker shook his head, Nass continued, "He's a Vietnam vet. Did two tours there. You know anyone who volunteered for an extra tour in Vietnam?" The tall biker shook his head again. "He's fuckin crazy. I've heard stories about him. If that old bastard says he's gonna run over our bikes, he ain't lyin."

Nass started off toward his motorcycle. The other Disciple stood up slowly but stayed on the bleachers. "Let's just beat the hell out of him. That old bastard runs over my bike, I'll fuckin kill him."

Nass stopped and turned around. Speaking slowly, as though explaining something to a child, he said, "First of all, I ain't gonna beat up a Vietnam vet. You know how much shit will rain down on us for that? Second, do you really think that old man is afraid of dying?"

Seeing that Rivard had almost reached his truck, Nass hurried off toward his Harley. With a last glare at Coach Zim, the tall one followed. Coach Zim smiled as they hurried away. When he turned back around he saw that the entire team had stopped practicing to watch.

"Okay, show's over! Get back to practice!" He then added one of his better lines. "If Coach Rivard and I could get you guys to hustle like that, we'd have a championship year."

Now the bikers had returned, and this year he wasn't available to run them off. Neither was Paul Rivard, at least not for a few more days. For now all the team had was a whistle-blowing fool in short-shorts, who at the moment stood off to the side with his arm around April Spring while the team practiced. When the bikers decided to get rowdy – and it was only a matter of time – Nutsack and Donna Reno, the girls' softball coach, were the only adults available to keep them in line and drive them away. Given a choice of which one he'd put up against the bikers, Coach Zim would choose Donna Reno. The thought of Nutsack Horne trying to intimidate the bikers by flexing and posing made him wince.

From Coach Zim's vantage point atop the hill, Nutsack Horne appeared to be deep in conversation with April and wasn't even watching the players. He watched practice – not much more than a bunch of guys playing an unorganized game at the local sandlot – for a while longer, then headed back along the trail to see if the new tires were installed on his truck.

The jack was being lowered as he approached. His truck sported two new Hercules tires. A young man with a buzz cut and a tattoo on his neck put the jack away and began washing the blue off the tires' white lettering with a spray bottle and a sponge.

"You don't need to do that," Coach Zim said. "Looks like you've worked hard enough. I'll wash the tires."

"I gotta clean them myself," the young man said. Don, according to the name patch on his stained jacket. "Willie says it's good customer service."

"Willie's right about that. How's business?"

"Busy as hell." Don stood up and looked over the tires. "I like these local jobs. Willie's had me doing road calls all over the place. I was down in Saugus this morning, working on a tractor trailer." He wiped his forehead with a greasy hand. "We got twenty people working at the shop now."

Coach Zim whistled. "Wow, twenty. It doesn't seem that long ago that it was just Willie working in the shop. I'm glad to hear you guys are doing well." He reached into his back pocket for his wallet. "What do I owe you for this?"

Don leaned inside his service truck – lettered with **Willie's Tire Shop**, along with the phone number and address, on each door – and came out with a bill. $475.00 for two aggressive tread tires and the roadside call.

"Not bad," Coach said. "But more than I have on me, unless you can take a credit card."

Don shook his head. "Don't worry about it. Most road calls are for bigger accounts, but Willie said to just give you the bill and you can pay whenever." He began to get into his truck, then paused. "Mind if I ask you something?" Without waiting for an answer, he continued, "You're a pretty popular guy around here. I ain't never heard nobody say a bad word about you. So who slashed your tires?"

"I don't know. But whoever did it owes me four hundred and seventy-five dollars."

He waved goodbye to Don and got into his truck. The new tires hummed as he drove across the empty parking lot. The practice field was visible through the bare trees as he drove past. He fought the temptation to watch more of baseball team's practice and instead headed home.

9

Tom Collins returned to school a couple of days later with a shaved head and a swastika tattooed over each ear. The tattoos were the talk of the school, even dominating conversation in the teacher's lounge.

Coach Zim sat at a table during his free period, reading the sports section of the newspaper while snacking on a bag of chips and a soda. He didn't give a shit about Tom Collins's fashion choices and didn't want to get drawn into a conversation about him. Judging by the chatter going on around the room, he was the only one who felt this way.

"Do you think he's a white supremacist?"

"I heard his father also has swastikas tattooed on his head, you just can't see them because of his hair."

"I heard someone dared him to do it for fifty bucks."

Every time the conversation drew closer, Coach Zim leaned his head over the newspaper in hopes that nobody would ask his opinion. His nose was an inch away from an article on Tommy John surgery when Harold Iannucci, the biology teacher, sat down across the table from him.

"So, Coach, wasn't there a recent incident between you and Tom Collins?"

Coach Zim kept his nose in the paper, hoping Iannucci would get the hint. He didn't. He was the type of guy who'd been ignored so many times in his life that he hardly noticed anymore. Iannucci had a pretty good-looking wife and Coach Zim was willing to bet that she'd ignored him at first, too. Probably still did.

First Iannucci cleared his throat. Then he did it again, louder. He tapped on the table. After wondering out loud what would possess a young man to do something so stupid, he leaned forward and tugged at the corner of the newspaper.

Finally, Coach Zim could take no more. He didn't mind Iannucci, which was the only reason he didn't tell him to beat it. But the guy could be as clingy as a freshman cheerleader. Looking around the room, he noted that the handful of other teachers sat in pairs or small groups. He didn't want to join a group of gossipers with nothing better to talk about than a teenager's haircut and tattoos. He also didn't want to get up and sit somewhere else by himself – Iannucci would just follow.

Then he spotted Eileen Campbell, sipping a coffee and staring into space. Eileen taught Home Economics and spent a good deal of her day staring into space. She had long, straight hair, good-looking in a Joni Mitchell hippie girl sort of way. She wasn't known to be a gossip and kept mostly to herself. He'd probably be safe with her.

Grabbing the newspaper, he stood up, avoiding Iannucci's gaze, walked over to Eileen Campbell's corner. She didn't even look up when Coach Zim sat down. He relaxed, glanced at the clock on the wall, and leaned back to read the paper for the final ten minutes of his free period.

"I went on a date last night. A guy I met on an online dating site. For Christians."

Coach Zim glanced up. She was still staring off, and Coach wondered if they'd been making pot brownies in her class. He smiled, just to be polite, and resumed reading.

"I used to believe that nothing could be more uncomfortable than an old-fashioned blind date," she went on. "I was wrong. Last night was my second and last date with someone I met online." Eileen paused for a moment, presumably to allow Coach to ask why. He didn't. "The first guy was thirty-two years old and still lived with his mom. Never moved out. Goes to church every morning, works from home. Creepy."

At this point Coach Zim glanced up, prepared to make a hasty exit. Then he saw Iannucci look over with a hopeful expression. He sighed and hid behind the newspaper as Eileen Campbell told him about her most recent date, a bespectacled man named Bruce with a comb-over and bad breath. Bruce believed that most Christians spend a large amount of their lives fighting the urge to fornicate with others. This, Bruce believed, was unhealthy and brought negative energy into people's lives. Fighting sexual attraction was a waste of such a short lifespan, Bruce reasoned. If God didn't want people to fornicate, he wouldn't have made the desire so strong. Instead, Bruce opined, people should all have sex on the first date. Positive energy, positive vibes, less time fighting an invincible foe.

"Then I asked him, 'What about venereal disease? Do you consider herpes to be part of that positive energy?'"

Coach Zim deliberated making a mad dash for the doorway and roaming the hallways aimlessly until next period, but the bell saved him the hassle. He smiled at Eileen Campbell, nodded to Harold Iannucci, and ran for the door like a fullback hitting the goal line.

He got his first look at Collins less than two minutes later while standing in the hallway outside his classroom, alternately greeting students with a pleasant smile and barking threats at those who misbehaved. Collins walked down the hall like a king to his coronation, surrounded by his gang of delinquent sycophants and turning his head this way and that so that everyone could get a clear view of the swastikas. Most of those who viewed the tattoos appeared disgusted, but several, Coach Zim was disappointed to see, gave Collins high fives and fist bumps.

Noticing Coach Zim, Tom Collins leaned over and whispered something to a few members of his group. They looked over at Coach and burst into laughter as they walked past. A couple of them made jabbing motions. Coach Zim was certain they were referring to his slashed tires. Try as he might to ignore it, Coach Zim felt himself growing angry at the punks. As a teacher he was not supposed to sink to their level – after all, they were a group of immature teenagers and he was a middle-aged man. Even so, it took a great deal of self-control to avoid a confrontation. He imagined squeezing Collins in a headlock and removing those offensive tattoos with a magic eraser. It worked. By the time the bell rang and he entered the classroom, there was a smile on his face.

After the final bell, Coach Zim went to see Principal Craggy. Emma smiled when he entered the outer office. A short plump girl with purple hair tapped and swiped her phone frantically from a chair against the wall.

"He in?" Coach Zim asked.

Emma nodded. "Should I tell El Principal you'd like to speak with him?"

"Nah." Coach Zim opened Craggy's door. "He'll figure it out."

Principal Craggy stood up halfway, then froze when Coach Zim walked in. With a quick wave, Coach Zim plopped onto the couch and stretched out his legs. As expected, Craggy did not look appear happy to see him. He glared for a moment and then sat back down behind his desk.

"What are you doing here, Jim? I'm a very busy man."

"Yes, I saw Anna Dylan outside. Got caught stealing from the cafeteria again, right? Well, you should take it easy on her. Her old man hurt his back at the factory and there's no money coming in."

"How I deal with disciplinary issues is none of your business, Jim. Why are you here?"

Coach Zim held up his hands in a conciliating gesture. Craggy arched his eyebrows. It wasn't like Jim Zimmerman to not meet every contradictory statement with some sort of wiseass response. His behavior was typically more juvenile than that of the students who were sent to Craggy's office every day.

"I'd like to know what you are going to do about Tom Collins."

Craggy sighed and leaned back in his executive chair. "The tattoos. You aren't the first one to come to me with this today. Vice Principal Simon has been here at least five times today demanding that the young man be expelled."

"For possibly the first time ever, I am in complete agreement with Simple Simon. I'm not easily offended, but the swastika is the most evil, offensive symbol in history."

"I agree, Jim. Although many Americans may argue that the Confederate flag is equally offensive, or even more so."

"The Confederate flag is seen by some to be a reminder of slavery and black oppression, but it is also considered a symbol of southern pride by many people. I don't know of anyone who considers the swastika to be a symbol of pride. Imagine the Dukes of Hazzard with a swastika on their car. Sort of adds a different vibe, wouldn't you say? The swastika is a symbol of evil and death. Nothing else."

"You'll get no argument from me," Craggy said.

"So are you going to expel him?"

Expelling Tom Collins was not an option, Craggy explained. For one thing, his father seemed quite serious about pursuing legal action against the school because of the alleged locker incident. And, although freedom of speech was being crushed by the government and the media in most of America, it was still alive and well in the hallways of Apple Brook High. He could send a student home if he or she wore a particularly profane shirt to school, but tattoos were something else. Because tattoos on teenagers was a relatively new occurrence – twenty, even ten years ago, very few teenagers had even one tattoo – there were no real rules regarding their content.

"It's not like I can tell Collins to go home and remove his tattoos," Craggy said helplessly.

"Too bad they weren't Confederate flags," Coach Zim mused. "Luther would remove them for him."

"That would save me a lot of hassle," Craggy agreed. "Here's what I'll do: Tom Collins will have to wear a hat to cover the tattoos. If not, he cannot attend school until his hair has grown in enough to hide them."

"I'd rather you expelled him, but that sounds fair," said Coach Zim.

"Anything else?"

Yeah, he wanted to say. Your idiot nephew is going to singlehandedly ruin the proud baseball program this school has built up over decades in a matter of weeks. Kids that have a chance of doing something they can take pride in their entire lives are instead going to feel nothing but embarrassment because they were a part of the worst team ever at Apple Brook High. Players with a chance at college scholarships, kids like Adam Nass, who otherwise wouldn't be able to attend college, are going to miss out because Todd Horne isn't teaching them anything. Give the job to somebody more deserving. Paul Rivard. The JV coach. The softball coach. Luther the janitor. Eileen Campbell the home economics teacher. Anyone.

"No, that's it."

"Good. On your way out, tell Ms. Dylan I'm ready to see her. And Jim," Craggy said, as Coach Zim stood up, "I'd appreciate it if you would knock before you enter my office. I am the principal here, and I deserve some respect."

"I'll do my best to remember that," Coach Zim said. "Just to be safe, though, I'd avoid whacking off in here. I tend to be forgetful."

In the outer office, he smiled at Anna Dylan and informed her that Principal Craggy would see her now. And, he added, there was no reason to knock on the door. Just go right in.

10

Paul Rivard entered Coach Zim's classroom a half hour before classes began. He sat on the edge of Coach Zim's desk and said, "I attended my first baseball practice with Coach Dipshit yesterday afternoon."

It had been a particularly bad practice, even by Todd Horne's standards. An extra half hour of calisthenics before practice, on top of the usual half hour, because somebody farted and the team burst into laughter while Horne was trying to talk. Added to five laps around the practice field, that left about fifteen minutes for actual baseball practice. The players did their exercises at half-speed, the laps at slightly more than a walk.

On top of that, there were half a dozen bikers, members of the Grim Disciples, lying around in the bleachers, smoking pot and drinking beer and yelling insults at anyone within shouting distance. According to Rivard, Coach Horne's way of dealing with this threat was to pull his sleeves all the way up and flex his arms for the entire practice. Since he flexed his legs about ninety percent of the time, the additional flexing sapped his energy and left him largely immobile. It didn't much matter, though. He really had nothing else to do, with the team spending most of their time jumping and squatting and running.

Coach Zim listened and observed Rivard growing angrier with every passing minute. "What did you do?" he asked.

Not much, he explained, because it was his first practice under a new head coach and he wanted to get a feel for how things were run. After the first half hour – dedicated exclusively to jumping jacks, squat thrusts, push-ups, sit-ups and wind sprints – Rivard knew they were in big trouble. Half an hour after that, he was tempted to punch Horne in the face – "the only part of his body that wasn't flexed" – and take over. But Paul Rivard was a man who obeyed the chain of command and rarely bucked authority, and so he stood by and quietly seethed.

"You know, my first CO in Nam was this guy named Lenny Fish. Funny name, right? He even looked like a fish – thin face, big eyes, no lips. I'll never forget him. Guy thought he was King Shit of Turd Island. Bossing everyone around, making us do useless, petty shit. Dig holes after humping five miles in the jungle and fill them in the morning for no reason, shit like that." He gazed out the window at the morning sunshine. "We put up with it, but then he got four guys killed during a firefight. He got it in the back of the head during the next firefight. From our side."

Coach Zim stared at him, wide-eyed. "Did you do it?"

"Shit, no. He was an asshole, but I wouldn't shoot a commanding officer. I didn't feel any anger toward whoever did it, though." He turned to look at Coach Zim. "My point is that Horne is more incompetent than that CO, and judging by the looks in most of these kids' eyes, he'd get it if they were holding rifles."

"I guess that's why they don't hand out guns to the players."

Rivard went on to describe how Horne blew his whistle after every exercise to signal the beginning of another one, and how he was going to jam the whistle down Horne's throat if he did it again at that afternoon's practice. The new coach was also very close to April Spring, the team manager. April often sat in the bleachers to observe practice, but with the Grim Disciples taking up residence there it wasn't a good idea for a cute eighteen-year-old girl to be anywhere near them. As it was, they yelled and whistled at her, asking if she'd like a ride on their hogs. Horne responded by putting his arm around her protectively. A good reaction, except that he never let her go. The entire practice he stood with his arm around the girl. At times his hand drifted down to her waist, rubbing her lower back. Rivard said it was unclear whether the girl minded or not.

When the players finally picked up gloves and bats, they were either worn out from all the exercises or too discouraged to care. The result was a team that, in Paul Rivard's words, "couldn't run, hit, or throw worth a shit." Almost every pitch thrown by Brock Cooke hit the dirt in front of the plate; Robert Williams tried a head-first slide – the Black Barracuda, he called it - and slammed into the bag so hard he ended up with a fat lip and bloody nose; Dallas Thompson, shagging flies, caught one. Out of fifty. And on and on. Adam Nass was distracted, not surprising with his father's gang harassing him. Devin Krane, normally the most positive, upbeat player on the team, a cheerleader in a baseball uniform, moped around like his dog had died.

Worse than anything, though, was the sound of practice. Or rather, the lack of sound. Balls slapping heavily into gloves, the clink of an aluminum bat and the crack of a wooden one making contact with a fastball, the encouragement of a coach to run faster, throw harder, focus, the sound of players joking around. Most importantly, the laughter. That was it, Rivard said. There was no longer any laughter. The bad throws and catches weren't the problem; they'd coached teams that were horrible during spring practice. The 2008 team was probably the worst practicing team ever, and they'd won the state championship. Bad practices happen. But even when practice is going badly, it should still be fun. The sound of teenaged boys laughing and goofing off should always be there, even during the worst practice.

Coach Zim nodded. There was no denying that he felt a trace of enjoyment watching Craggy's replacement for him fall flat on his face. However, any pleasure he got from Nutsack's struggles was wiped away by the knowledge that good, hard-working, talented kids were losing out on what should have been a fun, valuable experience. There was nothing like the bond formed by those belonging to a good high school team. Coach Zim would be willing to bet that many professional athletes remained close to their high school teammates, maybe even more so than their professional teammates, because high school is such an impressionable time of life.

Two girls walked into the classroom. Coach Zim glanced up at the clock above the door. 7:45, ten minutes before the start of the first class. Most students avoided the classroom until the last possible moment, but there were always those who arrived early, whether it was to study, avoid trouble, or just find a quiet place. Coach Zim often found himself enjoying early morning conversations with these students, but today he was glad to see the girls take seats in the back row. He was also glad to see them lean their heads toward each other in deep, quiet conversation, instead of having them bent over some sort of small screen.

"I don't think I can assist this dipshit for an entire season," Paul Rivard was saying. "I'm not even sure I'll make it through the week. Our first game is Thursday. That's the day after tomorrow. We don't have a chance in hell of winning a game with that bozo coaching."

"Stick with it," Coach Zim advised, as he had the players. "You're a good coach and those kids are good players. Don't let Nutsack ruin that. You are the only one who can prevent him from completely destroying what we built."

Rivard gazed out the window, a determined expression settling on his face. Coach Zim knew he had him and tried hard not to smile. This was a call to action, a mission to accomplish, and there was no way an old soldier like Rivard could say no. The future of those kids, of the entire program, was his to save. It wasn't exactly engaging the Vietcong in a firefight in the middle of the jungle, but at least the objective was clear.

"Damn, you're right. That leg shaving idiot isn't going to ruin this season for those kids, not if I have anything to say about it."

"Just don't go getting yourself fired," Coach Zim said. "If Horne goes running to Uncle Garth, Craggy wouldn't think twice about letting you go. Then those kids will be helpless."

"Right, right." Rivard slid off the desk and made his way to the doorway that connected their classrooms. "This situation calls for stealth. He won't even know what hit him, that leg shaving, shorts wearing fairy." He was mumbling to himself as he opened the door, but within seconds he barked, "Page! Get your butt away from my desk! If I catch you leaning against my desk again it's a week's detention! And if I end up getting poked, prodded, pricked or blown up by anything you put in the area, your own mother won't recognize you when I'm finished with you! Oh, I have your attention now, do I?"

His yelling was still audible with the door closed. The girls in the back row stared at the door with frightened expressions and then glanced at him appreciatively. Coach

Zim smiled. Coming across as a good, kind teacher was much easier with a man like Paul Rivard in the next room.

The sun shone warm and bright that afternoon, the temperature right around sixty degrees. The spring air smelled as clean as a freshly scrubbed room, and Coach Zim felt the surge of joy that presented itself every year as spring took hold after a long cold winter.

That feeling quickly faded as he approached his truck. Another tire had been slashed, one of the new ones on the back. The first time he'd dealt with it well. He'd been angry and wanted to find out who slashed his tires, but chalked it up to the risks associated with teaching high school. Instead of interrogating everyone he suspected might be involved, he'd counted himself thankful that it didn't happen more often.

This time he was pissed off. He looked around the parking lot for anyone who appeared suspicious but saw nothing. He scanned the forest along the edge of the parking lot and again found nothing. Grumbling, he tossed his jacket and bag onto the seat and kneeled down behind the truck to lower the spare tire. He was thankful for the warm weather. A few weeks earlier and he would have been kneeling in snow.

The spare was corroded to the bottom of the truck, but after some wiggling and grunting and swearing it came loose. He took the jack and tools from beneath the back seat and within half an hour had the spare mounted and the slashed tire in the bed of the truck. He stared at it for a few moments and then slammed the tailgate closed. Now he had to bring the truck into the shop to have a new tire mounted and the spare replaced. He glanced up frequently while he worked, expecting to see Tom Collins or one of his flunkies watching and laughing, but there was nobody. For all he knew it could have happened at eight o'clock that morning.

The parking lot was empty save for a few cars scattered here and there like random pieces on a checkerboard. He drove away and made it as far as the front of the school, where he pulled into a parking spot. He knew he shouldn't do it, but he got out, locked the door, and walked down the nearby trail to the hill overlooking the practice field. The trees were still bare, with leaves just beginning to bud, and his truck was visible from the top of the hill. If anyone messed with it, he'd be able to see them.

The smell of marijuana hung heavily in the air. Coach Zim saw a group of three teenagers – two boys and a girl - sitting about fifty feet away, passing a joint. He cleared his throat, loudly. The teens looked hazily in his direction, then bolted to their feet faster than startled dogs. The girl deftly slipped the joint into her bag while the boys picked up their backpacks. They walked past him single-file – the first boy mumbling hello, the girl flashing a bright stoner's grin, the other boy staring at the ground, saying nothing – and disappeared up the trail toward the school.

Coach watched them go and took a seat. The smell of pot still hung in the air. To his surprise he found it comforting, the way the smell of a blueberry pie always brought back memories of his Aunt Dorothy. He'd never smoked much and it had been over twenty years since he'd last done so, but when he was younger he'd had good times at parties and concerts where a haze of pot smoke hung in the air.

Of course pot back then was a lot more organic and weak than what the kids smoked today. And pot was the least of their worries nowadays with meth and heroin taking over and destroying young lives. A couple of towns over, in Bryant Falls, there had been six deaths already this year from heroin, with many more sent to the hospital. Apple Brook saw its share of addicts, but not as many as Bryant Falls.

Coach Zim prayed it stayed that way, but he'd heard rumors that the Grim Disciples were selling heroin. Sitting atop the hill like a sports Buddha, gazing down as the teams practiced, he wondered if that was why they hung around the high school practices and games. He resolved to keep an eye on them.

Not today, though, because the bleachers were empty of bikers. In their stead sat April, the varsity team manager, with Coach Horne right next to her. On the field, the varsity appeared to be scrimmaging the junior varsity. Paul Rivard umpired – even this far away Coach Zim recognized his squat, angry form – and Emilio Fernandez, the JV coach, stood on the first base line, occasionally barking orders.

Things looked bad, at least for the varsity squad. Coach Zim watched three innings, and by his calculations the JV team was ahead by seven runs. He felt a great sadness watching the young men he had molded into a sharp, attentive squad play as though they didn't want to be there. Coach Rivard tried his best to encourage the team, but it was as though they didn't hear him. Like they didn't want to hear him.

For his part, Nutsack Horne did next to nothing. He blew the whistle every time a new player was due up at bat, as though the kids didn't know. After half an inning, Paul Rivard walked over to the bleachers and ripped the whistle from around Nutsack's neck before returning to the field. From that point on, so far as Coach Zim could tell, Horne didn't pay any attention to the game. Instead, he talked with April and a few other female students sitting on the bleachers.

Coach Zim had seen enough. He stood up and walked slowly down the trail, feeling a bit guilty, like a scorned lover who'd spied on his ex and her new lover. He couldn't let go of the team, and what he'd seen on the practice field hadn't helped matters any. It occurred to him, as he emerged from the trail and gazed at the brick facade of Apple Brook High School, that Craggy was most likely still in his office, sipping booze and making some poor kid's life miserable. Maybe he should pay the principal a visit. After all, this was all his fault.

A blond girl in a short skirt sat by herself on one of the benches at the front of the school. She was bent over, head in hands, obviously crying about some terrible high school malady that would be replaced by something just as dreadful tomorrow. Best to leave her alone, Coach Zim told himself.

But the girl looked up, and Coach Zim recognized her as one of the top students in the junior class. He also noticed the swollen eyes and cheeks smeared with glistening tears. Stuffing his keys back into his pocket, he approached her.

"Hi, Iris. Something wrong?"

She looked up, sniffed, wiped her cheeks with the back of a hand, and tried to smile. "Hi, Coach Zim. I'm just having a bad day, that's all."

He nodded toward the bench. She slid over. He glanced at her scrawny legs and realized he weighed more than twice what she did.

"I wish I'd run into you about an hour ago," he said. "I had a flat tire when I came out of school. You could have helped me fix it."

She smiled for a moment, and then it faded. "I've got a C in Creative Writing because my last paper was two days late and Mister Beaudoin won't accept it. I tried to tell him my grandfather got really sick and we went to see him at a hospital in Connecticut and I didn't bring my iPad and our car broke down and we didn't get back until yesterday, but he doesn't care!"

She covered her face and started bawling. Coach Zim sat silently for a moment, trying to figure out what he could say to stop her from crying. Forty-eight years old and he still didn't understand women, and teenagers were the worst.

"Well, is a C so bad?"

Wrong answer. She lowered her hands and stared at him in disbelief.

"Are you kidding me? I've never even had a B. In my life!" She sniffed and continued, "I have it all planned out. Finish in the top five in my class and get a scholarship to an Ivy League school. Do you know what a C will do to my grade point average? You think any good school will want me then?"

The tears again began to flow. These poor kids are under so much pressure, Coach Zim thought. Whether from teachers, parents or of their own making, it was too much. But, that's how the world worked. You're nothing without a college diploma nowadays.

"You explained all this to Mister Beaudoin?"

"Uh-huh. Just now. He's so mean!"

He couldn't disagree with that. Bruce Beaudoin was a real asshole, apparently unhappy with his lot in life as a high school writing instructor instead of the best-selling novelist he believed – without a shred of proof – he deserved to be. In perhaps an effort to appease his ego, Beaudoin enjoyed a reputation as the school lothario, rumored to have bedded several female faculty members. Judging by the fact that she was still married to him, Mrs. Beaudoin was most likely unaware of her husband's extracurricular activities. Normally Coach Zim wouldn't consider blackmailing a fellow teacher, but Beaudoin was a jerk who enjoyed having the power to make teenage girls cry.

"I'll have a talk with Mister Beaudoin for you. We'll see if we can get this straightened out."

"Oh, thank you, Coach Zim!" Iris leaned over and gave him a hug. "You're the best!"

He accepted the hug awkwardly – these days it was dangerous to reciprocate – and asked if she needed a ride home. She nodded, but her tear-streaked face grew concerned as she approached the passenger side of the pickup truck. He noticed her staring at the rusty fenders.

"She don't look like much, but she rides great," Coach Zim said, unlocking the passenger door. He smiled. "New tires."

11

Todd Horne awoke early Thursday morning and saw the sunlight stretching across his blankets. He tried unsuccessfully to wipe the sun away and then swore at it. First game of the season, and he'd been hoping for a rainout. He got out of bed – he slept naked because clothes felt restricting over his massive muscles – dropped to the floor and did fifty push-ups.

After going to the bathroom, he returned to the bedroom and, still naked, lifted a pair of forty-pound dumbbells and banged out three sets of curls, eight reps each. Then he posed in front of a mirror that took up almost an entire wall of his bedroom, the shades open because the morning sunlight helped his muscles appear more ripped.

In the shower he shaved his legs, arms, and chest. He dressed in his favorite pair of white shorts (he owned fifteen) and an extra small Apple Brook Warriors polo shirt, so tight around the biceps that it restricted his blood flow and made the veins in his arms pop freakishly. He stared at himself in the mirror for a few minutes, turning and flexing at different angles. Then he went to the kitchen, ate a bowl of plain oatmeal with blueberries and honey and washed it down with a protein drink.

After brushing his teeth, Horne returned to the bedroom. He put on his Apple Brook baseball hat and gazed in the mirror one more time. I look like a baseball coach, he told himself. The look would be complete when he got to school and slipped one of the dozen whistles he kept in his desk drawer around his neck. That asshole assistant coach Paul Rivard had ripped one off his neck the other day without even saying why. Pretty brazen for an old man, but word was he was half-nuts from Vietnam. After having his whistle removed Horne had stood up and flexed, but Rivard hadn't even flinched. The old guy had obviously lost touch with reality.

He wanted to win today. The team had a pretty good chance, in his opinion. The pitcher who'd somehow benched more than him was on the mound, and a couple other kids were looking good. He didn't know any of their names yet, but it had only been a few weeks and he recognized most of their faces, which was the important thing. They'd certainly be fitter than the other team, thanks to his heavy calisthenics regimen. And he was undoubtedly thicker and more ripped than any other coach in the state, so the intimidation factor was in the Warrior's favor before the game even began. Horne flexed again in the mirror, imagining the opposing coach shaking in his cleats, scared shitless.

After they won, Horne planned to throw a party. Not for the players – they were supposed to be on their best behavior during the season. But April and her friends could come over and celebrate the win with him in his hot tub. He imagined April stripping naked in the hot tub, felt himself becoming hard, and dropped to the floor to bang out another fifty pushups. He was tempted to fill a syringe with Winstrol and jab it into his ass, but he wasn't due to take it for a couple more days and didn't want to screw up his cycle.

He jumped up and did a most muscular pose until curly veins popped out and crawled down his forehead. He was ready. Come on. *Come on*! He grabbed his bag and left the house, pumped to win his first game as head coach.

Coach Zim stood slightly slumped, staring at himself in the bedroom mirror. Polo shirt, khakis, a thin LL Bean fleece pullover. For the first time in twenty-five years he wasn't wearing an Apple Brook baseball hat and windbreaker.

"This doesn't feel right. It's like Superman without his cape."

Angela sat in a nearby chair, wearing a robe, painting her toenails bright green. "You're a great coach, Jim. But Superman?"

That got a small smile. "You know what I mean. I always wear the same thing, every game day. Khakis, red shirt, red underwear, red socks, red Apple Brook hat and jacket, white sneakers. This doesn't feel right."

"So change. Wear the clothes you always wear when there's a game."

"But I'm not the coach anymore." He sat down heavily at the end of the bed. "You think Tom Landry continued to wear his Fedora every Sunday after he retired?"

"Not sure who Tom Landry is, but I imagine he wore his Fedora if he felt like it."

"You gonna listen to me announce the game this afternoon?"

"Of course. I have an article to finish, but the radio on the desk will be tuned to MBL." She looked up. "How do you feel about it?"

"Uncomfortable. What if I want to tell Krane to move to the left, or yell to Thompson to play deeper? The umpire'll probably frown at my instructions coming from the PA system. Or what if I swear on the air? I tend to do that when I watch games."

"You'll be fine. You're announcing with a student, right?"

He nodded. "Charlie DeMar. Funny kid. Smartass funny. Not sure how he got this job."

"You don't usually swear around students. You'll be fine."

She was right, of course. Usually was. This was just another transition, from player to coach and now to announcer. He'd succeeded at the first two; announcing shouldn't be any different.

He left the windbreaker at home but decided to wear the Apple Brook baseball hat. Nothing wrong with having a little school spirit, even if he was just an announcer now.

"Coach Zim, can I talk to you for a minute?"

He was on his way to the cafeteria – Steak-ums, his favorite – but he nodded to Ackerson and moved to the side of the hallway. "How's it going, Brandon?"

The boy shook his head. "Not too good. I got into some trouble with Miss Folger today."

"Really?" Coach Zim was surprised. Ackerson was the best artist in the school, including Kate Folger, and never seemed to cause trouble. "Did you mouth off to her?"

"No, nothing like that. She gave us an assignment, draw something meaningful to you. That's all she said. Didn't give any other instructions or specifics."

"Uh-huh. And what did you draw?"

"A group of couples holding hands. Gay couples and straight couples."

"Well, that may make someone of Miss Folger's age uncomfortable, but you can't get into trouble for that."

"That wasn't the problem."

Coach Zim's eyes narrowed. "What *was* the problem?"

Blushing slightly, Ackerson said, "The couples were naked. Holding hands, naked. She said it was pornography and wouldn't give me credit for the assignment. Said I'll have to go to the principal's office if I show up with pornography again."

Coach Zim was confused. "She's been an artist for a long time. A *long* time," he added, unable to help himself. "She's seen nudity before. What's the big deal?"

"Because some of the couples were gay. Nudity is fine, but gay nudity isn't."

"Ah. I see. But she must have known gay artists. I'm sure there are gay artists. That famous guy who painted the soup cans, he always seemed pretty gay to me."

"That's not very politically correct."

"Boo-hoo, Ackerson. You know I didn't mean anything by it."

"Anyway, I was hoping that you might have a talk with Miss Folger." Ackerson looked uncomfortable. "Maybe convince her to give me credit. At least partial credit. I mean, I did the assignment."

Coach Zim sighed. "When did I become everyone's intermediary?"

That morning, before classes began, he'd walked to the English wing to have a talk with Mr. Beaudoin about Iris Dore's late assignment. The conversation had begun pleasantly enough – Beaudoin had a set of four Patriots tickets that he'd won in a radio contest but would never use, tenth row on the forty yard line, and asked Coach Zim if he'd like to buy them for fifty dollars. Hell, yes. He pulled two twenties and a ten from his wallet. Beaudoin handed him the tickets. So far, so good.

But then Coach Zim mentioned that he'd spoken with Iris about her late assignment. He described Iris as an exemplary student – among the best in the school – and said he believed the story about her grandfather. In fact, he'd called Iris's house the previous evening and her mother had corroborated the entire story. The girl had completed her work, he told Beaudoin, but had no way to turn it in. If nothing else she deserved partial credit, and maybe a chance to do some extra credit work to make up the full grade.

Beaudoin leaned back in his chair, fingers crossed behind his head. "So I'm just supposed to give away free grades because a girl has a good reputation? When I was at Columbia, a paper not turned in on time was a zero. No excuses. And that's how I run my class."

"This isn't college, Beaudoin. This girl wants to go to a good school like Columbia but might not have a chance if you give her a zero on this paper. She said this assignment is worth as much as the final exam, and if she gets a zero the highest grade she can earn for the quarter is a C."

"That's correct. And she should have thought of that before going away without her school-issued iPad if her assignment was saved on it. Being prepared is half the battle. You as a baseball coach should know that."

Was everyone saving up their assholeness specifically for him? It was too early to argue with this jerk. Instead, Coach Zim got right to the point. He explained that he knew what Beaudoin and Eileen Campbell had been up to twice a week after school behind the maintenance shed the previous fall (before she got into online dating, apparently). If Iris did not receive full credit for her paper, Mrs. Beaudoin might get an anonymous phone call regarding her husband's afternoon trysts. There were witnesses to other infidelities as well, he told Beaudoin.

"As you said, being prepared is half the battle," Coach Zim said.

The smirk disappeared from Beaudoin's face. It gave Coach Zim more pleasure than he cared to admit. Beaudoin nodded, agreed to change Iris's grades, and said he wanted his Patriots tickets back. Coach Zim shook his head, waved the tickets and left the room.

Now he looked down at Ackerson. "Can I see the picture?"

Ackerson shrugged. "Miss Folger kept it. You can see it if she has it. She probably threw it away."

Coach Zim's stomach growled. "I'll talk to her, because I don't think you did anything wrong. But I can't promise it'll help. Miss Folger can be stubborn."

Ackerson nodded, but seemed distracted. Coach Zim followed his gaze down the hallway, where Collins and a couple of his friends were staring at them and laughing.

"That idiot still hassling you?"

"No more than usual, I guess," Ackerson said. He shrugged again.

"If it makes you feel any better, he may be laughing at me and not you. Pretty sure he's slashed three of my tires in the past week. And there's a good chance he's going to sue me or the school for allegedly stuffing him in a locker."

Ackerson smiled. "I heard about that."

"But don't worry, Ackerson." Coach Zim clapped him on the shoulder, causing the boy's knees to buckle. "Guys like that usually get what's coming to them." His stomach growled again. "And now I need to get to the caf before they run out of Steak-ums."

He glanced back at Collins one more time before hurrying off to the cafeteria for lunch.

He ran into Ackerson again after school, on his way out the door.

"Brandon, you want a ride to the baseball game?"

"Baseball's not really my thing, Coach. Sorry. Besides, I have an art club meeting."

"Oh, come on. You can sit up in the booth with me. Best seat in the house. I think." He paused and scratched his chin. "I've never actually been up there."

Ackerson shook his head. "Another time, Coach. But good luck."

Coach Zim waved goodbye and hurried out the door. He didn't notice Tom Collins and his friends waiting around the corner, watching.

12

The game didn't start until 3:30, an hour and a half after school got out, but Coach Zim finished up in his classroom and made the ten-minute drive to the baseball stadium by 2:30. He wanted to be there early, try out the announcing equipment and get a good feel for the booth. Also, he wasn't exactly sure where the booth was located. He parked in the lot across the street from the park.

Paul Rivard pulled in next to him. Rivard hefted a large, heavy mesh bag full of helmets and baseballs from the bed of his pickup. He carried it easily over his shoulder as they walked toward the stadium.

"Got a feeling about this one, Paul?"

"My hope is that Coach Horne gets a foul ball to the nut sack and has to leave. Because, honestly, that's the only hope these kids have."

"Anything you can do?"

"Yeah, I could kick him in the nuts before the game. Other than that, we're fucked." They reached the end of the parking lot and crossed the street. "Jesus, it's gonna seem weird being in that dugout without you."

"You're telling me. I've dreamt of that dugout every night for the past week."

They reached the sidewalk and noticed Luther strolling toward them, slow and dangerous, like walking thunder. They waited. Since Coaches Zim and Rivard were two of the only teachers the janitor liked, he said hello and fell in with them.

"Hey Luther. Early today, aren't you?"

"You know me, Coach Zim. First game of the season always gets me excited."

"Plus the ticket booth isn't open yet, so you get in free," Rivard said.

"There's that too."

"You usually punch in right about now, don't you?" Coach Zim said. "Principal Craggy doesn't take well to tardiness."

"Craggy can kiss my black ass. He ain't never said nothin bout being late to me yet."

Rivard looked up at Luther. "Yeah, I have a feeling he's probably not going to."

They arrived at the front gate of Duke Vincent Field, named after Coach Zim's predecessor as Apple Brook High's head baseball coach. In the years when Jim Zimmerman played and up until fifteen years ago, the field had been a joke. The infield was rough and lumpy and the outfield dipped down so far in left field that the ground would remain sopping wet two days after a rain storm. The stadium, simply known as Apple Brook Field back then, seated about two hundred people on wooden benches so old and worn that more than one person had left a game and gone straight to the emergency room to have a large splinter removed from their backside.

And then, fifteen years ago, on Halloween night, a smoldering cigarette butt left by a group of teenagers who'd gone to the field to get drunk and high caught one of the dry old benches on fire. The place burned in less than half an hour, just enough time for the town's fire department to arrive and watch the old wooden canopy collapse and crush the benches and dugouts beneath.

The fire was the talk of the town for weeks. Townspeople pointed fingers at the teenagers responsible for the fire, calling for long jail sentences for the kids and large fines for the parents. Cooler heads – led by Coach Zim – finally prevailed, and people realized that the teens may have actually done the town a favor by destroying the old place. As Coach Zim said, "The place was a tinderbox; better it happen now than in the middle of a game."

The town applied for and received a grant to rebuild the bleachers. The new building stretched from first base to third, with a brick exterior facing the road and new, comfortable seats with drink holders in place of the old wooden benches. Instead of seating two hundred the place now held seven hundred fans, with a large announcer's booth up high in the center. A net spanned the entire seating area from third base to first, eliminating the risk of catching a foul ball to the face, always a danger in the old bleachers. The new building even had restrooms, eliminating the old porta-potties which once lined the right field fence. The town took the remaining money left from the grant to level the outfield and install an irrigation system.

A sign atop the front of the building, sixty feet in the air, announced it as Duke Vincent Field. There had been some debate about what to name the stadium – many wanted to name it Jim Zimmerman Stadium. Coach quickly put an end to the debate by throwing his support behind naming it after the late Duke Vincent. Maybe, he said, after he was retired he'd consider having something named after him. But that was a long, long way in the future.

Not so long as he'd imagined, turned out. He gazed up at Duke's name and hoped they never changed the name of the stadium. Coaches who got fired didn't deserve to have fields named after them.

The gate was already open. It was wide and led to a small parking lot next to the field. Coach was always baffled when people parked there because vehicles tended to end up with smashed windshields, courtesy of foul balls. Kept the local glass companies in business, at least.

They stood and talked by the gate for a few minutes as adults and teenagers working the ticket booth and concession stands arrived. They eventually made their way inside, stopping at the small gate in the chain link fence along the first base line that opened onto the field.

"Guess I'd better get set up," Rivard said, lifting the latch. He gazed at the empty field. "If we're lucky Nutsack won't show up."

"Yeah, and I should get up in the booth. Want to come up, Luther?"

"No thanks, Coach. I like my seat in the bleachers."

A small car with rap music pounding from the open windows raced through the gates and squealed to a stop next to the fence. Five young men in clean red and white Apple Brook uniforms piled out, hats and gloves in hand. As they approached, Rivard opened the gate.

"Good luck, boys," Coach Zim said.

"Wish you were out there with us," Dallas Thompson said. He led the others onto the field.

"I'll be up above, watching. Like God, but much less powerful."

The players nodded sadly as they filed through the gate.

"Jesus, you guys ain't going to a funeral!" Coach Rivard barked. "Get your asses in there and warm up!" He watched them, shaking his head. Then he looked up at Coach Zim and smiled. "As bad as this might get, there's still nothing better than a baseball game."

Watching Rivard follow the players onto the field, Coach Zim nodded in agreement. Nothing like it. From the distance came a deep rumble, different from the dead pounding thud of rap music through a subwoofer. This was powerful, like approaching thunder.

Three Harley Davidsons rolled through the gate. They pulled to a stop against the chain link fence, not far from the gate. The elderly man in the ticket booth scowled at them but didn't leave his seat.

"Afternoon, Coach," said Tyler Nass. He got off his bike and leaned against the fence, running a tattooed hand through his long hair. Like the two other bikers he wore sunglasses and a leather jacket with a Disciples patch on the back. "Or should I say, ex-Coach."

Coach Zim smiled.

The bikers turned their gazes to Luther.

"You boys got somethin you wanna say to me?" Luther stepped forward. The bikers continued to stare but said nothing.

Two small cars, low to the ground and whining like lawnmowers, zipped into the parking lot. More Apple Brook players. Tyler Nass looked over, recognized his son, and whooped. "Hey Nass, kick some ass!" he yelled.

Adam smiled, looking embarrassed. The players greeted Coach Zim sadly as they passed through the fence. On the other side, Coach Rivard barked that they were late, called them dipshits and ordered them to begin warming up.

"Hey son," Tyler Nass said as Adam walked past, "don't fuck up or I'll take it out on your hide. I got money riding on this game." He laughed. "If you win, Sexy Sherri said there's a blowjob in it for you."

Adam avoided his father's gaze and glanced up at Coach Zim, who winked and wished him luck. The players jogged into the outfield and began stretching and throwing baseballs back and forth.

"You've got a good kid there, Nass. I have no idea how, but he is a good kid. Why don't you leave alone? You're embarrassing him."

"Know what's embarrassing? Getting fired from coaching a high school team." Nass coughed and spit a glob near Coach Zim's feet. "Where do you go from there? Coaching Little League? Quite a career you've got there, *Coach.*"

"And what's your career, Nass? Rapist? Drug dealer? Yeah, you've made your family real proud."

Nass straightened up from the fence and stepped forward, his fellow Disciples falling in behind him. Coach Zim stood his ground, Luther beside him.

"Somebody don't step back soon, they's gonna be so much leather lyin on the ground it'll look like someone run over a cow," Luther growled.

The bikers looked at one another but did not back off.

"Coach! Coach Zim! Up here!" Charlie DeMar's happy round face looked down at him from the bleachers. "I've been looking for you. The game starts in half an hour. You coming up to the booth soon?"

Coach Zim nodded to him, then turned back to Nass. "Enjoy the game, boys. You coming, Luther?"

Luther glared for another moment at the bikers, then followed Coach Zim up the stairs to the bleachers. Finding his favorite seat in the back row, Luther wished Coach Zim good luck. Coach waved a thank you, found the stairs leading to the booth and headed up.

From his seat in the booth, Coach Zim watched the teams warm up. The Augusta Tigers wore purple and grey uniforms and were coached by Mike Dumont, who stood only a couple inches over five feet tall but had a voice like a circus barker. He should be an announcer, Coach Zim thought while eyeing the microphone.

The Tigers weren't a very good team because Mike Dumont wasn't a very good coach, but Coach Zim had always gotten along very well with him. He went down to the front row of the bleachers near the visitor's dugout to say hello. They chatted for a few minutes and then wished each other luck. They shook hands as Todd Horne jogged onto the field in short shorts, blowing his whistle. Mike Dumont could only stare in wonder as Coach Zim said goodbye and returned to the announcer's booth.

Charlie DeMar had welcomed Coach Zim into the booth like a king greeting a visiting dignitary, complete with grand sweeping motions with his arms while showing Coach around. The booth was basic – a table with microphones, laptop computers, a couple of chairs, and a tray of food (grapes, twinkies and soda) off to the side. Charlie explained how everything worked while he set up. He typed a few things and viewed a screen that made no sense to Coach Zim and made a phone call to WMBL's station, where his uncle sat during the game, monitoring the broadcast and making any necessary changes to the equipment there. Once the signal was verified and they were given the okay by his uncle, Charlie showed Coach Zim where he'd sit and gave a quick explanation of how the broadcast would work.

"I'll do the play by play stuff," Charlie said, sitting next to Coach Zim and setting up a second microphone. "You know, introduce the players by name and number as they come to bat, maybe give a batting average or something like that." There was a second laptop opened next to him and he pointed at the screen – players' names and numbers, it looked like, but he was clicking too fast for Coach Zim to be sure. "Your job, Coach, is to be the expert – share a little info that people might want to know about our players, the field, the opposition, stuff like that. I'm the robot giving basic statistics. You're the expert."

Coach nodded. It was discomforting to receive instructions from a teenager, especially Charlie DeMar, whose round face almost always wore a mischievous smile. He hoped the kid wasn't going to prank him to make his friends laugh.

"How many people are listening, do you know?"

"Yup, we have that info." Charlie rolled his chair to the first computer and hit a few keys. "Last year we averaged about forty-two listeners per game."

"Are you kidding me?"

"No. Most people who want to hear the game just come to the home games. We only broadcast away games during the playoffs. We get more listeners then."

Not exactly the big time, Coach thought.

"Plus," continued Charlie, "Mister Carey was doing the commentary with me last year. I had him for algebra and he's the only person who can make baseball sound more boring than math. Most people would rather listen to static. Or even country music."

"I like country music," said Coach Zim.

"Of course you do."

There was a sharp burst of rap music. Charlie picked up his phone and walked to the back the booth. Coach Zim wondered if the comment about country music was an insult, assumed it was, and gazed out at the field. The view really was fantastic from the booth. Still, he missed being out on the field, under the warm sun and surrounded by the sweet smell of fresh cut grass. The umpires walked onto the field and the two teams jogged back to their dugouts. Charlie sat back down beside Coach Zim.

"That was the old lady," Charlie said.

"Your mother?"

"No, my girlfriend, Morgan. Going on two weeks." He shoved an entire Twinkie into his mouth, chewed for a moment, added a large swig of Mountain Dew to the mix, chewed a little more, and swallowed. "Game's about to start. You ready?"

Todd Horne's sharp whistle repeatedly pierced the air as he tried in vain to gather the team together in the dugout. Paul Rivard ripped the whistle from around Horne's neck and tossed it into the trash can next to the dugout, earning a burst of applause from fans of both teams.

Coach Zim nodded. "I'm ready."

At the same time as the Apple Brook Warriors took the field, Brandon Ackerson heard footsteps and laughter behind him while walking home from school. He knew those voices. Keeping his head down, he walked faster. When something hit the back of his leg he cried out and dropped to one knee. Someone grabbed him in a full nelson, pushed his head down until his chin was against his chest, and wrestled him into the woods.

In a tree-shaded clearing he was flung onto the ground. Cold brown leaves slid and crunched as Ackerson tried to stand. There was quiet laughter as he was kicked back to his knees. He rolled onto his butt to face his attackers, though he already knew who they were.

Five teenagers stared down at him. Tom Collins stood in the center. His hair had grown in enough that the swastikas were little more than dark shadows. One of the gang drank from a pint of whiskey. Tom Collins held out his hand while staring down at Ackerson. When the pint was handed to him, Collins surprised Ackerson by holding out the bottle.

Collins smiled when Ackerson shook his head. "You should take some. It might help with the pain."

A steel-toed boot flew toward his face. Ackerson jerked his head back just in time. Collins signaled to the others to hold Ackerson down and sipped whiskey while each boy grabbed and knelt on a limb. Ackerson struggled, eyes wild like a pig being led to slaughter, but he was not a strong boy and soon gave up. Lifting his head, he watched as Collins took one last sip and stuck the bottle in his back pocket.

"Well, you little faggot," Collins said. He stepped forward and stood over Ackerson, one foot on each side of the boy's hips. "I hear you're drawing pictures of naked faggots having gay sex and showing them around at school. You're quite the fucking artist, aren't you?"

His friends laughed. Ackerson shook his head, too frightened to speak.

"You like drawing peckers, huh? You seen many peckers? I guess you wanna see my pecker."

Collins unzipped his jeans and pulled out his penis. Filled with terror, tears welled up in Ackerson's eyes. He didn't notice when his bladder let go. But scared as he was, Ackerson made an observation – it was small, about the size of a C battery. He'd never actually seen a penis up close, but Collins's was smaller than his own. The thought also occurred to him that pulling out one's penis in the middle of a group of young men could be construed as far gayer than drawing a picture of nude couples. But he said nothing, not wanting to anger his attacker even more.

"You want it, don't you?" Collins said. "Want me to put it in your mouth?"

And then, without warning, he began urinating on Ackerson's face. The taste was warm and putrid. Ackerson closed his mouth and eyes and turned his head. He struggled to get loose and was startled when the strong hands released his arms and legs.

"What the fuck, Tom!" one of the boys yelled. "You pissed on me, man. I've got your piss on my hands!"

"Me too!" said another. "It splashed in my face!"

Ackerson rolled onto his side, wiping his face on his sleeve. He opened his eyes. Two of his attackers were faced off with Collins, hurling insults and threats back and forth. Fists started flying, and then the other two boys jumped in. It was a full-out brawl. None of them noticed when Ackerson slid away, grabbed his backpack and hurried off through the trees.

"Leading off the season for the Apple Brook Warriors is Adam Nass. Nass batted .285 last season and almost broke the Maine state record for stolen bases. Think he'll do it this year, Coach Zim?"

"I do, yes. Nass is fast and has a gift on the base paths."

"Rumor has it he's quite gifted with the ladies, too. Let's face it - this guy's fast anyway you look at it, Coach."

Coach Zim chuckled. Half an inning into his broadcasting career, he was already getting the hang of it. Charlie gave a statistic about a player, Coach made an observation, and then Charlie replied with something that had little to do with baseball and was sometimes insulting. He'd heard Charlie DeMar described as a wiseass and a slacker by other teachers, and these seemed like reasonable observations. Nevertheless, he'd already found himself growing fond of DeMar. The kid enjoyed life and wanted to have fun, something adults often forgot about.

Adam Nass grounded out. The next batter failed to get on base, as did every other batter until the bottom of the sixth inning, when Nass was walked with two out. High school games last seven innings, and with the score 12-0, things were not looking well.

"Finally, Coach, Apple Brook has a baserunner. The runner is Nass, which is good news. What will Coach Horne do?"

"I have no idea what Coach Horne will do."

"Well, one thing I hope he doesn't do is tear his shirt off again."

In the fourth inning, after a bases-loaded double drove in three runs for the Tigers, Todd Horne began yelling at the other dugout, calling them cheaters and demanding to have their bats checked. The umpire warned him to be quiet, and Horne's response was to point at his legs and flex them. When the ump turned back to the field and yelled "Play ball!" Horne ripped off his shirt and flexed, doing a most muscular pose until his face turned cherry red. After a couple minutes of being ignored by the umpire and heckled by the crowd, Horne struggled back into his extra-small shirt.

Nass took off for second on the first pitch as the next batter, Robert Williams, swung. Williams made contact, a bullet that reached the shortstop on one hop. He tossed it to the second baseman just as Nass slid. It was close – real close – but the second base umpire jerked his thumb back dramatically, calling the runner out. Nass got up, dusted himself off, and ran back to the dugout to retrieve his glove.

On his way he passed Coach Horne, who was going ballistic. Horne ran to home plate to argue with the umpire. Then he ran back to the dugout and threw a helmet against the back of the dugout. The helmet shattered, throwing shards of plastic everywhere. Then it was out to the on-deck circle, where Horne did his best Lou Ferigno impression, grabbing his shirt around the collar and tearing it off until it was nothing but a torn little rag, which he then threw toward the opposing dugout.

Finally, in the midst of his rage, Horne lifted a bat over his head with one hand on each end and slammed it down on top of his head. Bo Jackson used to break them this way. There were two differences, however. First, Bo Jackson wore a batting helmet. And second, Bo Jackson used a wooden bat, which allowed it to break when slammed down onto his head. This was not the case when Todd Horne did it. Horne dropped like he'd gone boneless.

"Oh, Dude, did you see that?" Charlie DeMar yelled into the microphone. He whacked Coach Zim repeatedly on the arm. "Coach Horne just smashed himself in the head with an aluminum bat, knocking himself out! That may be the coolest thing I've ever seen in my life!"

Charlie stuck his phone out of the booth, pointed it at the field and took a picture. Then he began texting and posting it on every site he knew of. Meanwhile, the paramedics – there were a minimum of two at each game, along with a police officer – rushed onto the field and began working on Horne.

"Apple Brook is losing badly, but wow, this is exciting. I mean, this is how you liven up a baseball game," said Charlie. "Coach Zim, why didn't you ever do anything like this when you were losing?"

"We rarely lost."

"Ha. Good one. And true. There's the stretcher. Oh, and Coach Horne is getting to his feet! Nope, he's back down. Hit the ground like a sack of turnips, as my grandfather says. You ever see a bag of turnips hit the ground, Coach Zim?"

"I don't like turnips."

"Well, who does, right? Except my grandfather, of course. Coach Horne is now being carried from the field. I have to say, he didn't look too good when he tried to stand. What do you think, Coach Zim? A concussion?"

"Most likely, yes. At least. Hopefully nothing more serious."

They watched as Todd Horne was carried off the field by two EMT's. The crowd cheered enthusiastically – maybe a bit too enthusiastically. He was carried past the jeering bikers and loaded into the ambulance.

"Okay, here we go. The Warriors are back on the field after the unfortunate demise of Coach Horne."

"I don't think you mean demise, Charlie. That would mean Coach Horne died. He didn't look dead to me."

"Hard to tell from this angle, but I'll go with your expert opinion, Coach. I must say, that bat doesn't look any worse for wear. And coming to bat for the Tigers is…"

Fifteen minutes later, the first game of the season was over. Final score: Tigers 12, Warriors 0.

He sat in the study that evening, sipping a beer and watching footage of the previous day's Sea Dogs game on his computer. Some of the players were incredible – strong, fast, athletic in the way one thinks of when looking at statues of Greek gods. Their talent stood out even more after the debacle he'd witnessed from the booth that afternoon.

What would it be like to work with these guys, he wondered. A hell of a lot easier than coaching high school ball, that's for sure. They wouldn't need to be repeatedly reminded to hit the cutoff man, take the pitch on a 3-0 count, and all the other little things he drilled his teams on until his throat was sore.

It wouldn't be as much fun, though. He was a high school coach. No getting around that. He'd been offered several college head coaching jobs over the years, the next step on the ladder leading to the pros. He'd turned them all down because he *liked* the mistakes. Mistakes were an opportunity, and Coach Zim relished the repetitive hitting and fielding and running drills that taught the kids discipline and gave them self-confidence. High school kids played for love of the game, not money.

He watched the screen. Most of these players didn't need his advice, and the ones that did probably wouldn't take it. With a sigh, he realized that he'd had more fun broadcasting the game earlier that day than he did working with the Sea Dogs.

13

Coach Zim hid behind a tree at the edge of the woods near the school parking lot. Fifty feet away, his pickup sat in its usual spot in the back corner of the lot. He'd been standing there for half an hour, watching for Tom Collins or whoever slashed his tires. He planned to do this every morning until the slasher was caught and coughed up the six hundred and fifty bucks they owned him for tires. Upon hearing his plan that morning over breakfast, Angela frowned and told him he was acting irrationally. Maybe he was. It wouldn't be the first time.

The ground was covered in dew and the temperature was in the mid-fifties, not bad for early morning in May. Even so, after a half hour in the shade Coach Zim was stamping his feet and blowing on his hands. Tomorrow he'd wear an extra sweatshirt under his windbreaker, along with thicker socks and a pair of gloves.

The bell rang across the parking lot, signaling that classes would begin in five minutes. After making sure nobody was looking, he emerged from his hiding spot. He grabbed his bag out of his truck, locked it, and scanned the parking lot again to make sure nobody was watching him. Paranoid. That was the other word Angela had used to describe his plan. He preferred to think of himself as vigilant.

While walking through the parking lot, he noticed Brandon Ackerson standing on the grass along the side of the school. He watched Ackerson unzip his backpack and pull something out. Coach Zim was close enough now to see a handgun.

He quickened his pace while walking as softly as a man his size could. Ackerson stood rooted to the same spot for several moments, seemingly hypnotized by the gun in his hand. Then he resumed walking, holding the gun stiffly by his hip.

"Brandon!" Coach called. "Hey, Brandon! Wait up!"

Ackerson kept walking. Coach moved faster, jogging now, and called out again. This time Ackerson paused and looked over. Seeing Coach Zim fast approaching, he made a clumsy attempt to stuff the gun into his backpack.

Without saying a word, Coach Zim grabbed the backpack and opened it up. Nestled between a sketch pad and an iPad was the gun. Coach set the bag on the ground and knelt down. He checked the gun inside the bag, where no one could see. Loaded.

Most people panic in critical situations. Coach Zim had always been the opposite. Circumstances which caused sweating and shaky hands and dry throats in most people left him feeling calm, as though he'd just swallowed a warm shot of whiskey. This coolness had earned him a reputation as a clutch player when he was younger, and it was the same way now. With his hands still inside the backpack, he quickly emptied the chamber, released the clip, and zipped the bag closed.

"Come with me." He grabbed Ackerson roughly by the arm and led him across the parking lot to his truck. He unlocked the doors, threw his bag and Ackerson's backpack in the back, and pushed Ackerson into the passenger seat. Then he got in on the driver's side.

The 8:00 bell rang. Neither of them noticed.

Coach Zim felt confused, wondering if he'd just thwarted another of the school shootings which had become so commonplace in America. He looked at Ackerson. The boy trembled from head to foot. Tears streamed down his face.

"Am I going to jail?" he whispered.

"Probably. Before I call the cops I want you to tell me what just happened. Were you going to shoot someone? Because that's a real fucking gun, Brandon. Please tell me it was for show and tell."

"Yes. No." He sobbed loudly. "I don't know."

Coach glanced at his watch. "You have one minute to explain to me what happened. Then we go inside and call the police. Maybe I can help you. I don't know."

Ackerson took a deep breath. As tears rolled down his cheeks, he told Coach Zim that it had been Tom Collins who'd beaten him in the parking lot. Then he described what had happened the previous afternoon when Collins and company had dragged him into the woods.

Coach Zim shook his head in disbelief. "He pissed in your mouth? On your face?"

"Yeah. But I turned my head pretty fast. Not much went in my mouth."

"Jesus. Fucking animal," Coach mumbled.

He looked over at Ackerson, at his red cheeks and glasses and shaggy hair and slight frame. The kid would get eaten alive in jail. Even if he just went to a youth facility, he'd probably come out feeling closer to Tom Collins than to his old self.

"I don't think I could have shot him." Ackerson sniffed. "I just wanted to scare him, make him feel the way I felt yesterday. The way I feel every day, really."

Coach Zim turned and gazed out the windshield for a long time, absently tapping his thumbs against the steering wheel. The correct thing to do, what the school district had taught them to do since Columbine, was immediately alert the school police officer if it's even suspected that anyone on the grounds has a gun. He was breaking the rules right now by not turning Ackerson in right away. He could lose his job, although if he brought Ackerson in right now he'd be fine. In fact, he'd likely be hailed as a hero.

Finally, he reached down and pulled out his ancient cell phone. While punching in a phone number, he said to Ackerson, "Keep your mouth shut. Got it? Don't say a word."

Ackerson nodded. Coach Zim stared out the window, phone to his ear, wondering if he was doing the right thing.

"Hi Linda, it's Jim Zimmerman." He nodded. "That's right, Coach Zim. Listen, I hate to call so late, but I won't be coming in today. A last minute emergency came up." He paused. "No, I'm fine, thank you. I hate for you to have to find a substitute so late, after the day has already begun, but…Okay, thanks Linda. You too. Bye.

"She's had a crush on me for twenty years," he said, after hanging up. His seat creaked as he turned to Ackerson. The kid was still afraid but now appeared confused as well, like a prisoner wondering how his captives were planning to execute him. He shifted again in his seat and started the truck.

"What are we doing?"

"We're taking a ride, Ackerson. Unless you'd rather go inside and see Officer Farrell."

Ackerson shook his head no. Coach Zim drove slowly through the parking lot, toward the exit.

Half an hour later they pulled into a small dirt parking lot on the east shore of Willow Pond. Coach Zim got out, reached into the back and pulled out a fishing pole and tackle box. Then he walked around the truck and opened the passenger door.

"Grab your backpack," he said.

Ackerson did as told and followed quietly as Coach Zim made his way down a narrow footpath. It was still early enough in the year that leaves were just budding on the trees and shrubs, allowing sunshine through, and the ground was covered with brown, crisp leaves leftover from fall. Neither said a word as they followed the path along the water's edge.

About a quarter mile from the parking lot they came to a small open peninsula. A single tall pine tree stood near the far end like a sentry watching over the water. In contrast to the trail, the ground of the peninsula was soft and spongy and covered by rust-colored pine quills.

"This is known as The Finger," said Coach Zim. He walked to the edge of the water and dropped the tackle box next to the pine tree. "Best fishing in the area. Not a lot of people know about this place, so I'm trusting you to keep your trap shut."

He dropped to his knees, the joints cracking like dry twigs, and opened the tackle box. He took out a purple rubber worm, grabbed the fishing pole, and fastened it to the end of the line. Then he slowly stood up, groaning and holding out an arm for balance.

"I swear that gets harder every day." He nodded toward the pine tree. "Don't lean against that. Covered in pine pitch. It'll take days to get that stuff off your hands." He held out the fishing pole. "Ever been fishing?"

Ackerson shook his head.

"You'll love it. I usually don't get to fish this early in the year because of baseball, but I've made it out here a few times this year. Here, take the rod."

Ackerson grabbed the rod awkwardly and followed Coach Zim around the tree, to the far edge of the peninsula.

"What we have on the end of the line is called a Kelly worm. Great bait. Like catnip for bass." He looked at the water and scratched his head. "If bass were cats. Aw, hell, you know what I mean." He looked at Ackerson. The boy held the fishing pole in both hands like a piece of firewood.

"First thing you need to do is learn how to cast. I learned in my backyard with a lead weight on the end, but you'll be doing on the job training."

The rod was old, with a Zebco reel. Coach Zim gave a quick tutorial on how it worked – push the button as the arm begins to move forward. Ackerson's first cast flew approximately two feet. The next one ended up behind them, hooked on a branch of the pine tree. Luckily it wasn't high and Coach Zim got it free without ruining the worm. The third one landed about ten feet out in the lake.

"Not bad, Brandon. Now reel it in. Not so fast, not…okay, well, that's a good start. You want to reel it in slowly. Not so slow that it will sink, but slow enough to give the fish a look. Think of it as an ice cream truck driving slowly through a neighborhood so the kids can catch it."

Ackerson nodded and tried again. Within five minutes all of his casts were going forward and gaining distance, and a couple of minutes later he got his first tug on the line. Excited, he reeled in as fast as he could. Soon the line went slack, and when it broke the water there was no fish and half the Kelly worm was missing.

Coach Zim took the rod from him, unhooked what was left of the worm, and tossed it into the tackle box. Then he fastened a new worm to the swivel on the end of the line.

"Can you guess what your mistake was?" he asked, handing the rod back to Ackerson.

"I reeled it in too fast?"

"Exactly. Just give a little tug and reel it in nice and steady. If not, you'll tear the hook right out of the fish's mouth."

Half an hour later he'd caught five bass. Small, six to eight inches, but when they're the first fish you've ever caught it doesn't matter if they are the size of tadpoles. The first one he held up to Coach Zim, who slapped him proudly on the shoulder, removed the fish from the hook and set it back in the water. He showed Ackerson how to remove the second fish from the line and set in back in the lake gently, placing it underwater before releasing it. Some people frown when touching and removing a fish from the hook, but Ackerson did it with a smile.

While watching the teen reel in his line, Coach Zim said, "So, about the gun."

Ackerson hesitated for a second. "I'd forgotten all about it, to be honest."

"Yeah, fishing will do that for you. I truly believe that fishing is the best meditation known to man. Whenever I feel stressed, I come here."

"It's great," Ackerson agreed.

"So where'd you get the gun?"

"It was in the stuff my dad left behind when he left. I found it a long time ago. Loaded. I don't think my mom ever saw it." He cast out again. "I didn't know how to unload it. I could have Googled it, but the gun kind of scared me."

"You got a problem with us getting rid of it?" Coach Zim pulled the gun and clip from the backpack.

"Nope. I want you to."

Coach Zim tossed the gun and the clip, one after the other, into the lake. Each landed with a dull plop about a hundred feet from shore, leaving nothing but round ripples where they'd hit.

"You probably shouldn't have done that, Coach. Littering and everything. It can't be very good for the environment."

"Damn. You're right. I probably should have thought that out." Coach Zim scratched his head, feeling like a total ass. "That was really stupid."

Ackerson shrugged and reeled in another bass. The morning was growing warmer and the black flies had found them. Coach Zim found a can of bug spray in the tackle box and sprayed both himself and Ackerson.

"You realize how stupid you were?" he asked a little while later. He was sitting on a large rock nearby. "How your life could have changed? Everybody's lives?"

"Are you going to tell anyone?"

"No." Of course he wasn't. A student came to school with a loaded gun and he saw it and did nothing? He wouldn't just be fired, he'd probably be thrown in jail. No, he wasn't going to tell anyone.

"What are you going to do?" Ackerson stopped fishing and turned toward him.

"Nothing, I guess. I just hope you realize what could have happened. I believe you weren't going to shoot anyone, you just wanted to scare them. But you would have gone to jail for a long time. Collins and his friends would have just laughed about it. And can you imagine what it would have done to your mother?"

Tears welled up again. "I know. But he just won't leave me alone. I didn't do anything to him but the asshole won't leave me alone!" His voice echoed across the lake. "I can't tell the police, because that'll just make it worse."

Coach Zim realized he was probably right. "I mean it when I say guys like that usually get what's coming to them. And I'm sorry, but I am going to the police with this."

Ackerson's eyes grew wide. "The gun?"

"Jesus, Ackerson. Don't you listen? I never saw any gun, because you never had a gun. I'm talking about what those guys did to you yesterday."

"No, no, no." He shook his head several times. "Then they'll really hurt me. I know they will."

"I'm sorry, son. I can't let them get away with this. I'll tell you what – I know the chief of police. I'll talk to him and see what he says."

Ackerson nodded but didn't say anything.

"You gonna keep fishing or do you need me to take over?"

"How much longer can we stay?" asked Ackerson as he cast out.

Coach Zim leaned his head back, soaking up the sun. "As long as you want, son. I took a sick day, remember?"

"Have you gone crazy?"

He'd told Angela everything that had happened, from watching his truck before school from behind a tree – which she again called irrational – to spotting Ackerson with a loaded gun and the trip to the fishing hole. They'd stayed until about noon, when they'd left for a lunch of cheeseburgers and Cokes at a local diner. Then they stopped at a convenience store near the boat launch for another package of Kelly worms and a cheap fishing rod for Coach to use, and spent the rest of the afternoon fishing off The Finger. The fish weren't biting quite as well in the afternoon as they had been that morning, but they still caught a few.

The Zimmermans sat now at a table near the window of Delano's, their favorite restaurant in Apple Brook. They ate at Delano's most Friday evenings. Coach Zim had dropped Ackerson off at home late in the afternoon, then gone home to shower and change. The days were growing longer and the sunlight was still bright on Main Street outside Delano's large picture window.

"I haven't gone crazy at all. In fact, I think I behaved quite rationally."

"Really?" They were silent as the server brought their food to the table. Angela glared at her husband when he smiled at the server. Then she continued, in a quiet voice. "A student brought a loaded gun to school. A loaded gun, in Apple Brook! People could have died! And what did you do?

You played hooky and took the gunman fishing! And to you this is rational."

"Well, no, not the way you describe it." He finished cutting his prime rib and took a large bite of mashed potato. "First of all, it was Brandon Ackerson. He had a loaded gun, yes, but he wasn't going to shoot anyone."

"How do you know?" Angela hissed. "You don't know what was in his head at the time."

"But I do know," he said, a little louder than he intended. He glanced around and lowered his voice. "Brandon is a good kid. It's his dad's old gun, he left it behind when he took off. The gun was already loaded and Brandon was scared to unload it. I'm telling you, I understand kids. Not all of them, but most of them. And there is no way this kid would have shot anyone. He was scared and hurt and wanted Tom Collins and his friends to feel the same way. That's all." He stuffed another piece of steak into his mouth and said, "He's an artist. He's sensitive."

"Not all artists are sensitive, you know."

"This one is."

She chewed her salad while her husband crammed steak and potatoes down his throat and washed it down with beer. A couple they knew stopped by to say hello. Angela chatted with them briefly while Coach Zim waved, nodded and chewed.

When they were once again alone, Angela said, "Regardless of the boy's sensitivity, do you realize how this looks?" Without waiting for a reply, she continued, "I'll explain how it could look to a lawyer. You could be an accomplice to commit murder. He had a loaded gun and not only did you not inform anyone, you covered for him."

Coach Zim rolled his eyes. "Enough, Angela. I told you, nobody will ever know there was a gun, because there is no gun. Unless they want to dive down into the muck at the bottom of Willow Pond and look for it. It was an incident, and now it's over. The boy was pushed to the breaking point. That's all."

She looked like she wanted to say more, but stayed silent for a few minutes. Coach Zim finished off his steak, leaned back and rubbed his stomach. He glanced across the table at his wife and frowned.

"We're not finished, are we?"

"I just want to be sure that you understand the seriousness of today's actions. You could lose your job, forever. You could go to jail. You could be a felon."

"I could, but I won't. You know what this kid is going through. What kind of man would I be if I just turned my back on him?"

Angela swallowed the last of her salad and took a sip of wine. "Did Collins really pee on his face?"

Coach Zim nodded. "While his friends held Ackerson down. A month after they beat him unconscious in the school parking lot. For no reason that I can see, except they might think he's gay."

"Is he?"

"I don't know." Coach shrugged. "I think so. I'm not even sure he knows, but it shouldn't matter."

Angela thought for a minute. "It could be a hate crime, if he is gay."

"He doesn't want to go to the police, but I told him I'm going to talk to Chief Walsh about it. See what he has to say."

The conversation moved on to other topics, and by the time dessert arrived they were laughing about something they'd seen on television the previous evening. When they left the restaurant the sun had set. They went home and had a couple more drinks. Around nine o'clock Angela asked her husband if he was ready for bed. He said he was going to stay up a little longer and watch TV. Then he looked over, realized that she was wearing her skimpy maid outfit, and almost tripped in his haste to reach the bedroom.

14

Monday morning. Todd Horne's head hurt, partially from the concussion he'd suffered the previous week and partially from the sunlight shining directly in his face through the window behind his uncle's desk. He squinted and tried to shift the small seat away from the light, but it was a large window. Despite the sensation of sharp glass entering his skull through his eyeballs, he had to admit that the warm sun felt good on his bare legs. The temperature outside was cool, and he should have worn warm-up pants over the shorts and taken them off when he got to school, like he sometimes did in the winter. But he'd overslept that morning. Effects of the concussion, most likely.

He pulled his Apple Brook cap down further, hoping the visor would shield the sunlight from his eyes. Instead, the pressure of the hat squeezing against his temples and touching the lump on top of his head only made the headache worse. If he removed the hat the sun would seem brighter. Plus, the lump was visible on top of his head, looking like an egg balancing atop his skull.

He pulled the hat back up, reducing the pressure on his temples and skull, and cupped his hand in front of the bill of his ball cap. That shaded his eyes some. His uncle was now visible behind his desk, leaning back in silence, staring at him while shaking his head and frowning. The silence made his head hurt more. Horne considered asking if he could close the blinds, but decided it would only make his uncle angrier.

"You don't look good, Todd. I suppose that's what you get for slamming a baseball bat into your own skull."

"I saw Bo Jackson do it on a documentary."

"With an aluminum bat?"

Todd shook his head miserably. "I want to thank you for the homemade soup. I was pretty nauseous this weekend and it was the only thing I could eat."

"That was your aunt. She loves everyone, no matter how idiotic they are."

Horne continued to squint but said nothing.

"I'm going to get right to it, Todd. You embarrassed yourself by throwing a temper tantrum and knocking yourself out with a baseball bat. Normally I find that sort of stupidity in others humorous. Not this time, though. Do you know why? Of course you don't. You're an idiot. It's because you embarrassed this school, and you embarrassed me. I hired you, and you are my nephew. That's two strikes against me. And two strikes against me is two strikes against you, Todd. Are you following me so far?"

Horne nodded.

"Excellent. And do you know what happens when you get three strikes, Todd?"

Tentatively, Horne replied, "You're out?"

Craggy pointed at him. "Exactly! Coaching baseball *has* taught you something. So if you do anything stupid again regarding the baseball team, you are out as head coach." Craggy's voice rose. "Not only will that make me look like an incompetent idiot for hiring you in the first place, but it will probably result in my getting a divorce. And you know what? I don't give a shit!"

Outside the office, a couple of people started laughing. Inside, Horne winced.

"Could you please not yell, Uncle Garth? My head is killing me."

Craggy stood up, considered rushing around the desk to strangle his nephew. Instead, he turned his back, walked to the window and stared outside. Behind him, Horne leaned to the right, where his uncle's shadow blocked the shards of light from piercing his eyeballs. He doubted that Uncle Garth obstructed the sunlight out of kindness but was nevertheless grateful.

After a minute or so of silence, Horne began daydreaming about that afternoon's game. It was an away game, at nearby Rockport. He was thankful – a fifteen-minute bus ride, he could handle. Anything longer and his skull would probably feel like a watermelon dropped from a tall building. He'd demand total silence on the bus, tell the players that they should take the time to concentrate on the game, not talk about girls.

Speaking of, he'd have April give him a gentle head massage on the bus. Maybe in the dugout, too. She'd visited him in the hospital, brought him a nice teddy bear. She was the only one to visit, he thought. Couldn't quite remember. He'd only been there one night, for evaluation. The doctor said he had a concussion and it could take weeks, even months, before he felt back to normal, and that he should avoid any physical activity for at least a week, until his reevaluation. But the doctor was a scrawny geek who'd obviously never lifted a weight in his life, so on Sunday afternoon Horne decided to get in a short back and bicep workout at the gym. He took some Tylenol for his headache and washed it down with a protein drink before heading out.

Ten minutes into the workout, during his third set of lat pulldowns, his headache returned, worse than before. He finished the set, moved on to dumbbell rows, and felt a thick rush of dizziness and nausea, as though he were standing on a rocking boat. Sweating heavily, on the verge of vomiting, he finished his set and left the gym. The rest of his Sunday was spent lying in bed with the shades drawn. He felt miserable. Maybe the geek with the stethoscope had been right.

From pain had come knowledge, though. Lying in bed, he'd had time to think about baseball. He was embarrassed about the outcome of his first game as a head coach, and not only because of the mishap with the bat. He'd wanted to win, to make his uncle proud of him. Instead he'd lost by double digits and ended up in the hospital.

But lying in his room, in and out of consciousness, Horne had come up with some changes for the team. Changes that only he, a new coach, could come up with. Other coaches, like that know-it-all Coach Zim, had been around the game too long, become set in their ways. Nobody saw what he saw – a different way to play the game. It would be revolutionary, probably change the game forever, the way the west coast offense had changed football. A new term would be brought into the game's lexicon – The Horne Method. In baseball circles his name would be as big as Mantle and DiMaggio and what's-his-face, the fat guy who hit all the home runs a hundred years ago. Baby something.

Despite his discomfort, he couldn't wait to implement his changes during that afternoon's game. The thought made him smile.

Principal Craggy turned from the window to see his nephew leaning sideways in his chair, grinning like a buffoon. He momentarily wondered if the blow to the head – which he'd unfortunately failed to witness but planned to view later on YouTube – had scrambled Horne's brain. Looking at him, though, he didn't seem any more stupid than usual.

"What are you still doing here?" he asked.

"I didn't know we were done."

"We are. Get out." He sat back behind his desk. "And please, Todd; don't do anything stupid at this afternoon's game. Just try to win."

Horne stood up slowly and grinned again. "Don't worry, Uncle Garth. I have a feeling you're going to be pleasantly surprised at the results."

"Uh huh." Idiot. "On your way out tell Miss Duggan I'd like to see her, please."

A few seconds later Emma walked in.

"Could you please tell Mr. Zimmerman I'd like to see him after period one?"

"Sure." She turned to go, then paused. "Who is Mr. Zimmerman?"

"Jim Zimmerman. History teacher." She stared at him. "Coach Zim!"

"Oh, okay. Why didn't you just say Coach Zim to begin with?"

Because he's not a fucking coach anymore! That's what he wanted to say, but the door was open and he was under enough pressure without blaspheming the town hero. Besides, he liked Emma, despite the snarky comments and obvious fondness for his old rival. She was a nice girl and a good secretary.

He sat back behind his desk and put his head down. It was going to be another long day.

Craggy's cell phone rang. The wife. Answering it would ruin an already bad day. Not answering might be worse. On the third ring he answered. For the next five minutes he listened as his wife berated him like a little kid because he hadn't woken her up on time for her nine o'clock dentist's appointment. He had tried waking her, but the sleeping pills kept her in a near coma and there was only a slight change in her bear-like snoring as he shook her. Arguing would do no good, however, so he listened to her scolding in smoldering silence until she'd run out of things to say.

Craggy set the phone down and gave it the finger. He pulled out a pint of vodka from his bottom desk drawer. Ordinarily he drank whiskey, but this required something that couldn't be smelled on his breath. He wasn't in the habit of drinking so early in the morning, but this day had started badly and might get worse. A little pick-me-up might be the only thing to get him through the day.

The vodka burned on the way down, warming his chest from the inside like a furnace. He screwed the cap on after only one sip – after all, it was nine a.m. The sound of someone giggling came from outside his office. Emma. And he knew who always made her giggle. He'd barely closed his desk drawer when Coach Zim burst into the room.

"Hey Craggy, you wanted to see me?" He sat heavily onto the couch. "Make it snappy, though. I put Rivard in charge of my class and who knows what the hell will happen. He's in a bad mood this morning. Game today. He doesn't like losing but he says it's unavoidable with Nutsack in charge."

"I thought I told you to knock before entering my office."

"Was that you? Hey, did you see the video of Nutsack knocking himself out on YouTube? I'll bet you fifty bucks it's on ESPN by the end of the day."

Craggy's hand twitched, and his mind drifted to the vodka in his desk drawer. One sip wasn't going to be enough. "I wanted to tell you that Lester Collins, Tom Collins's father, hired a lawyer and has filed a lawsuit claiming that Tom was stuffed inside a locker. He's sticking with the story that you stuffed him in."

"Is he suing me?"

"No, the school district. But you are named in the lawsuit. If they find in favor of Collins, there's a slight chance you could lose your job, pension, everything." The thought was like a sliver of sunshine on Craggy's cloudy day.

"The school district has lawyers. Let them handle it." He stood to go. "Is that all?"

"That's all. Just wanted you to know."

Coach Zim left the room without another word. Craggy could tell the news had upset him, no matter what he said. This brought a big smile, his first of the day, and caused him to flush with optimism. Maybe he could hold off on that bottle of vodka until the end of the day.

Students yelled and laughed and jostled their way down the hall between classes. Coach Zim stood near the doorway to his classroom, greeting some students and shouting warnings to those who misbehaved. Brandon Ackerson shuffled past on his way into the classroom and gave a shy hello. Coach Zim gave a friendly nod and patted him on the shoulder.

A few yards back down the hallway, Tom Collins and his friends lurked like sharks trailing a raft full of shipwreck survivors. Collins made an obvious attempt to find Ackerson inside the classroom on his way past, bending forward with a malicious grin across his face. Then he looked up at Coach Zim and said something about seeing him in court.

Coach Zim ignored him. He'd like nothing more than to throttle the little shit until he was little more than a bloody heap to be mopped up by a custodian. But he was in enough trouble, from what Craggy had said earlier. A lawsuit was serious. If they fired him over this, not only would he lose his job and pension, but he'd never get hired to teach, or coach, anywhere again.

Inside the classroom, most of the students were bent over their iPads and phones. The entire generation looked they had scoliosis, in his opinion. Seated or standing, they were always bent over, as though unable to lift their heads. They say that humans change over generations to adapt to their environment. Coach Zim imagined that within two generations human beings would have longer, thinner thumbs and curved backs and necks for better texting ability. Humans spent centuries learning to walk on two feet and now appeared to be heading back down, head first.

Ackerson was among those bent over, swiping away. Coach Zim had called Chief Walsh Sunday morning. Coach Zim was one of the few people in town who had the chief's home phone number and was welcome to call at any time. The Chief had been waiting for his wife to get ready for church – "God doesn't care what necklace you wear, Betty" – and seemed happy for the distraction.

After the preliminaries – how's the wife, been hotter than normal, Red Sox aren't looking so good – Coach Zim got down to business. Without using any names, he asked what would happen to a group of seventeen-year-old boys who'd allegedly restrained another boy against his will and assaulted him. He left out the urine, for the time being.

"Do these boys have records, Coach?"

"For now, let's say they don't." Incredibly, Tom Collins had never been arrested.

"Well, we'd investigate, take statements from the alleged victim and the boys being accused of the crime. Then we'd decide whether or not to make arrests. In the end, considering they are only seventeen, they'd probably all end up with probation."

"Yeah, that's what I thought."

"You said this is for a class, Coach?"

"Yup," Coach Zim replied quickly.

Chief Walsh had been a cop long enough to smell a lie, even over the phone. "I thought you taught English."

"History. It's not for my class. It's for a criminology class."

"Oh, that must be Wally Bernier's class. I think it's great that they have a criminology class in high school now. But why didn't Wally call me himself?"

"Probably embarrassed about having to ask. You know Wally, he likes to pretend he knows it all."

"That he does," agreed Chief Walsh.

"Don't tell him I asked you about it, okay? It's just something we were discussing one day in the teacher's lounge."

"No problem, my friend. Gee, it's too bad you're no longer coaching. I don't ever remember an Apple Brook baseball team getting beaten as badly as we did Thursday."

"It wasn't good, but I think things will get better."

"I hope so. Listen, the wife's finally ready so I guess we're off to church. But hey, have you seen the video of Nutsack Horne knocking himself out? My granddaughter showed it to me yesterday on the YouTube. Funny as hell, I must have watched it five times. Goddamn fool." In the background Mrs. Walsh scolded her husband. "Well, at least now I can ask forgiveness for my foul language. It'll give me something to do in church," Chief Walsh replied, then whispered into the phone, "I gotta go, Coach. Look for that video. It's on the YouTube."

Now Coach Zim walked into classroom and watched the electronics disappear. A few weeks earlier he'd assigned the book *Killing Lincoln* to the class. It wasn't on the curriculum but was the best book on the subject he'd read, written at a level that teenagers could understand and enjoy. The class had begun having discussions about it the previous week. He liked class discussions, enjoyed seeing the students begin to think for themselves and form their own opinions instead of listening to a supreme leader dictate what they should learn and what they should think from that most powerful of pulpits, the front of the classroom. He enjoyed the thought of himself as a supreme leader, but lecturing and dictating wasn't going to teach these kids nearly as much as discussions and debates. This was something he understood instinctively and wished other teachers did as well.

"Okay," he began, "I'd like you to think about the White House in Lincoln's day. Anybody could walk in or out of the White House. Just walk in, like it was a public library. You could walk around the grounds and even picnic on the lawn. Compare that with the White House as we know it today – basically a barricaded fortress, with the highest security known to man. Not only are citizens not allowed on the grounds, but the area around the White House is prohibited airspace. You with me so far?"

Most of the students nodded.

"Good. My question to you is, which do you think is better? Having an open White House, where people can walk on the grounds, or at least walk up to the grounds without being threatened by law enforcement personnel? Or a White House where not only the grounds but the streets around it are blocked off?"

"That's kind of a stupid question, Coach Zim," said Eddie Dumont. Tall, skinny, headed into the Navy in the fall. "If anyone can go to the White House, the President will get assassinated. The White House has to be closed off to the public."

Several students nodded in agreement.

"Then consider this, Dumont. In almost two hundred and fifty years only four Presidents have been assassinated, and none of those men were killed within the White House grounds. This tells me that being outside the White House is more dangerous than being inside. And consider that there hasn't been an assassination in over fifty years. There have been attempts, of course, the most famous being the attempt on Reagan's life in eighty-one. Which took place outside of the White House grounds, I should add."

"Good points," said Dumont. "But in this day and age, I still believe the President needs as much security as can be provided."

"I don't know," said Meadow Angers. Short, pretty, bound for sunny University of Florida in the fall. "It seems like more and more of our rights are being taken away every day. Maybe, you know, we shouldn't be walking into the White House or picnicking on the lawn, but, like, we should be allowed on the grounds somehow. I mean, we are American citizens."

"I heard Willie Nelson smoked a joint on the roof of the White House," said Michael Barrow, and most of the class laughed.

"But think about it," said Meadow. "I mean, like, just really think, you know? We were a better country when we had more freedom."

"Things have changed, honey," said Eddie Dumont.

And they were off. Coach Zim sat on the corner of his desk and observed, interjecting only when asked or when the debate got too off track. A few times he snapped at a student if the profanity got out of control, but in general he let them swear and give each other the finger. It pleased him to see them become involved, batting ideas and opinions back and forth like a political tennis match.

About halfway through class, Coach Zim saw from the corner of his eye a shadow fall and linger in the doorway. He casually made his way along the side of the room to the back while his class engaged in their debate. He glanced at Ackerson and saw that he was laughing at something Michael

Barrow had just said. Something about the history of pot smoking in the White House.

He stepped into the doorway and there stood Tom Collins, as he expected. He was staring into the room and jumped back in fright when Coach Zim's large frame suddenly filled the doorway. Coach Zim walked out into the hall, toward him. Collins backed into the lockers on the far wall, fear in his eyes. But when his back hit the lockers and the steel clanged the insolence returned, spreading like a rash across his face.

"Gonna stick me in a locker again? Go ahead. We've already got one lawsuit against you."

"Where's your pass?" Coach Zim calmly asked.

Collins pulled a wrinkled piece of paper from his front pocket and jabbed it like a dagger at Coach Zim.

"Says you left Mr. Greer's class ten minutes ago," Coach Zim said. He handed back the pass. "It doesn't take ten minutes to go to the bathroom."

"I had to take a shit."

"There's a bathroom in the corridor near Mr. Greer's classroom. What are you doing down here?"

"Toilets are plugged."

"Uh huh. I'm not going to waste my time checking. Let's take a walk to the office."

"I'm not going to the office," Collins said. He smiled and leaned against the lockers.

Coach Zim sighed loudly, and then his hand shot out toward Collins's ear. His reflexes were still very fast and Collins never had a chance. By the time the teen's head jerked back, slamming painfully against a locker, Coach Zim already had ahold of his earlobe. Squeezing the soft, spongy flesh between his thumb and forefinger, he led Collins across the hall to the doorway of his classroom and was pleased to see his students still debating. He cleared his throat loudly. A few students looked his way. Among them was Ackerson, whose eyes grew wide at the sight of Coach Zim holding onto Tom Collins in what had to be a very painful manner, judging by the way Collins was moaning and his knees buckling.

"I'm going to the office for a minute," Coach said quietly, so as not to disturb the debate. "Be right back."

He started away, dragging Collins and wearing the satisfied expression of a priest dealing out corporeal punishment at a Catholic boarding school. Collins, nearly in tears, dug into Coach Zim's forearm with his sharp nails. Coach Zim squeezed the earlobe harder, causing Collins to cry out.

"I'm going to sue your ass again! First you stick me in a locker, then you drag me down a hallway against my will, like a dog! I'm gonna get rich off your ass, man!"

"Let me know how that works out for you," Coach said.

"Hey! Hey! Help! I'm being assaulted by a teacher in the hallway! Help!"

Miss Jacobs, head of the history department, opened her classroom door and looked worriedly into the hallway. Coach Zim twiddled his fingers and smiled as he passed. Confused, she glanced down and saw a bent-over Tom Collins being led by the ear down the hallway. Her eyes narrowed as she stared at the shadow of a swastika slightly visible beneath his short hair. She nodded at Coach Zim and closed the door to her classroom.

"Shut your mouth, Collins." He lowered his voice. "Before I piss in it."

Collins stopped walking and looked up. This caused his earlobe to be nearly ripped from his head because Coach Zim never broke stride. Coach felt the flexible skin around the earlobe tighten like a leash and did what any dog owner would do – gave it a firm tug. Collins yelped in pain and moved forward quickly.

"I've got one," Coach Zim announced, entering the office with Collins in tow. "Where do you want him?

The middle-aged women behind the counter in the office stared at Collins in disgust. One of them pointed to a line of plastic chairs against the wall. Two of the chairs were already occupied by surly-looking boys.

"Join the queue. Vice Principal Simon is a very popular man this morning. Lots of kids here to see him."

Only when Collins was seated in one of the chairs did Coach Zim release his ear. Collins gingerly touched his ear and again threatened to press charges for assault and file another lawsuit. Coach Zim ignored him and explained that Collins had a pass but was wandering the halls and causing a disruption outside his classroom. He also explained that Collins had used improper language and threatened him. Mrs. Dubrow, the youngest of the office workers, wrote it all down.

"Thank you, Coach," she said as he left the office. From his seat Collins gave Coach Zim the finger, which Mrs. Dubrow saw and added to the list.

Laughter, sharp and full, rolled toward him from a side corridor. Not the giggling, untamed laughter of teenagers, the sound gangly puppies joyfully rolling over each other would make. This was the thicker, more controlled amusement of adults. He sometimes wondered why adults lost the ability to laugh uncontrollably as they aged, as those were the years when they most often needed to laugh.

Had to be the teacher's room. Sounded like they were having a good time - it started as one low chuckle and quickly grew into a chorus of laughter, high and low, male and female. He poked his head into the room. Several teachers – everyone in the room – were gathered around a small television. He'd never seen such joy and happiness in the teacher's room. Usually a somber, miserable mood hung over the room like a cloud thick with despair. An uninformed visitor to the room would have the immediate impression that someone had passed away, not realizing that he was witnessing the unpleasant consequences of trying to educate groups of teenagers. He imagined the teacher's rooms in most American high schools were much the same, like a funeral on a cloudy day.

Several teachers were gathered around the room's small television. Phil Carlson, laughing along with the rest, noticed Coach Zim standing in the doorway and waved him in. "Coach, you have to see this. It's hilarious."

Coach Zim entered and, because he was the tallest in the room, stood behind the others. On the screen, two ESPN hosts were banging on the studio desk and wiping tears of laughter from their eyes. One of them regained his composure long enough to sob, "Roll it again." And there on the screen was the video of Nutsack Horne knocking himself out by slamming a bat on his head, slowed down for extra effect. Shown immediately after was a clip of Bo Jackson snapping a wooden bat on his batting helmet, and then, again, Todd Horne trying it with an aluminum bat and dropping like an empty sack.

Although he'd already seen it on YouTube, the clip was funnier on ESPN. Maybe because of the uncontrollable amusement of the hosts, or the teachers giggling together in the lounge. Coach Zim laughed along with the rest of them and watched as they replayed the clip again and again. Then he remembered he still had a class to teach.

"Hey, I gotta go," he said with a last chuckle. He headed for the door, hoping the debate in his classroom hadn't gotten out of hand.

"You know, Coach," Harold Iannucci called after him, "even with all the championships, Todd Horne did something you never did. He got Apple Brook High on ESPN."

Coach gave Iannucci the finger and couldn't help but smile as laughter chased him down the hall.

15

As Coach Zim drove to Portland to meet with Sparky, the Sea Dog's manager, on the team's off day, the Apple Brook Warriors walked onto the home field of the Rockport Rockets. Rockport was a terrible team, perennial bottom dwellers, and Apple Brook hadn't lost a game to them in almost twenty years. This information alone should have given Coach Horne confidence, had he bothered to learn anything about his team's opponents. Rockport should have been an easy win, a way for his team to get back a bit of swagger after the previous week's embarrassing loss.

But Coach Horne rarely looked at the schedule and showed no interest in scouting other teams. He was confident of a win, though. He'd have felt the same way if they were playing the Red Sox that afternoon. His changes, the ones that would make him a legend and make the players stop saying, "but Coach Zim never had us do this", were going to make losing a thing of the past. He took another pain pill and team manager April Spring rubbed his head until the bus pulled into the parking lot outside the ball park.

Paul Rivard bounded down the steps first and stood by the door of the bus, barking at the players as they exited. "Move it, Nass; tuck in your shirt, Williams; Cooke, if I see your hat sideways again I'm gonna pull it down to your neck; where the hell's your glove, Krane; move it, dipshits, move it!"

Todd Horne stood next to the visitor's dugout on the third base side, soaking in the warm afternoon sun and watching his team warm up. While he felt slow and foggy due to the pain pills he'd been downing the past couple of days, his headache was reduced to a dull, almost rhythmic throb. Balls slapped into gloves and music played from the PA system and Paul Rivard barked orders to the players. Nutsack Horne grinned stupidly and soaked it all in through a dull haze. In his hand was the lineup card, the one with the revolutionary changes that had come to him while in his concussed state.

The team gathered in the dugout before their first at-bats. Coach Rivard growled, "Shut up, ladies" and all was quiet. Coach Horne walked to the top of the dugout stairs and held up a piece of paper.

"Men, here is tonight's lineup." He could barely suppress a grin. "You'll notice I've made some changes. Changes that will no doubt lead to the most successful season in Warrior history!" He waited for cheers. None came. Poor kids were dense. No wonder they'd lost the first game. "Thompson, you're batting first. Nass, you'll be batting cleanup, in Thompson's usual spot."

Nass, who'd been in the on-deck circle swinging a bat, stopped and stared.

"Agolli, you're batting second. Krane, you're batting third. Williams, you'll be batting eighth."

Anderson Agolli was a great fielding third baseman with a cannon for an arm who couldn't hit his way out of a wet paper bag. He'd hit .190 the previous year and since junior high had always batted eighth or ninth. He could only stare at Horne, as confused as the rest of the team.

"Horne, you moron," Paul Rivard snapped. "You hit yourself in the head again? You've got the fastest guy on the team batting cleanup, the next fastest batting eighth, your power hitter leading off, and the worst hitter on the team batting second. No offense, Agolli."

"Thanks, Coach," said Agolli.

"Once again, Coach Rivard smothers us with love and encouragement," Krane remarked.

Todd Horne held up his hand toward Coach Rivard, cutting him off. Nearly quivering with excitement, he announced, "I've got a few defensive changes, as well. Thompson, you'll be starting at catcher today."

"I've never caught in my life," Thompson said, looking very worried.

"Are you kidding me?" Rivard said. "Thompson can't catch anything! It's like his glove has a hole in it! He's the last person who should be catching!"

"Thanks, Coach."

"Krane and Nass," Horne continued, "you're swapping positions. Krane, you'll play second and Nass will move to shortstop. Williams, you'll be in center field playing shallow, almost in the infield. In fact, I want the left fielder and the right fielder playing shallow, too. We'll dare them to hit it over our heads."

"Why?" demanded Coach Rivard. "Why would you make such stupid moves? I realize you ain't the sharpest knife in the drawer, Horne, but this is ridiculous. Do you know anything about baseball? Are you trying to lose?"

Horne smiled at Rivard the way a teacher smiles at a simple student. At this point he couldn't control his excitement and flexed each pectoral alternately, like two small balloons bouncing under his extra small polo shirt.

"You see, Paul, a guy like you has been around the game for so long that you can't imagine how anything new can work. But because I've never coached, or even played baseball before this year, I can see newer and better ways to play the game. You're old-school, and there's nothing wrong with that. But it's time to shake things up."

Rivard stared at him, hands hanging at his sides, clenching and unclenching. His face went from pink to scarlet to almost purple, like a man being choked. The team watched, transfixed, as Coach Horne grinned and bounced his pectorals while Coach Rivard clenched up and slowly changed colors. Finally he picked up a bat, cocked it up at his shoulder and glared at Horne for a moment as though considering walloping him, and instead swung at a row of batting helmets. The helmets scattered everywhere with a loud crash. Several players flinched, and April screamed and dropped her scorebook.

"That's right!" yelled Coach Horne. "Let's get mad! Let's get pumped! *Come on! Do it*!"

And he broke into a most muscular pose, turning back and forth like an oscillating fan so the entire team could have a look as he flexed in front of the bench. The team sat in silence, most of them staring in awe at the thick blue veins bulging like worms from his forehead, hoping one would burst. Only April's clapping and squeal of delight as he pointed at a quad and flexed it broke the silence. Horne didn't see or hear the umpire signal for the game to begin, so Dallas Thompson walked slowly past his flexing coach toward home plate to bat lead off for the first time in his high school career.

"We lost nineteen to two? To Rockport? But they used to stink."

"Oh, they still stink," said Paul Rivard. "But nobody stinks worse than us."

Coach Zim sat on a stool at his kitchen counter, drinking a beer and eating from a bowl of peanuts. He listened as Rivard told him about the changes that Nutsack Horne had implemented, both offensively and defensively. The game had started out well – Dallas Thompson had crushed the game's first pitch over the left field wall, causing

Horne to break into such an outburst of flexing that he became lightheaded and had to be led back to the bench by April Spring.

That was the high point of the game. It wasn't as though the Warriors were outplayed, not really. They could have won the game, had it been played the way baseball has been played for over a hundred years. But with the outfielders pulled up to the edge of the infield – the Dipshit Shift, Rivard had taken to calling it – routine fly balls dropped in for doubles and triples while the outfielders raced out to chase them. A deep drive to the warning track in center field, normally a guaranteed out with the fleet Williams running under it, resulted in an inside-the-park home run. And moving Dallas Thompson to catcher resulted in four errors and countless passed balls. It got to the point where the umpire put on an extra padded vest as a result of being hit by so many passed balls. And when a Rockport player got on base, "there may as well have been a green light flashing from second base", according to Rivard. Twelve stolen bases.

"It wasn't the big oaf's fault, neither," said Rivard. "He doesn't know how to play catcher. Hell, he was just learning to play right field by the end of last year. It's all that dipshit Horne's fault."

"How did we only score two runs?" Coach Zim asked. He crunched on a peanut and gazed absently at Angela, seated in front of her laptop at the table, her latest article reflecting off her glasses. Behind her, the darkness outside was divided into six-inch squares through the kitchen window. "I know our kids can hit. And Rockport's pitcher, Jamison, has a good fastball but nothing else. We nailed him last year."

"We got a lot of hits this year, too. But Horne had Thompson batting first and his two home runs were solo shots. At one point we got the bases loaded with two outs and

Thompson up. Thompson, who hit two home runs. Horne had him bunt. With the bases loaded. And two outs."

"Why did Horne do all this? And what did he have to say afterward?"

"Ol' Nutsack was inventing a revolutionary way to play the game. And when the massacre was over he blamed the players and said they obviously needed to do more calisthenics. Then he said he had a headache and spent the ride home in the back of the bus with April Spring rubbing his head. I think he's porking her."

Coach Zim choked a little on his beer. "But she's a student."

"No shit, Sherlock. But if he ain't porkin her, he's trying to. Would you put it past him?"

Coach Zim had heard the rumors about Nutsack Horne and some of his female students. "No, I suppose I wouldn't."

"You know, last week's game was my worst experience ever in baseball. Until today."

"How did you keep from punching him?" Paul Rivard was not the most even-keeled, level-headed person. Coach Zim had seen him swing at men for much less.

"I punched my thigh and bit my lip the entire game." Rivard chuckled. "Now I have a bloody lip and a big bruise on my thigh."

Coach Zim laughed. "What are you going to do Thursday? You're playing Bedford High. Defending state champs."

"I'm praying for rain."

They talked for a couple more minutes before hanging up. Coach Zim was eating the last of the peanuts in his bowl when he noticed Angela looking at him over the top of her laptop. He smiled at her and she smiled back.

"The team lost, huh?"

Coach Zim nodded and repeated what he'd heard from Paul Rivard – the lineup changes, the fielding changes, the loss to a team that they hadn't lost to in almost two decades. He skipped the part about Rivard's suspecting that Nutsack Horne was sleeping with April Spring. It was only a rumor based on no proof, nothing more, and he hated spreading rumors. Besides, Angela would want to call the police and have Horne investigated, proof or no proof. Over the years Coach Zim had seen the lives of several young men ruined because of false accusations of rape, and he refused to be a part of that.

"They're going to demand your return to coaching the team soon."

"They? Who are they?"

"Everyone. I'll bet half the town has talked to Principal Craggy about it by now."

"Doesn't matter, even if they did. Craggy's wanted me out for a long time, and he's not letting me back in."

"That's okay. You've got your job with the Sea Dogs to look forward to, right?"

He'd met with Sparky Webster earlier that day to discuss a couple of players he'd been asked to observe. After a cup of coffee and a short discussion, he and Sparky went down to the batting cage to talk with the players. Coach Zim showed them what he'd noticed they were doing wrong. The players thanked him politely and went back to their workouts.

"Nice fellas, but it's weird. They were polite, but they didn't really want to hear what I had to say. I'm not teaching them anything. My job is to observe, not teach."

"And you're a teacher," Angela said.

"Well, I always have been. It's just different, that's all. Just something I'll have to get used to."

Angela nodded and didn't say another word. She'd let her husband figure this one out for himself.

16

Both Coach Zim and Angela were early risers, six o'clock on most weekday mornings. On weekends they often enjoyed a lie-in until eight, sometimes nine on a rainy or snowy Sunday. Once or twice a week they had breakfast together at George's Diner, always ordering the same things – a mushroom and cheese omlette with a side of fried hash for Coach Zim and a blueberry muffin for Angela. On the other days Coach Zim stopped at Aroma Joe's on his way to the high school for two chocolate donuts and a coffee.

At seven in the morning most people prefer the comfort of their vehicle while they wait in line, half asleep, for that all-important first coffee of the day. But not Coach Zim. He enjoyed getting out, stretching his legs, joking with the girls behind the counter, most of whom he remembered as students. This, as much as the coffee, helped kickstart his day. Plus, the drive-thru line was usually a dozen cars long with a ten or fifteen minute wait, and chances were about even that half a mile up the road you'd discover they'd gotten your order wrong. By walking inside, he could laugh and joke while watching them fill his order.

Entering Aroma Joe's, he noticed a white sign in the front window. Written in red marker was ***Bring back Coach Zim!*** He'd never noticed the sign before, but there were a lot of things he didn't notice. The girls behind the counter were friendly, as usual, but did not mention the sign and so he assumed it had been there for days, maybe even weeks.

The faster service inside Aroma Joe's was also beneficial when in a hurry and today he was, because the person who'd slashed his tires was still out there, on the loose. It had rained the previous day, Tuesday, but this morning was sunny and mild, a perfect day for lurking behind a shaded tree at the edge of the high school parking lot, watching the kids like a pervert. That was Angela's description, not his. To Coach Zim, it was a covert operation, something James Bond might do. When he mentioned this to Angela, she reminded him that he was a middle-aged American high school teacher and former baseball coach with a bit of a paunch who was faithfully married and drove a rusty pickup truck.

It didn't matter what she said. Stealthily sliding out of his truck at the back of the parking lot, crouching low as he hurried to the trees with a bag of donuts in one hand and a coffee in the other, he felt like Bond. In the shade of the trees, he looked down at his watch and wished it could take pictures or videos or give him the exact coordinates of his location, or a location anywhere in the world. Then he remembered that he had a cell phone which did those exact things sitting in the glovebox of his truck. He reached inside the bag, stuffed half a donut in his mouth and watched the parking lot.

Half an hour later, he no longer felt like James Bond. Instead, he felt like a teacher who was going to be late for class if he didn't hurry up and get his butt out of the woods.

In the school's front lobby two more signs, exactly like the one at Aroma Joe's, were taped to the tile walls. Coach Zim didn't notice them and walked right past. He did notice the t-shirts, red, with white lettering – ***Bring Back Coach Zim!*** It seemed that half of the students in the school were wearing them, and with the swarm of red and white flooding the hallways it looked like the day of a pep rally.

He'd reached the doorway to his classroom when Vice Principal Simon came up from behind and grabbed him by the arm. Coach Zim stopped, looking down at the hand on his arm for a moment and then at Simple Simon.

"Are we dating?" he asked.

The vice principal released his arm. "Principal Craggy would like to see you. It's about all this." He gestured to the students in the hallway.

"It's about you moving your index finger in a circle?"

"Now, see here! I'm tired of these sarcastic remarks from you! I am the vice principal here and I demand a little respect."

"Simon, I don't have time for this today. Were you or were you not moving your finger in a circle while wordlessly explaining why Craggy wants to see me?"

"You know what I meant!"

A group of three junior girls, all wearing ***Bring Back Coach Zim!*** shirts, said hello as they walked past. Coach Zim nodded to them and smiled.

"I really don't, Ed. I never do. When does Craggy want to see me?"

"As soon as possible."

"Tell him I'll be there next week."

"Sooner than that."

"Tell him I'll see him after school." The warning bell rang. Five minutes until school began. "I could go now, if you'd like to take over my first class."

Ed Simon looked inside the classroom, where half of the students stared like acne-riddled zombies at their iPad screens and the other half sat on desks and threw things and laughed. Terror filled his eyes.

"I think after school will be fine."

Coach Zim smiled as Simple Simon hurried away, but his happiness didn't last long. Coming in the other direction was Tom Collins. He wore a black Lynyrd Skynyrd t-shirt with the sleeves cut off. Other students stared and nudged each other as Collins passed. Coach Zim watched, curious. As he approached a tattoo became visible on Collins's scrawny left bicep. A confederate flag. Coach Zim groaned and shook his head. The idiot was using his pale skin as a billboard for hate.

Collins saw Coach Zim watching him and glared back. Then he drew his fist up to his chest and flexed his bicep. It looked like a bone with a small tumor. "Like my ink?"

"Nice. Did you join the Dukes of Hazzard fan club?"

"It scares you, doesn't it? Scares a lot of people. But you'd better get used to it," Collins sneered. He approached slowly, surrounded by the rest of the Hitler youth. "This'll be here forever."

"Or until Luther sees it. Then it might become a removable tattoo. I'd invest in sleeves if I were you."

A flicker of fear passed over Collins face, and Coach Zim's smile returned. He walked into the classroom and walked to his desk. As he took of his jacket and got things in order, he listened in on the loud conversations going on throughout the room. It was how he usually found out the latest gossip – who was dating, who might be pregnant, where the party was that weekend, etc. Teenagers were loud and had no filter. That was one thing that had not changed over the years.

Most of the talk this morning was about the confederate ink decorating Tom Collins's skinny arm. It seemed everyone had an opinion about the tattoo, most of them negative. When his desk was in order, Coach Zim whistled sharply and the class immediately went quiet.

"Good morning," he said. "You guys seem especially talkative this morning."

"Just talking about tattoos," said Alfred Lemay, a junior whose mother taught chemistry at the school. Thus far, Alfred had shown absolutely no gift for science, mathematics (his father was a professor at a junior college) or any subject other than pot smoking. There were rumors he was heading to military school for his senior year. "I'm thinking of getting one this summer. It'll be sweet. You have any tattoos, Coach?"

"None that I'll show you, Lemay," he replied, and the class laughed.

"Did you see Tom Collins's new tattoo?"

Coach nodded. He wanted to tell them that tattoos were stupid, that most young people who get them regret it within a few years, that having a tattoo removed is a painful and expensive process. But they were teenagers. On certain subjects, he might as well be Charlie Brown's teacher – "*Wa wa wa wa.*"

"What do you think about the confederate flag?" asked a student from the back row.

"I don't think it's the best choice for a tattoo in today's United States," he replied.

"Yeah, but what do you think of the flag itself?"

Coach Zim thought carefully before answering. "I think it can be construed as a symbol of racism. But I also think it can be seen as a symbol of southern pride. A good example of this is the Dukes of Hazzard." He stared at their blank faces and sighed. "It was a television show on long before you were born. A very bad, but very popular, television show. Two southern cousins drove a car with a confederate flag painted on it and raised hell. Nothing racist about it. Just southern pride."

"So you think the flag is okay some of the time?" Lemay asked.

"I didn't say that. As I said, it's not a racist symbol for some southerners. Maybe even most. But it does offend a lot of people, particularly blacks, and with good reason. To them it represents something else, something horrible. Put it this way – it's a matter of southern pride for some white people. You don't find many African Americans going around waving the Confederate flag. In my opinion, we need to seriously consider the rationality of any flag or symbol which offends an entire race or other segment of society."

"So you think it should be banned completely."

"Well, that's where it gets tricky, because when you try to eliminate something, you can run into problems. Erasing history doesn't work. We learn from history, both bad and good. We often learn more from the mistakes we've made. So to try to erase slavery, or the confederate flag, or the word nigger – yes, Hatch, I said it. Stop covering your face. I said the N-word. It's just a word, and the more attention you give it by trying to eliminate it, the more power it will have. Most of you guys have read Harry Potter, so you know about the fear and power involved with saying Voldemort's name. It's similar to that."

Several students nodded, and Coach Zim saw that he was getting through to them. This wasn't always the case. This wasn't today's lesson plan, but it may be more valuable than what he had scheduled for the class. And so he asked, "What do you think?"

And they were off, just like the discussions from the *Killing Lincoln* book. He sat back in his chair, propped his feet up on the desk, and acted as moderator for the next forty-five minutes. When the bell rang he congratulated the students on their excellent verbal and cognitive skills, and then watched them hurry for the door as though the room had caught fire.

He stood outside the doorway, greeting students entering his second period class as well as those passing in the hallway. Someone called his name – "Yo, Coach Zim" – and he smiled as Charlie DeMar approached. In one hand was his iPad, while the other arm was wrapped snugly around a pretty blond freshman whose body had peaked way too soon. They both wore *Bring Back Coach Zim!* shirts.

"Morgan, right?" Coach Zim said, and the girl's bright smile faded. Charlie shook his head rapidly back and forth behind her.

"Morgan?" The girl stepped away from Charlie and glared at him. "Who's Morgan?"

"My old old lady." He smiled at her and then at Coach Zim, the smooth bullshit artist at work. "Coach, this is my new old lady, Lacy. My new and improved old lady."

Lacy's cheeks flushed as though she'd never been so flattered. She nestled back in under his arm.

"Coach, I was just telling Lacy that I might be losing you in the booth. People are talking about you going back to coaching." He pointed to his shirt. "Sounds like it's a done deal."

"This is the old guy who works for you at the baseball games? Wow, you weren't kidding. Usually it's the other way around, the old guy is the boss."

Now it was Charlie's turn to blush. "Naw, I wouldn't say I'm his boss. You know, we're sort of partners. Right, Coach?"

Charlie's eyelid fluttered as he winked about a dozen times in rapid succession. Coach Zim had to fight back the laughter. He nodded until he had it under control. "Charlie's just being modest. He's taught me a lot so far. He's a heck of a guy. But I'm not going anywhere. I don't know where the t-shirts or posters came from, but nobody's asked me to coach again."

They didn't hear the last part of this, because as soon as Coach Zim said that Charlie had taught him a lot, Lacy had gazed dreamily into Charlie's eyes and they immediately began making out.

Coach Zim cleared his throat. Nothing. Public displays of affection by teenagers tended to nauseate him, and he tapped Charlie on the shoulder. Nothing. Only when he pried their heads apart – like removing a plunger from a stuck drain – did they separate. Charlie smiled sheepishly, adjusted his pants, and they moved away as though conjoined at the pelvis.

As they walked on down the hallway, Coach Zim heard Lacy say, "That was kind of mean, but don't fire him, Charlie. He seems like a nice old guy."

As the school emptied of students at the end of the day, Coach Zim sat at the desk outside Principal Craggy's office, playing tic-tac-toe with Emma. She'd beaten him two straight games and was on her way to a third victory when Craggy announced on speaker phone that he would see Mr. Zimmerman now.

Emma hung up. "Principal Craggy will see you now, Mister Zimmerman."

"Not until this game is finished," Coach Zim grunted.

She marked her third diagonal O. "Tic-tac-toe, three in a row." She drew a line through them. "You lose again. Or I win again. Whichever makes you feel better."

"What the hell," he said, standing up. "Do you sit here practicing tic-tac-toe all day?"

Emma smiled. "Good luck," she said. Then she lifted her sweater. Coach Zim wasn't sure if he should look away, but then saw the red ***Bring Back Coach Zim!*** shirt she wore underneath. He shook his head and entered the principal's office.

Craggy sat behind his desk wearing his usual grim expression. He gestured for Coach Zim to sit in the small chair before his desk. As usual, Coach Zim plopped down onto the couch and stretched his legs out across it. For a minute, Craggy stared at Coach Zim and said nothing. Coach Zim didn't notice. He gazed out the window, watching students freed for another day walk past and wondering how Emma could have beaten him three games in a row. He sometimes played against students who finished early on the day of a test or during a detention, and he almost never lost. What were the odds of him losing three games in a row?

Craggy finally spoke. "Something you'd like to tell me, Jim?"

"Yeah, there is. I was wondering if you've ever played tic-tac-toe against Emma. She's unbelievable. If there's a tic-tac-toe world championship tournament, I say we sign her up."

With a slightly shaking hand, Craggy took a slow, deliberate sip from a plastic cup. He closed his eyes as he swallowed, and set the cup back down on his desk. Coach Zim wondered what was in the cup. He'd have been willing to bet it was something stronger than soda.

"I think you know what I'm talking about and are being deliberately obtuse, as usual."

"Garth, I honestly don't know what you're talking about. I don't even know what obtuse means. My wife would know. She's the smart one."

Craggy's face twisted into a humorless smile. He opened a desk drawer, reached inside, closed it. Then he held up a red ***Bring Back Coach Zim!*** t-shirt.

"Oh, not you too, Garth," said Coach Zim. "Are you the one who started passing these around to everyone?"

Garth Craggy's face slowly changed color, going through the entire spectrum of reds until it closely resembled the shirt in his hand. If steam had begun shooting from his ears, like Elmer Fudd in an old Bugs Bunny cartoon, it wouldn't have surprised Coach Zim. He watched as Craggy shakily picked up his cup, tipped it back and gulped it all down. Whatever was in the cup, it seemed to be working. Craggy closed his eyes and exhaled heavily. His face gradually faded from Alabama crimson, little by little, until all that remained were flushed cheeks. Coach Zim watched, fascinated, wishing he had a soda and popcorn for the show.

Craggy sat silently for a few moments, eyes closed, his breathing slow and steady. His back was perfectly straight, hands folded gently across his stomach. I may as well have walked into a yoga class, Coach Zim thought. Before long he was bored and tired of having his time wasted. The couch creaked as he swung his legs off it, and he was about to stand when Garth Craggy spoke.

"Don't get up, Jim. We aren't finished yet." He hadn't moved, and his eyes were still closed.

"Yes, yogi master," Coach Zim replied. He slung his legs back onto the couch and sat through a few more minutes of silence. "Hey Garth, did you confiscate someone's bong today, or visit the Maharishi, or what?"

"I'm just trying to remain calm. It's been a long day." He finally opened his eyes. "A very long day. Because, besides all the other shit that comes with my job, there were several phone calls – some quite angry – about my choice for the school's baseball coach. From little old ladies to firefighters to fellow teachers, everyone seems to have an opinion on how I do my job. And, on top of that, every time I moved, no matter where I turned today, all I saw was *this fucking shirt!*"

He shouted so loud that the large windows behind his desk rattled in their panes and the old bell on the wall hummed. Coach Zim saw students outside the window pause in their hasty escape to see where the yelling had come from. They looked up toward the second floor, where a few of the windows were open. The windows in Craggy's office were closed.

In the rooms and hallways outside the principal's office, the noise and commotion that comes with the end of a school day abruptly came to a pause, replaced by a cautious silence. Directly outside the office, there was absolutely no sound. Coach Zim imagined Emma at her desk, leaning toward the door, trying to hear what was being said.

Inside the office, Craggy had lost all pretense of calm. His eyes were wide and crazed. One hand banged repeatedly on his desk, steady as a metronome, while the other whipped the ***Bring Back Coach Zim!*** shirt around and around above his head like a Steelers fan waving a Terrible Towel. Finally, he stood up, squeezed the shirt into a ball and whipped it as hard as he could at Coach Zim, who caught it with one hand.

"About time somebody offers me one." He held it up by the collar. "Hey Garth, this isn't going to fit me. It's a medium. I take an extra-large."

"Explain this to me!"

"Well, I'm six foot four and weigh between two-twenty and two-forty, depending on-"

"Why? Why can't you give me a straight answer?"

"Garth, you aren't doing so well at remaining calm. Maybe you need to refill that cup."

Craggy gripped the edge of the desk and slowly lowered himself into his chair. He took a deep breath, leaned back, and began to look like his usual calm, menacing self.

"I'm sorry, Jim," he said at last. His voice was level and composed. "That was uncalled for. It's been a long day, and I'd just like to know who is behind half the student body wearing those t-shirts. I was hoping you might be able to help me."

"Honestly, Garth, I have no idea. I saw a sign at the donut shop this morning, noticed a few in business windows on the drive here, and saw them in the hallways. And the t-shirts, I just don't know. I'd like to know who organized all this, though. It's a little flattering but it's also embarrassing."

"Well, if you find out who's in charge, tell them they may as well stop because there is no way in hell you will be brought back to coach baseball at this high school."

"Gee, Garth, don't sugarcoat it." He folded his hands behind his head. "Hey, I can understand how satisfied you must be with Nutsack. After all, he did get on ESPN."

Craggy slumped a little. "I've had a talk with Todd. I think we're about to get the baseball program turned around."

Their talk took place during lunch period. Todd Horne had avoided the cafeteria and the teacher's room – anywhere he might run into adults - since the video began playing on ESPN. With kids, if he even suspected they were talking about or laughing at him, he'd threaten them with detention and confiscate their electronic devices. But he had no control over teachers. They'd make jokes and laugh and tease him. Some were polite enough to at least try and keep a straight face, until fucking ESPN played the clip again. Then they'd laugh like they were at a comedy show. The TV in the teacher's room was always on ESPN now, it seemed.

It had been less than a week but it seemed like the video would never go away. During lunch period on Tuesday Horne, tired of the laughter at his expense, walked into the teacher's room fully flexed, face beet red, trembling with effort and lack of oxygen. There was silence in the room, until tiny Miss Jacobs said that he was in the wrong room and the bathroom was three doors over. That broke them up, and they laughed even harder when Horne deflated and slinked out of the room.

So now he ate lunch at the desk in his small office outside the gym, next to the boys' locker room. When Craggy walked in unannounced, Horne had been staring at a muscle magazine and flexing a bicep like the juice monster whose picture took up an entire page.

"Christ, give it a rest, Todd."

"Sorry, Uncle Garth." He closed the magazine. "Just doing some isometrics until I can start lifting weights again. My head's feeling better, so hopefully soon." He crossed his fingers and held them up.

"Yes, we all anxiously await that day. In the meantime, let's discuss baseball. Are you planning to win any games at all this season?"

Horne nodded eagerly and proceeded to show Craggy his detailed plans, written on a pad with Gold's Gym letterhead. Craggy looked them over and decided the concussion was more serious than he'd thought. He had Dallas Thompson pitching, Nass and Krane playing first and third, no shortstop, and four outfielders. At random areas of the page *The Horne Shift* and *Do it!* were scrawled.

Craggy handed the pad back to his nephew and considered firing him right there. Unfortunately, that left him with Rivard as head coach and that was almost as bad as having Zimmerman in charge. Instead, he left the room without a word, giving Todd Horne the idea that his uncle was happy with his ideas. He opened the magazine back up and resumed flexing his bicep, harder than before.

To Coach Zim, Craggy now said, "Yes, I believe Todd's just about to get the team back on the right track."

"Would that be the same right track I've had them on for the past twenty years, when we won all those championships?" Coach Zim asked.

Craggy ignored him. "Aside from this, I've also got that little shit Collins walking around my school with a new racist tattoo. Is he trying to use his body for hate group advertisement? This is the kid that's suing the school."

"I wouldn't worry about him too much. The swastikas were one thing – we don't have any angry Jews walking around the school – but we do have a large, angry black janitor who may not take kindly to a confederate flag. I wouldn't be surprised if he ripped Collins's arm off and beat him with it."

"One can hope." Craggy leaned forward. "Well, thank you for meeting with me, Jim. I'm glad to hear that you aren't behind this shirt operation. One less thing for me to worry about, although I still would like to find out who is behind it."

Coach Zim's knees popped as he stood up. "Good luck with that, Garth. Hey, can I keep the shirt? My wife might like it."

As soon as the door closed, Garth Craggy opened up his bottom desk drawer and took out his half-empty pint of whiskey. He was out of Pepsi and considered walking to the vending machine to get one. In the end, he decided to just take a swig of whiskey straight from the bottle. It burned and the taste was awful, but it was fast and easy. At this point, fast and easy sounded great.

17

Paul Rivard may have prayed for rain, but the day of the Bedford High game arrived sunny and warm, with temperatures expected to be around 70 degrees at game time. Coach Zim was amused to see even more ***Bring Back Coach Zim!*** posters lining the walls of the school. He'd discussed it the previous evening with Angela and she'd convinced him to just go with it, accept the shirts and posters as a compliment. When he'd left the house that morning, he noticed she was wearing the shirt he'd given her.

The Bedford High game was a big deal. Bedford was a perennially good team, finishing second to Apple Brook several times. In the past few years, the two had switched places, with Bedford first and Apple Brook second, or even third. The way the Apple Brook team looked this year, they might finish last. Bedford, on the other hand, looked unstoppable, with three senior pitchers – two lefties and a right hander - who'd given up a combined two runs in the three games they'd played thus far.

Though he wasn't coaching, Coach Zim was nervous about the game all day. Bedford was the team he most wanted to beat every year. Bedford was a good team but they played dirty. The reason for this was because Max Dutch coached his team like he was running the Cobra Kai dojo. Pitchers were head hunters, baserunners were taught to kick out at anyone within range when sliding into base, and opposing baserunners learned to duck quickly or risk being decapitated by thrown balls. It was dirty, but effective – many teams were visibly afraid of Bedford.

There wasn't a coach that Coach Zim hadn't gotten along with well during his entire coaching career, with the exception of Max Dutch. The two had been rivals in high school, when Jim Zimmerman's Apple Brook Warriors twice defeated Max Dutch's Bedford Patriots in the regional playoffs and went on to win the state title. Even as a teenager Dutch was a dirty player. He was a good player, one of the best in the state, but nowhere near as good as young Jim Zimmerman. Problem was, he believed he was as good a player as Zimmerman. And when both became coaches, Max Dutch believed he was a better coach. That wasn't true either, but Dutch never stopped trying to prove that he was better, no matter what it took.

Coach Zim actively disliked Max Dutch. Dutch was the only person Coach Zim came close to fighting on the baseball field, and it happened more than once. Dutch taught his kids to hurt other players and there was no room for that in high school baseball as far as Coach Zim was concerned. Every time he wanted to punch Dutch in the mouth – there had been many over the years – he thought about what the players would think of him. They might find it cool, yes, but it would also open a door that the players might want to follow him through. And if any of his players ever crossed that threshold to violence and cheating he wouldn't be able to stop them because he'd stepped through that door first. On Coach Zim's team, character came first. Character was everything. And character usually led to winning.

He wasn't overly surprised when several players visited his classroom immediately after school. He'd been hurrying, wanting to get to the field early – a habit he couldn't shake – but the players were faster. He was pushing the chair in behind his desk when they walked in – Krane,

Nass, Thompson, Williams, a few others. They were worried about Bedford's tactics, as well as what their own coach had in store for them.

"I talked to Coach Nutsack a little while ago," Krane said. "When I told him about the way Bedford plays, he flexed and said if they want pain, they're gonna get it. Then he walked away, yelling *Come On!* over and over."

"Yeah, that idiot's gonna get us killed," said Williams. "Not to mention we're gonna lose again."

Coach Zim didn't bother telling them to treat their coach with respect. That sort of flew out the window when Nutsack belted himself with the bat and completely disappeared with the Horne Method, or whatever the hell he called it. At this point, a team full of monks would have been calling him Coach Nutsack.

"You beat them last year. Nothing's changed, except you guys are older, stronger, and more experienced."

"We beat them once," Krane said. "The second time we played, they killed us. And they've given up two runs in three games. We've given up about a hundred in two games."

Coach Zim narrowed his eyes. "Is that it? You guys are going to roll over and die? If I'd known I had such a team of babies I'd have quit coaching before this."

"You didn't quit, Coach. You were fired."

"Thank you for correcting me, Krane. The point is, you guys are giving up before the game even starts. You can win this game. Cooke's pitching for us, and he's as good as anyone they've got. All you guys need to do is score some runs and eliminate the errors. And play hard. Don't let these guys intimidate you, and don't lower yourselves to their level."

"Nutsack'll do something to screw us up," said Thompson.

"Coach Horne does have some original tactics, I'll admit," said Coach Zim. "But he's not on the field. You are. And you decide who wins or loses. It's all on you."

"I wish you could help us," said Krane.

"Well, I am announcing the game, so listen to what I'm saying. I may be able to help." The players smiled. "And listen to Coach Rivard. He's coached against these guys enough, he won't put up with any nonsense from their players or coach." He looked each boy in the eye. "Now get to the field and show these guys that they can't beat you by cheating. You are the better team." The players nodded. "I know you are. Coach Rivard knows you are. And by the end of the game, Bedford will know that you are."

The players gave a cheer and he high fived each of them. He sent them on their way and stayed in the classroom a moment longer, pleased with himself for inspiring the young players. Then he turned off the lights and followed them to the field.

The stands were nearly full when he arrived and both teams were on the field warming up. Coach Zim walked to the chain link fence on the first base side. Tyler Nass and another Grim Reaper sat nearby on their Harleys, talking to a couple of teenage girls. Coach watched the girls protectively and scowled at the bikers. Tyler Nass glanced up, smiled, and flipped him off.

He leaned over the fence. Paul Rivard was looking over something in a notebook with a look of dismay. Coach Zim called out and waved to get his attention. Rivard walked to the fence, still glancing at the notebook.

"You can come out on the field, you know. You'd probably get a standing ovation if you did," Rivard said.

Coach Zim nodded toward Max Dutch, standing near home plate talking with the umpire. He was a large man, almost as tall as Coach Zim, with a bald head under his Bedford cap. "I don't want that asshole to see me. He'll make some smartass comment about me losing my job, I'll say something about him losing his hair, and then the ump will need to separate us. The kids don't need to see that."

"It might fire them up," said Rivard. "Take a look at this."

He held out the notebook. Coach Zim looked at what he assumed was the batting order. It was almost the same as the previous game's lineup. Coach Zim frowned, then scanned the field.

"Where is Nutsack, anyway?"

"Gone home. Hopefully he won't come back. He was leading the team in calisthenics when his shorts ripped in the seat. He's gone to put on another pair. And this is what he's left me with." He looked at the notebook as though it were dipped in feces. "I'm not doing it. I'm not letting Thompson bat first and putting Agolli at cleanup. I like Agolli – he's a nice kid and he could drop a moose with that arm – but watching him at the plate is like watching a blindfolded little girl swing at a piñata."

"The kids are nervous," Coach Zim said. "A few of them came to see me after school. I told them to listen to what you had to say."

"Kick them Bedford pansies in the balls if they try any of their shit, that's what I'd like to say. But if I say that then I'll get fired and they'll be stuck with only Nutsack as their coach. So I'll toe the line."

"You're a good man and a good coach, Paul. Good luck. I hope you crush Dutch."

Rivard tore the lineup sheet out of the notebook, crumpled it, and tossed it at Coach Zim. "Get that shit away from me, will you? Throw it in the trash or something." He turned and walked toward the infield. "Nass, you dipshit, what the hell are you doing?"

Coach Zim turned away and saw Tyler Nass glaring at Rivard.

"That old prick talking to me?"

"No, he's talking to the other Nass dipshit," Coach Zim said. "The one with talent."

He walked up the stairs to the stands and observed that at least a quarter of the fans were from Bedford. He also noticed that most of the Apple Brook fans were wearing **Bring Back Coach Zim!** shirts. A few of them clapped when they saw him walk past. He ignored them. Luther, he noted, was sitting in his regular seat near the back, wearing his janitor's uniform. Coach Zim said hello as he walked past, and Luther nodded in return. It was more of a greeting than he gave most people.

The clapping grew as Coach neared the booth. He kept his eyes down until he reached the stairway. In the booth, Charlie DeMar stood in front of the microphones, making out so enthusiastically with Lacy that neither of them heard the door open. Coach cleared his throat, loudly. Nothing. Again, he placed a hand on each of their heads and physically separated them. Charlie looked up sheepishly, and Lacy looked annoyed. They gazed lovingly into each other's eyes as they said goodbye. Coach Zim sat down, grabbed a can of Coke and a slice from two large pizzas on the side table, and sat in front of his microphone. Lacy left soon afterward. Coach Zim was glad to see her go. The sight of them staring at each other made it difficult to eat.

"Poor thing can't keep her hands off me," Charlie said.

He sat down next to Coach Zim and adjusted his microphone. He called the radio station and spent a couple of minutes on the laptop. Then he hung up and slapped Coach Zim on the arm.

"Ready for the big game, partner?"

Coach Zim nodded. "If you value your hand, you won't slap me again."

"Sorry, Coach. I've been doing some crazy things lately. I guess love will do that to you."

Coach Zim grunted and got up for another slice of pizza.

"When did you first know you were in love?" Charlie asked.

"It wasn't the first day I met my wife, I know that. Love takes time."

"You were never in love before you met your wife?"

"Anyone I may have ever loved before was forgotten as soon as I met my wife. Marriage is a lot easier that way." He paused. "There's lust, and there's love. It's easy to get the two mixed up at your age. At my age, too. Give it a few months, see how you feel then."

"I think Lacy might be the one."

Coach Zim ignored him.

For the next few minutes they sat in silence, watching the teams finish their warm ups and jog to their respective dugouts. Charlie started the broadcast by introducing himself and Coach Zim, then said hello to his grandmother and her friends at the Sunny Fair development, Apple Brook's only over-55 adult community. During the national anthem he pointed toward the home dugout. They watched Todd Horne pass through the gate and jog to his team.

The Warriors took the field. Immediately, Coach Horne appeared agitated. He waved his arms, pointed and yelled. The players completely ignored him. Horne stomped his feet and reached for his whistle, which Coach Rivard had already ripped off his neck and thrown in the trash. He flexed, to no avail. Then he picked up a bat and held it in the air.

Charlie covered his microphone. "Why's he doing that?"

Coach Zim told him about the lineup sheet and mused that Coach Rivard must have put the players at positions other than where Horne wanted them.

"Now this is exciting," said Charlie DeMar. "Coach Horne has picked up a bat and is holding it over his head. Might we see a new ESPN clip before the game even begins?"

There was some laughter from the crowd, many of whom pulled out their phones and pointed them at Todd Horne. He'd obviously learned his lesson, though, because he didn't smash the bat into his head. Instead, he threw the bat straight down at the ground, where it bounced back up into his crotch. Horne instantly dropped to his knees and rolled onto his side, gently cupping his tenders.

"Play ball!" cried the umpire.

While Brock Cooke was busy striking out the first batter, Horne writhed on the ground, gasping for air, while the players on the bench more or less ignored him. Finally, the team manager, April, jogged from the dugout and knelt beside him. It wasn't pretty. He was covered in dirt, his face blaze red as if he'd been doing a most muscular pose. With April's assistance, Horne got to his feet and hobbled to the dugout. A couple of people clapped, but most jeered and laughed and continued to record it on their phones.

By this time Cooke had struck out two batters and walked one. The runner on first took a big lead, almost daring Cooke to try and pick him off.

"Think he's going to try and steal second, Coach?" Charlie said into the microphone, chewing on a mouthful of pizza.

"Looks that way, Charlie."

"I hope Nass is wearing a protective cup under his uniform. These Bedford guys like to slide with their spikes up." He burped without covering the microphone. "Excuse you, Coach Zim."

Coach Zim glared.

"Say, Coach, wasn't Ty Cobb famous for sharpening his spikes?"

"That's what they say, yes."

"You ever see him play?"

"He played at the beginning of the twentieth century, Charlie. A hundred years ago."

"Huh. So, you ever see him play?"

Coach Zim had already learned to take nothing which escaped from Charlie's mouth to heart. The kid was either one of the sharpest wits he'd ever come across or a complete buffoon. He hadn't yet decided which it was, but either way, the kid wasn't to be taken seriously.

The game went on, scoreless into the fourth, when Dallas Thompson hit a long double, scoring Adam Nass, who'd singled and stolen second. Coach Zim and Charlie were as excited as everyone else in the stands, standing up and shouting as Nass crossed home plate. Coach Zim looked down toward the home side and saw Paul Rivard standing outside the dugout, clapping and encouraging the players. He gave Nass a pat on the butt as he disappeared into the dugout. There was no sign of Nutsack Horne.

This was because Nutsack Horne's nutsack was swollen to the point where it appeared he'd shoved a large bag of coins down his tight white shorts. He sat to one side of the bench, moping, sweat on his brow and a bag of ice on his balls. April sat close, rubbing his shoulders. The players stayed on the other side of the bench and laughed quietly about Nutsack's nutsack until Coach Rivard told them to knock it off. He was just as happy as the rest of them to see the idiot out of the way, but there was a game to be won. The only excuse for smiling was scoring a run. And even then, it'd better be quick.

"This could be it," Charlie said excitedly as Apple Brook took the field at the top of the seventh. "Brock Cooke has thrown a three-hitter so far against the defending state champions. All he needs is three more outs. What would you do, Coach? Leave him in, or take him out?"

"No. Leave him in, definitely," Coach Zim said, almost to himself.

For one of the first times he wished he had his cell phone with him, so he could call Rivard down in the dugout and make sure he left Cooke in. But after a decade of coaching together, Coach Zim knew Rivard would do exactly what he himself would do. He'd coached a great game so far, gotten as much out of the kids as anyone could have. It was his game to win or lose now.

It was the right decision. Cooke's arm had to be tired after throwing almost a hundred pitches, but the adrenaline pumped through him and kept his fastball over eighty miles per hour. The first two batters grounded out and the third struck out, giving Cooke seven strikeouts for the game.

The players on the field rushed to the mound after the third strike to mob Cooke. The rest of the team ran from the dugout to join them. They jumped on top of each other and threw their hats and gloves into the air as though they'd just won the state championship. Normally, Coach Zim was against excessive celebrating, but this was a huge win, something the team needed. The celebrating was completely spontaneous, with the enthusiasm and joy that can only come from teenagers. No, he wouldn't mind it at all if he were coaching.

He stuck his head out the front of the booth. Coach Rivard obviously felt the same way. He stood, beaming, giving high fives and slapping butts as the players made their way to the dugout. They'd attempted to end the celebrating long enough to line up and shake hands with the Bedford players, but Max Dutch's team was already headed for the bus. Coach Zim shook his head but wasn't really surprised. They were poor sports both on and off the field.

Charlie was already on the phone with his old lady Lacy, telling her how much he'd missed her over the past two hours and asking her to come up to the booth. Coach Zim wanted to get out of there before he witnessed another makeout session, so he shook Charlie's hand and said goodbye. He considered waiting around to congratulate Coach Rivard, but he didn't want to take attention away from the big win. Instead, he tried his best to keep a low profile as he made his way to the crowded parking lot. He'd give Rivard a call later.

In the dugout, while the players laughed and fist bumped and loaded up the equipment bags, Coach Todd Horne remained seated in a corner, icing his nuts. Seeing that it was putting a damper on the celebration – not to mention annoying the hell out of him – Coach Rivard grabbed Anderson Agolli and pulled him aside.

"How many hits did you get today, Agolli?"

"None," he answered.

"Right. Well, then, why don't you help Coach Horne to his car?"

"What? Just because I didn't get a hit? We only got five hits all game, and Dallas got two of them. Most of the team didn't get a hit."

Coach Rivard glared. "Agolli, how many times did you strike out?"

"Three. But I made a couple of really good plays at third."

"I know that, Dipshit. I watched you. And because of those good plays, I'm rewarding you by letting you help your coach to his car. And before you argue, just let me add, shut up."

Agolli cursed Rivard quietly and helped Coach Horne to his feet. Horne dropped the bag of ice, leaving his white shorts wet down the front. Horne threw one arm around Agolli's shoulder, keeping the other on his aching balls. The team moved aside but nobody said anything to him. Most didn't even notice him leaving. April walked close behind, carrying the bag of ice.

As he passed through the fence to the parking lot in a bent-over shuffle, Horne heard the Grim Disciples laugh at him. It was a testament to just how sore he was that he couldn't even flex at them. Not a calf, nor a tricep. Instead, he hobbled along, holding tight to the scrawny third baseman whose knees, in Horne's mind, had to be buckling under the weight of so much muscle. He kept his head down and stared at the size and symmetry of his slow-moving shadow on the blacktop. It seemed unbelievable that anyone would dare laugh at someone so perfectly proportioned. Had he looked up, Horne may have been surprised at the large number of people filming him on their cellphones.

Agolli deposited Coach Horne in the passenger seat of his car. April got into the driver's seat. Horne groaned deeply as he sat, which Agolli assumed was a thank you. He didn't care, either way. He shut the door, waved to April, and hurried back to the field.

The team sat in the dugout, looking like kids itching to be dismissed from school. Agolli slid in on the end of the bench as Coach Rivard told them he was proud of the way they'd played. They didn't let Bedford bring them down to their level, but instead won with clean play and teamwork. It was just one win, he stressed, but also an important one. Coach Rivard commanded their attention and respect, and while he spoke both he and the team forgot that he wasn't the head coach.

He finished up by ordering them to take it easy that evening, to not go out and celebrate and do things they shouldn't do and act like a bunch of dipshits.

"What's going on now?" Agolli asked as they left the field.

"Bunch of us are going to Applebee's," said Krane. "Then maybe a party in the game room at Barrow's house. You coming?"

"I've got a bunch of homework."

With an incredulous look, Krane said, "After this win, do you think any teacher will care if you're late with your homework?"

Agolli thought about it for a second. "I guess not. I'm in."

The players piled into small cars that sounded like lawnmowers with sound systems that pounded the air like approaching dinosaurs, and before long the parking lot was empty.

Almost empty. Adam Nass stood with his back against the chain link fence while his father jabbed a dirty finger into his chest. On the back of Tyler Nass's motorcycle, a fourteen-year-old freshman sat patiently, chewing gum and leaning forward to check herself in the mirror. On the back of the other motorcycle sat another fourteen-year-old girl. The Grim Disciple leaning against the Harley rubbed the young girl's thigh and watched with a smirk as Tyler Nass bullied his son.

"The fuck, baseball star! You too good to return my calls?"

"I had homework, I told you." After years of abuse, he knew that it was best to stay cool. Showing the slightest trace of fear to a Grim Disciple whipped them into the sort of frenzy blood prompts in sharks.

"You don't return my call again, I'll break down your buddy Krane's front door and beat his father so badly he'll never be able to go on TV again. What kind of father lets another man's teenage son live at his house? He a fucking queer, or what?"

Adam couldn't help it. He lost his temper. "He's a better man than you'll ever be, asshole."

Tyler Nass responded by throwing a left hook into his son's stomach. Adam exhaled a short groan and dropped to his knees. He collapsed and rolled onto his side, gasping for breath.

"Are you crying? Jesus, I barely hit you. Hey girls, look at the baseball star cry."

The young girls on the back of the bikes looked uncomfortable – Adam Nass was a cool, popular senior – but laughed. Tyler Nass left his son rolling back and forth and gasping like a fish on a dock. He straddled his bike and the engine roared angrily to life. The other Grim Disciple started his bike just as Paul Rivard walked off the field and into the parking lot.

Rivard had been cleaning up the dugout and hadn't seen the confrontation between the Nass's. He'd heard nothing, either, having tuned the dugout radio from the rap station that the kids preferred to his favorite country station. But now, as he walked through the fence opening, carrying over his shoulder a mesh bag of bats and balls, he saw Adam Nass lying on the ground, rolling in pain. Nearby, his father laughed and revved the engine of his motorcycle.

"Hey!" Rivard called, trying to be heard over the twin roaring Harleys. "What's going on here?"

He hurried to Adam and knelt down beside him. The heavy exhaust gave the air over Adam a blue, oily haze. Coach Rivard helped Adam to his feet, practically yelling in his ear to ask if he was alright. Adam nodded yes, said he'd just had the wind knocked out of him.

Rivard glared at the bikers. Tyler Nass and his friend smiled, while the girls on the back of the motorcycles turned away and pressed their faces into the Disciples' greasy denim jackets. The girls may have been with badass bikers, but they were young enough to be scared of a teacher.

"You do this?" Rivard yelled to Tyler Nass.

"Mind your own fucking business, old man."

"When you lay a hand on one of my players or a student at my school, it is my business. That includes the young girls you have on the back of your bikes. Just giving them a ride home, I assume?"

"I said mind your business, old man." Tyler Nass put down his kickstand and stepped off the bike.

Adam Nass, still holding his stomach, stepped protectively in front of Coach Rivard. Rivard gently pushed him out of the way.

"Call 9-1-1, Adam" he said. Adam nodded, pulled out his phone, and stepped away.

"Calling the police for help? I heard you were a tough old guy, but looks to me like you're a fucking pussy."

"Oh, the call for help isn't for me." Paul Rivard bent down and pulled an aluminum bat from the equipment bag. He took a couple short practice swings. "It's for you."

Nass laughed and pulled a switchblade from inside his jacket. "You think you can take on two of us?"

"I survived the Vietcong. They were a hell of a lot tougher than you pretty ladies."

"That was a long time ago, old man."

"Ty, we'd better get out of here," said the other Disciple. "I'm carrying. If the cops find anything on me I'm facing five years."

Nass hesitated, then put the knife away and got back on his bike. Both bikers gave Rivard the finger before pulling away. The girls on the back held on tight and screamed as they pulled out of the parking lot and into the road without slowing.

The roar of the Harleys had faded away when a police car pulled into the parking lot, lights flashing. Emerging from the car slowly, like a chicken from an egg – or, based on his build, like a sausage from a wrapper – Officer Kyle Bertrand hooked his thumbs into his already strained belt loops. He gazed around, accessing the situation, and waited for Coach Rivard and Adam Nass to approach.

They didn't. Kyle Bertrand had been a student at Apple Brook High a few years earlier, and Paul Rivard remembered him as a fat dipshit. Now, apparently, the town had seen fit to make him a fat dipshit with a badge and a gun. Rivard had respect for law enforcement, but not when law enforcement had no respect for itself.

Officer Bertrand finally ambled over, thumbs still resting in his belt loops. There was no fight going on, so far as he could see. Looked like it may have been a false report or, at the least, an exaggeration. He was a busy man. It was early evening, prime time for speeders. There were plenty of people doing thirty and over in the twenty-five-mile-an-hour zone on Main Street. He didn't have time to waste on this malarkey.

In his deepest voice, he said, "I received a call about a fight. Is it over?"

"Of course it's over. You don't see a fight going on, do you?"

Bertrand stared at Rivard from behind his mirrored sunglasses, unsure of how to reply. Yes, Mr. Rivard was a well-respected – and feared – teacher at the high school and a decorated Vietnam War veteran. But Kyle Bertrand was a police officer, and in his opinion a badge trumped a teaching certificate. But Rivard didn't appear the least bit afraid of the badge. And people who weren't intimidated by the badge scared Bertrand.

"So, uh, what happened here?"

"This boy was assaulted by a member of the Grim Disciples motorcycle club, to start with."

"Coach, I don't think we need to mention that," Adam said quietly. "It's just going to make more problems for me and the Kranes, and everybody."

Coach Rivard nodded. "You're right." To Bertrand he said, "Skip that. It was a family squabble. But two members of the Grim Disciples just left here with a couple of fourteen-year-old girls on their bikes, and at least one of them was carrying."

"One of the girls is carrying?"

"No, you moron. One of the bikers."

"Oh, I see." Bertrand pulled a pad from his shirt pocket. His tongue stuck out as he scribbled. "What is he carrying?"

"Jesus, Bertrand, do I have to do your entire job for you? I told you there are two bikers carrying illegal contraband riding around with a couple of girls who've barely hit puberty. They left here less than ten minutes ago, headed east."

Bertand nodded and took a quick description of the motorcycles. He squeezed back into the police car and took off at full speed, lights blazing. A couple of kids crossing the road on bicycles dove out of the way as the car pulled into the road. One of them flipped him off, but Bertrand never slowed down.

"It's a sad day when that guy's protecting our fair town," said Coach Rivard.

Adam Nass agreed with him. Picking up the equipment bag, he slung it over a shoulder and followed Coach Rivard to his car.

18

Coach Zim spent the next couple of weekends in Portland, working with the Sea Dogs. After spending time with and observing Sparky Webster, Coach Zim came to the conclusion that managing in the minor leagues is much different than managing a high school team. Easier in some ways, harder in others. Half of his job as a high school coach was being a den mother – making sure the players behaved in school, got good grades, were polite and respectful in and out of school, stayed away from drugs – basically helping to guide them toward becoming productive young men. The other half of the job was showing these kids how to actually play baseball. Most of them were raw and needed coaching on the basics of the game – throwing, hitting, running the bases, throwing a curveball. The kids were clay and he molded them. He was good at it, too – there were very few coaches who could do all parts of the job as well as Coach Zim. All those championship trophies could attest to that.

Coaching a professional baseball team was completely different. Professionals didn't need or want to be molded, and they certainly didn't want anyone watching over them. A manager's job at this level was little more than controlling egos and making sure the team didn't implode. The players already had the skills and talent. They just needed help keeping their focus.

He spent a lot of time sitting in the dugout next to Sparky, watching games and practices and trying to avoid flying sunflower seeds. Sparky, along with several other coaches and players, chewed sunflower seeds instead of tobacco. It was undeniably healthier – he'd never heard of anyone developing cancer from sunflower seeds – and thought by some to be much less disgusting. True, there wasn't a trail of brown slime all along the dugout floor and steps. Instead, there were clumps of soggy sunflower seeds. Coach Zim couldn't help but wonder, for the thousandth time, why people need to chew something during a game.

Meanwhile, the Apple Brook Warriors baseball team played five games over two weeks and won four of them. This was largely due to Todd Horne's missing four of the games due to injury. The morning after the Bedford game, Horne had noticed blood in his urine. This, combined with his swollen scrotum, sent him into such a panic that he dressed in loose sweatpants and left for the emergency room without once stopping to flex in the mirror. The diagnosis, according to the middle-aged, rumpled-looking emergency room doctor, was bruised testicles and a swollen nutsack. Lots of rest, loose clothing, heat and ice were recommended for the next week.

After writing him a prescription for painkillers, the doctor turned to leave the examining room. He paused and turned back. "Say, aren't you the guy from the video? The one with the baseball bat?"

Horne wanted to glare and flex at the doctor, but his head and balls ached too much. He sighed and nodded.

"I knew it. You're famous. I heard that video has almost ten million hits on YouTube." The doctor grinned. "You know what my kids did? They downloaded the video and added their own music to it. Classical, with a big buildup to the point where you knock yourself out. Funny as hell." He pulled out his phone and snapped a quick photo of Horne, slumped over, cupping his sore balls in his hands. "My kids won't believe I met you. Have a nice day, Mr. Horne.

Remember, lots of rest. I'd advise staying away from baseball fields. They don't seem to agree with you."

With a big smile, he closed the door. The most Todd Horne could do in reply was flex his bicep, and even that hurt.

Coach Horne spent the following week home from school, resting on his couch. He watched a lot of television but avoided ESPN, which had picked up the video of his nut smashing and ran it hourly, back-to-back with the video of his knocking himself out. They all had a good laugh with it, but thankfully the nut-bashing video didn't prove as popular as the head-smashing video. By the end of the week it was only showing up a couple of times a day on ESPN and the YouTube views, while higher the first day, slowed down to a trickle after just a couple million.

Though the doctor advised against physical exercise of any type and weightlifting in particular, Horne decided after three days that, while the swelling in his scrotum had gone down, his muscles were beginning to atrophy and needed to be worked. He did a set of light dumbbell curls and felt pretty good. He did another set, slightly heavier. The third set he bumped up to fifty pound dumbbells. After the last rep he flexed in his full-length mirror and felt pretty good. For about thirty seconds. Then the dull ache between his legs quickly grew to a hammering throb, and the swelling returned. At that point he decided to heed the doctor's advice. He popped another pain pill and returned to the couch.

While Nutsack Horne nursed his swollen nutsack back to health, his baseball team finally looked respectable. Under the guidance of Coach Rivard, they won four in a row and had a winning record by the time Horne returned. On the day of his return they promptly lost, but still held onto a winning record and a chance at making the playoffs.

Nutsack Horne was happy about the wins because it meant his team might make the playoffs in his first year of coaching. This would prove that he was just as good a coach as Coach Zim, and possibly better. The fact that all of the team's wins took place when he was absent never crossed his mind.

Principal Craggy was happy about the wins too. The angry, threatening phone calls had stopped coming in and students had, for the most part, stopped wearing those stupid **Bring Back Coach Zim!** shirts. This also made Coach Zim happy, although Angela continued to wear hers around the house.

Tom Collins began attending the games. Not because he'd developed a sudden interest in the game of baseball or been overwhelmed with school spirit. He hated school and found most sports except cage fighting boring. No, the reason he'd started showing up at the baseball field was because he'd heard the Grim Disciples were staying away due to several charges of drug trafficking and contributing to the delinquency of a minor, among others. This left an opening for a drug supplier to the town's youth. Tom Collins figured he was just the man to fill the job.

He wasn't doing anything else after school anyway. Most afternoons he liked to wait around and see if he could catch Ackerson alone, but the fag got a ride home every day with Mr. Ianucci. It was part of a deal between Coach Zim and Ackerson. Ackerson didn't want to take the rides home – said he felt like he was being babysat – but Coach Zim insisted, saying it was the only way he'd keep from going to the police about what Collins and his friends had done. Ianucci was happy to do it – Ackerson's house was on his way home. Collins considered jumping both of them, but even he realized that assaulting a teacher could land him in big trouble. Not to mention ruin his chances for a big settlement in the lawsuit against the school.

He hung out in the same area where the Disciples parked, near the stairway leading up to the bleachers. If he was making a deal he'd sometimes duck under the stairs, against the building and out of sight except from the field, and nobody on the field was looking his way. He sold mostly pot but also some heroin and meth. His father and a couple other guys made it in the back of his garage. Lester Collins was actually the supplier for the Grim Disciples. His father didn't like the idea of Tom selling at the games – too much risk involved – but with the Disciples out of business for a little while, there was nothing else they could do. Man's gotta earn a living, Lester Collins liked to say.

The first game, Collins made a couple hundred dollars. He sold mostly to younger hoodlums who found him cool with his swastika and confederate flag tattoos. For a sale, Collins was more than happy to part his hair and lift his sleeve and show them. He made twice as much at the next home game as word got around that he was selling. His clientele ranged from jocks and cheerleaders to dropouts and middle-aged addicts. There was only one or two cops at the field and they usually spent their time watching the game or talking to the prettiest high school girls. With the Grim Disciples out of commission, he had control of the drug trade.

Collins wasn't arrogant enough to believe that nobody knew what was going on. He'd seen the looks from Coach Zim and Coach Rivard. He just smiled in return. And he'd caught a glance from Luther the janitor a couple of times, but that may have been due to the tats on his head and arm. He looked away and tried to tilt his head and drop his shoulder in a way that the tattoos couldn't be seen. Luther didn't look very friendly and he didn't want to piss him off. But otherwise, Tom Collins didn't care who knew he was selling drugs. The more people who knew, the better business was. The way things were going, he'd never have to work a day in his life.

After two away games, the Warriors returned home for Nutsack Horne's first game coaching since hurting his balls. Everything seemed to be back to normal – no blood in his pee, no lemon-sized testicles, no more loose-fitting shorts and sweatpants. He was pumping iron again, although not at full strength because there was still a slight tug of pressure in his crotch when he lifted too much. And with the swelling gone, he was back to wearing tight shorts. When he first tried them on, he realized he hadn't shaved his legs in over a week. He promptly did so, as he didn't want to look silly.

While lying on the couch recovering, Horne researched baseball coaching techniques by watching Red Sox games on NESN. It appeared that most managers did the same things – sat around in the dugout a lot, scratching their balls and spitting tobacco or sunflower seeds; walked out to the mound once in a while to talk with the pitcher or pull him out; jogged out to home plate to argue what they considered to be a bad call. And yet, though they all did similar things, some managers won while others lost. This proved that it was the players who won or lost the game. It also reinforced his belief that he was not a bad coach, but instead was being brought down by a group of bad players.

His first game back, Horne decided to use what he'd learned from his research while sitting on the couch. Upon arriving at the field, he opened a pack of sunflower seeds and stuck a large wad in his mouth. He didn't want to use chewing tobacco, as it was very unhealthy and might stain his shorts. He folded up the rest of the pack and tried to stick it in his pocket, but his shorts were too tight. Instead, he stuck it in his sock.

"Welcome back, Coach," Paul Rivard greeted him in the dugout.

Horne tried to say thank you and wound up spraying half-chewed sunflower seeds all over the front of Rivard's shirt. Rivard swore under his breath and flicked seeds from his shirt. Nutsack Horne reached into his sock for the pumpkin seeds and refilled his mouth, as he imagined a professional coach would do. He watched the team stretch and toss a few balls around and resisted the urge to make them do extra calisthenics. While Coach Rivard stood along the baseline and shouted encouragement to the team, Horne sat next to April in the dugout and made out the lineup sheet. Tempting though it was, he didn't change the batting lineup or change the players' positions. For now, he'd put the Horne Method on the back burner while he tried his new professional managing technique.

For the first few innings, Horne did little but sit on the bench, spit sunflower seeds and scratch his recently healed balls. It was killing him to not pose and flex every time something went wrong, but he was dedicated to this strategy. And after four innings it seemed to be working – the Warriors were ahead, 4-2.

At the bottom of the fifth inning, Devin Krane received a called third strike on a fastball so inside and high he ducked to avoid it. He argued with the umpire, which sent Coach Rivard out of the dugout. Horne realized this was his big chance and jogged out to home plate.

From the announcer's booth, both Charlie DeMar and Coach Zim leaned forward at the site of Nutsack Horne in his tiny shorts hurrying to home plate. They weren't the only ones to show interest – fans in the bleachers pulled phones from their pockets and held them up like lighters at a Led Zeppelin concert.

"This is interesting, Coach Zim," said Charlie. "It appears that Coach Horne is going to argue the call. I would too – that fastball almost gave Devin Krane a lobotomy. Strike three, my butt."

"That's probably exactly what Coach Horne is telling the umpire right now."

"Coach Zim, did you ever let your temper get away from you when arguing with an umpire? You seem like such a relaxed, friendly guy," Charlie said sarcastically.

Coach Zim chuckled. "It probably happened once or twice, I have to admit."

"But you never wore short shorts while doing it, am I correct?"

"Yes Charlie, that's correct."

On the field, Horne was doing what he'd seen the managers on television do – yelling at the umpire and kicking dirt at him. For added emphasis he pulled up his shirt and flexed his abs. The umpire didn't seem impressed and warned him to get back in the dugout or he'd be ejected from the game. In response, Horne did a double biceps pose and spit at the umpire's feet.

Unfortunately, Horne wasn't a very accurate spitter. A large wad of sunflower seeds landed on the umpire's face. Embarrassed and slightly remorseful, Horne did what came naturally – he went into a most muscular pose and yelled as loud as he could, until his face was red and veins popped from his forehead.

It was at this point that the umpire, a popular deacon who had been a highly ranked amateur boxer in his younger days, punched Horne in the face. Horne blinked twice and fell over backward, frozen in his most muscular pose.

"Down goes Nutsack! Down goes Nutsack!" Charlie DeMar screamed into the microphone. "Wow! Do you think he's hurt, Coach Zim?"

"Looked pretty painful from here."

"Wow. Wow! Coach, no offense, but baseball seems a lot more exciting now than when you were coaching."

Coach Zim nodded. He couldn't argue with that.

Coach Rivard and a couple of players helped Todd Horne, who was confusedly flexing in all directions, from the field and into the dugout. In the stands, fans were chattering and laughing, all the while recording the action on their phones. By the time they got Nutsack settled in the dugout, the first video had been sent to ESPN.

The umpire was visibly upset about what he'd done. He called Coach Rivard and the opposing coach together for a conference near home plate.

"I wholeheartedly apologize," began the umpire. He appeared on the verge of tears. "I don't know what came over me.

"I do," mumbled Rivard.

"I am willing to call a halt to this game and you can continue it with a different umpire at a later date," he continued. "Or, if you prefer, we can have one of the other umpires take home plate for the rest of the game."

"Hell, no," said Rivard. "Except for that last boneheaded call, you've been doing a fine job. You always do. You're an honest guy."

"I agree," said the other coach. "Jesus himself couldn't have resisted the urge to punch that guy in the face."

"So we're all set?" The coaches nodded. "OK, then. I'll say an extra prayer tonight and at church on Sunday." He pulled his mask down and walked to home plate. "Let's play ball!"

After the game – which Apple Brook held on to win – Coach Zim watched from the bleachers as April Spring and Robert

Williams helped Todd Horne to his car. Fearing he'd suffered another concussion, April once again took the wheel as Horne slumped in the passenger seat, a bag of ice pressed to his face.

Coach wasn't aware of anyone standing beside him until he turned to leave and walked into a tree. He stepped back and realized it wasn't a tree at all, but Luther. He was wearing his janitor clothes.

"Sorry, Coach," Luther said. He nodded toward the parking lot. "You ever see a coach get injured more than the players?"

They laughed and walked down the steps together. As they reached the bottom, two glassy-eyed boys barely old enough to shave hurried from the shadow of the stairway. Behind them strolled Tom Collins. When he saw Coach Zim he smirked. Coach Zim watched the young boys walk away for a moment, then turned to Collins.

"I hope you aren't doing anything stupid like selling drugs, Collins. Because that's illegal."

"So is assaulting a student, asshole."

"Hey, Collins." Coach Zim nodded to Luther, who'd walked on ahead. "Why don't you show Luther those tattoos you're so proud of?"

Luther turned back at the sound of his name. Collins's face blanched. With a final glare at Coach Zim, Collins pulled a baseball cap from his back pocket, pulled it low on his head and walked away.

"What was that all about?" Luther asked as they reached the sidewalk.

Coach Zim shook his head. "Nothing. You want a ride back to the school?"

Luther shook his head. "Thanks, but it's a good day for walkin."

In the parking lot across the street, Coach Zim got into his truck and thought about the game he'd just witnessed. He enjoyed announcing the games but missed coaching. Not what Nutsack Horne was doing – that wasn't coaching. What he missed was being on the field with the players, smelling the grass and leather and sweat, feeling the warm sunlight, hearing the calls on the field and conversations from players on the bench, seeing the smiles and tears. He missed it all. But sometimes change happens for a reason, and he wondered if that was how he'd fallen so easily into the job with the Red Sox organization. It wasn't as fun, didn't give him the same thrill as coaching – not yet. But he hoped that if he stuck with it, it might.

19

"You're fired."

It was 7:30 in the morning. Todd Horne normally didn't arrive at school until a minute or two before the morning bell, but he had received a message on his cellphone at 5:30 a.m. The message was short but to the point – "This is Principal Craggy. Get your ass to school and be in my office by 7:30." The message was strange and left him uneasy, because Uncle Garth had identified himself as Principal Craggy. That sounded serious, and Todd treated it as such. He wore his most conservative shorts, which covered an extra inch of leg. There was a small cut and swelling under his left eye where the umpire had struck him, but there was nothing he could do about that.

"Geez, Uncle Garth, I'm sorry. But I'm the one who got punched. Were you at the game? Punched right in the face, for no reason! That guy should be arrested."

Confident that the matter was now settled, Horne looked up from his child's chair and into the face of his uncle. What he saw was not reassuring. Normally his uncle sat calmly behind the big oak desk when berating him. But now, Craggy paced back and forth behind his desk, staring daggers at him with every turn. This behavior made Todd uneasy. He flexed his calves and kept talking.

"I mean, it's not my fault I keep getting injured. Freak accidents. But look at my record, Uncle Garth. The team is doing better than last year, and this is my first year coaching. I don't want to brag, but I'm pretty awesome. I wouldn't be surprised if we added another trophy to the case this year." He smiled tentatively, but his uncle only glared. "You did see me get punched, right? You were at the game?"

Craggy stopped pacing. He placed his hands against the back of his chair and leaned forward. "Yes, I was at the game. But it doesn't matter, because ESPN has been playing it round the clock since early evening. It was the last thing I saw before I went to bed and the first thing I saw when I turned on the TV this morning. They have a compilation of your greatest hits that they've edited into a fifteen-second video. They're calling you The Flexing Fool and Conan the Self-Destroyer."

Horne brightened. "Really? They're calling me Conan?"

"Shut the fuck up, you imbecile."

Horne's jaw fell open. He unconsciously began bouncing his pectorals. "Uncle Garth?"

"As I said when you first walked in here, you are fired. Not from coaching. Well, yes, from coaching, but mainly from teaching. You are fired from Apple Brook High School. Fired from teaching, fired from coaching, and especially fired from fucking the students!"

Horne froze, mid-flex. He had to be talking about April. There had been others, of course, but most were one-time things and they'd promised never to tell. In the years he'd been teaching at Apple Brook there had been rumors – he'd heard them – but for the most part every girl had kept her mouth shut, and nobody in administration had ever questioned him. That the girls didn't talk because they were embarrassed about sleeping with him never once occurred to Horne.

But April was the one he'd slept with most often, at least a dozen times over the past three weeks. He'd never had such lust for a student. What a body, almost as good as his own. He'd tried his best to hide the way she made him feel, although every time she came near he felt himself getting a boner. This was difficult to hide in short shorts. On the baseball field, when she sat next to him in the dugout, he usually kept a clipboard in his lap to hide his erection. Just thinking about her now, her eighteen-year-old body lying naked on his weight bench, Horne felt something stir beneath his white shorts. He crossed his legs and mustered a look of total innocence.

"What are you talking about, Uncle Garth?"

"Don't Uncle Garth me. You know exactly what I'm talking about, you fucking pervert!"

Before Horne could reply, the door opened and Emma stuck her head inside.

"Excuse me, Principal Craggy. Should I turn on the intercom? I don't think they heard you in the Building Trades wing."

Craggy glared at her. His fingers were white from gripping the chair so hard. After a moment his face softened and he nodded. "Got it. Sorry."

Emma looked from Craggy to Horne, shook her head, and closed the door.

Craggy straightened up. He unbuttoned his suit coat and set it over his chair. Then he sat down. He gazed at a shelf full of awards while scratching his chin. Horne watched silently, unsure if he should speak or not. It didn't seem like a good time to flex. Sitting quietly, he tried to come up with a plausible denial about sleeping with April. Then his mind drifted to her doing naked bent-over rows, her tight, round butt up in the air, swaying back and forth. He wished there was a clipboard handy.

"Do you know how much shit you are putting me through?" Craggy finally said.

Craggy faced his awards while speaking, and Horne wasn't quite sure whether he was talking to him or just thinking out loud. So he said the first thing that came to mind. "Some weather we're having, huh?"

His uncle slowly turned to him. He stared for a moment, and then, to Horne's surprise, burst out laughing. This continued for a minute or so, until Craggy wiped tears from his eyes and settled back in his chair. By this time, Horne was laughing too.

"Do you know why I'm laughing, Todd?"

"Because this is all just a big joke?" he replied hopefully.

"No. No, this is not a joke. I'm laughing because, although I may end up losing my job because of you, at least now I can fire you without my wife hassling me about it. There's nothing she can say!" Craggy giggled.

Horne smiled, though a bit uncomfortably. "You aren't really thinking of firing me, are you, Uncle Garth?" His eyes went to the ceiling and the corners of the room, looking for cameras. "This is a joke, right? Am I going to be on America's Funniest Home Videos, or something like that?"

"Yeah, you're on a funny video, all right. Just watch ESPN for a few minutes and you'll see it." The thought brought Craggy back to the job at hand. "I'm not *thinking* of firing you, Todd. I *am* firing you. You are fired, effective immediately, for having sex with a student."

"Wha… wha..", Horne blustered, looking like a struggling pufferfish. He took a few slow, deep breaths, until he could speak. "It's not true. I've never slept with a student." Thoughts of April cupping and fondling her large breasts in her tiny hands invaded his thoughts. He struggled to sweep them aside.

"Ah, but you have, Todd. The girl's parents called me late last night. The father wanted to go by your house with his shotgun but his wife talked him out of it. Too bad, really," he said, gazing off thoughtfully for a moment. "Instead, they called my house to inform me that their daughter is pregnant by one of her teachers."

"April's pregnant?" Horne blurted.

Craggy arched an eyebrow and leaned forward. "Who's April?"

Horne tried to do the math in his head. Math was hard. He'd been screwing April for three weeks. A girl couldn't get pregnant in three weeks and already know about it, could she? He wished there was somebody in the room who could answer his question, but Uncle Garth didn't appear to be in the mood to answer questions.

He realized he'd been asked a question. "Huh?"

"I said, who is April? I didn't give you the name of the student."

"Oh, no, I meant the month. You know, the month of April."

"Do you believe that the month of April is pregnant, Todd?"

"Ha. No. Months can't get pregnant."

"No, they certainly can't. But female students can." He rested his elbows on the large desk and steepled his fingers. For a long moment, he said nothing. Finally, he spoke. "Are you sleeping with April Spring, Todd?"

At that very moment Horne had been thinking about the other night, April riding him while he bench-pressed a hundred pounds twenty times. "Huh?" He wondered if his uncle was psychic. "No, of course not. Who is she again?"

"The manager of your baseball team. The pretty girl you sit close to during every practice and every game. The girl who's given you a ride home after the last two baseball games."

"Right, right. Well, I'm not sleeping with her. If she says I am, she's lying."

He flexed his thighs to emphasize the point, slapping his hands down on them with a loud clap that echoed in the room.

"She didn't say anything, Todd."

"I thought you said she did. Or her parents did."

"No, Todd. The girl I'm speaking about is Victoria Purl."

Horne winced involuntarily. It figured. The chubby chick was the one he got pregnant.

He'd been in the middle of a dry spell that day at the end of February when he'd offered Victoria a ride home. She was a bit thick in the hips, but cute enough and very flirty. They'd stopped off at his apartment – he couldn't remember the excuse he'd used – and he'd ended up having sex with her. It hadn't lasted long – it had been a dry spell, after all – and he tried to make it up to her by putting on a posing demonstration, but she'd asked him to put his clothes on and take her home. As he dropped her off in front of her apartment building in one of the shabbier parts of town, he'd asked if they could keep what had happened between just the two of them. She'd agreed, maybe a bit too readily, now that he thought back on it. But she had agreed.

It just went to show what type of person she was that she couldn't keep quiet about it, he thought. True, she probably wanted to brag about it. He understood that. What girl wouldn't? But a promise was a promise. He'd kept his end of the bargain – he'd told no one.

And then it hit him – it was her word against his. He was a teacher, while she was a chubby teenager looking for attention. Would anyone believe that Todd Horne, with such a muscular, ripped body, would sleep with a plumper? Of course not. All he had to do was deny everything. He ran his hand over his massive bicep, hard as granite. Not only was he huge – Conan, they'd called him on TV – but he was smart. The thought brought a smile to his face.

"Do you find something funny about this, Todd?"

Horne returned from his thoughts, shaking his head. "No, Uncle Garth. But I don't know what you're talking about. I never slept with Victoria Purl. I mean, look at her –" he held his hands out wide and puffed out his cheeks –"and look at me." Standing up, he quickly went into a well-practiced side chest pose, holding it and smiling as though on stage at a bodybuilding competition.

Craggy watched for a moment. "Yes, as persuasive as that argument is, Todd – sit down, for Christ's sake – I don't believe you."

Horne exhaled and sat back down. Red-faced from lack of oxygen, he said, "It's my word against hers. I'm a teacher and she's a student. Who are you going to believe?"

"Her. I believe I just said that."

Thinking fast, Horne said, "She tried flirting with me once. Came into my office after school and lifted her shirt, flashed them big boobs at me." They were big, now that he thought about it. And surprisingly firm. He briefly wondered why he hadn't slept with her again. "But I said no. That's what this is all about, Uncle Garth. Victoria felt rejected and is now trying to frame me. Happens to attractive male teachers like me all the time. Probably happened a few times to you before you got old."

Craggy said nothing, just stared at him. Horne looked away, watched students outside the window walk past on their way into the building. The 7:55 bell rang, but Horne didn't notice. He wondered if Victoria really was pregnant. Then he began thinking about her large breasts, like warm, soft pillows. Before long he once again wished for a clipboard.

"Todd, Mr. and Mrs. Purl assure me that Victoria is pregnant, and that you are the father. Victoria was a virgin before you slept with her."

That would explain the blood and why she kept saying ouch, he thought to himself. He just figured he was huge. Outwardly, he exclaimed, "That's a lie! I've heard of her sleeping with other guys before me!"

Craggy shook his head wearily. "You have got to be one of the dumbest men on the planet. And I know it's not the steroids, because you've always been this dumb. Well, anyway, the Purls have a lawyer – a very good one, from what I hear – and they are going to make you take a paternity test. The police will escort you, if need be."

"When?" Horne asked, wide-eyed.

"This morning. You were smart enough to sleep with an eighteen year old, at least. She's not underage, so there are no charges. However, it is illegal to sleep with a student, no matter her age, and they will be pursuing charges for that." He gazed thoughtfully at his nephew, whose pectorals were bouncing up and down so quickly it looked like they were trying to take flight. "Chances are, your lawyer will claim you were blinded by love or some other bullshit and you'll get out of that charge. But you'll be done teaching. Anywhere. The Purls threatened my job, as well, although I've done nothing wrong except have an idiot for a nephew." He sighed. "But sometimes that's enough."

Horne looked like a spooked deer. "What can I do?"

"Go get the blood test. If you are the father – and chances are good that you are, judging by the panicked look on your face – you'll be making a hefty monthly child support payment. And stop being such a fucking moron." Craggy's knees popped as he stood and ambled over to the window. He stood in the warm sunlight, gazing out through the blinds. "You'll receive a call this morning from the Purl's lawyer. He'll explain everything."

"So I'm fired?"

"Officially, you are suspended. But very soon, unless by some miracle you aren't the father, you will be terminated."

"Does that mean I can't coach baseball?"

Craggy turned away from the window to frown at his nephew. "Of course you can't coach baseball, you imbecile."

"But those kids need me!"

"The only kid that needs you now is the one growing in Victoria Purl's uterus. And I have a feeling you'll be as much of a disappointment to him as you are to everyone else."

Horne suddenly jumped to his feet. "I don't need this school!" Pulling his shirt off, he went into a most muscular pose. "I'll go into bodybuilding full time. Look at me! *LOOK AT ME!*" His face and neck turned as purple as a fresh bruise, with thick veins appearing like worms during a rain storm. "Come on! *COME ON!*"

Still flexing, he turned to leave and fell over the chair he'd forgotten was directly behind him. The chair balanced on two legs for a moment and then slammed to the floor, delivering Horne face-first with it.

Craggy stood by the window and stared at his unconscious nephew lying face-down on the floor. His legs were bent back, sticking up in the air. He wished he'd known it was coming – he'd have gotten his phone out and filmed it. ESPN probably would have paid good money for it.

Oh, well. Pointless to dwell on what might have been. He went to the desk, pressed a button, and asked Emma to have the nurse and a janitor come to his office. Then he sat back in his chair and waited, contemplating who he could name as the new baseball coach.

20

Coach Zim sat behind his desk, munching on a ham Italian from Roscoe's, the local deli. The classroom was empty save for Brandon Ackerson sitting hunched over a front row desk, devouring a turkey sub. Once a week Coach Zim brought in subs from Roscoe's and he and Ackerson ate lunch together in the classroom. It was a chance for Ackerson to bring up any problems he was having, particularly with Tom Collins and his group.

The teenager wasn't very forthcoming, but after a lot of badgering Coach Zim found that Collins was still harassing Ackerson, though he'd toned it down considerably now that Ackerson was getting rides to and from school with Mr. Iannuci. The harassing was just typical high school bullying – mostly calling him names like Fagerson. Collins never once, while saying these words, considered the fact that it had been him and not Ackerson who'd straddled another guy and pulled out his penis.

If a kid had called him names back when he was a student in high school, Coach Zim probably would have shoved him into a locker. Which, come to think of it, was also how he'd reacted as a teacher. But Ackerson, with his fragile physique and quiet nature, wasn't going to counter name calling with intimidation or physicality. He seemed to have faith in Coach Zim's assurance that what goes around, comes around. He just wished it would happen soon, as did Coach Zim.

Ackerson had other things on his mind, anyway. His painting, *Beach Day,* had recently won the school district's student art contest. The painting, which depicted a teenage couple – a boy and a girl – kissing on a blanket on a half-empty beach while a younger boy crouches at the edge of the blanket and looks through the older boy's wallet, was now entered in the statewide student art contest. Ackerson told Coach Zim that Miss Folger had said it was the best student painting she'd ever seen and that it would easily win the contest. Coach Zim said he should be very proud of himself, because Miss Folger had been around a long time and had been working with students since the Eisenhower administration.

There was a knock as they finished up their sandwiches. They both looked toward the door as Devin Krane and Adam Nass entered. Ackerson threw his sandwich wrapper toward the trash can and missed by three feet.

"Don't try out for basketball, kid." Coach Zim leaned over, picked up the wrapper, and tossed it into the trash. "Stick with art."

"Yeah, hey, congrats on the painting," said Krane. He sat on the corner of Coach Zim's desk. "It's really good. My piece this year was a self-portrait. It kind of looks like Stewie Griffin. Miss Folger stared at it for a long time and told me we don't all have artistic talent."

"Get your butt off my desk, Krane," said Coach Zim. Krane stood and smiled at Coach Zim. "Have you heard the news?"

Ackerson stood. "I'm going to the art room," he said softly. "See you guys later."

Krane asked, "Hey, are you still having trouble with Tom Collins?" Ackerson shrugged. "If you do, just let me know. He tried to sell my little sister drugs at the last home game. As soon as the season's over I'm going to pound that asshole's face in. I'd do it before then but I don't want to get kicked off the team."

"Language," snapped Coach Zim. "And you aren't going to touch him, because you'll be the one in trouble if you do. I'm telling you guys, some sort of payback is waiting for that guy. It may take time, but I believe it's coming. It always does."

"Yeah, well, payback has until the end of the season. Then I'm kicking his butt."

Krane and Coach Zim said goodbye, and Nass nodded as Ackerson grabbed his backpack and left the classroom.

"So, have you heard the news?" Krane asked again.

"What news, Krane? That you haven't gotten a hit in two games? Yes, I've heard. I've witnessed it. It's ugly."

"Ha. Good one. No, I mean about Coach Horne."

Coach Zim shook his head. "What about him?"

"Nutsack's been sacked!" Krane said.

Coach Zim stared at him, unbelieving. He looked over at Nass. "Is this true?"

Nass nodded. "We just heard about it. Principal Craggy fired him this morning. From both teaching and coaching."

"For having sex with a student," Krane added.

Coach Zim sat back and whistled. He wondered where they'd heard this. He hated to ask, because the answer would be along the lines of somebody in the hallway heard a girl in Mr. Cash's Physics class say something to someone she was talking to on the phone, and so on. The source of news which travelled along the high school grapevine was occasionally reliable, but the information usually went through so many changes so quickly that nobody bothered to check the source. Still, this was big news and he asked how they found out about it.

"We heard VP Simon talking about it with Miss Heather, the new cafeteria lady. Then we overheard him asking her out," said Krane. "He tried using this really smooth voice, but she still said no. It was part sad, part disgusting, hearing such an old man get shot down."

Coach Zim frowned. Simple Simon was younger than him by a few years.

"If we hadn't been buying jelly donuts at the time, we wouldn't have overheard. I think we're the only ones who know about it."

"Glad to hear that healthy diet is paying off for you boys," Coach Zim said. He thought for a moment. He didn't want to get involved in solicitous high school gossip, but this was important. "Did Vice Principal Simon say who the girl was? I assume it was a girl?" he added. The idea of the narcissistic, muscle-bound Horne involved in gay sex with a student, while disgusting enough to nearly bring up his ham sub, didn't seem all that far-fetched.

"We didn't hear him mention any names," Krane said.

The bell rang, and the sound of slamming lockers and loud voices and sneakers squeaking on polished tiles carried in from the hallway. Coach Zim thanked Krane and Nass for the information and asked them to keep it to themselves until he could speak to the principal or vice principal. They agreed, and though he believed they honestly meant to keep quiet about it, he had a feeling that half the school would know by the end of the day. Keeping a secret in the confines of a high school was about as easy for these kids as sitting in a classroom and not thinking about sex every twenty seconds.

"Do you think they'll let you be our coach again?" Krane asked.

"I wouldn't get your hopes up," said Coach Zim, remembering recent conversations in Craggy's office.

The boys met Paul Rivard in the doorway. He gave a slight nod, which was all it took to get Krane asking, "Hey Coach Rivard, did you hear about Nutsack Horne?"

"Watch your language, little lady." He stepped into the classroom and jerked his thumb toward the hallway. "Beat it, you two."

"Way to keep it to yourself, Krane," Coach Zim called out as Rivard closed the classroom door.

"So, have you heard about Nutsack?" Rivard asked, sitting on Coach Zim's desk.

"Briefly, from Krane and Adam. They heard he got shitcanned for fooling around with a student. How close did they get?"

"Surprisingly accurate, especially for those two. I just left Craggy's office. Horne may have gotten a student pregnant. I didn't get a name but she's eighteen years old. He's suspended right now but it looks like he'll be fired soon."

"Wow." Feeling like a gossipy old woman, Coach Zim lowered his voice and said, "I wonder if it's April Spring?"

Rivard smiled, his face bursting into a weather-beaten map of deep cracks and crannies. "That's what I asked. Craggy assured me it was not, but he sounded like he thinks Nutsack may have been fooling around with her, too."

"I wonder how Craggy felt about firing his nephew."

"Didn't seem too broken up about it." He hesitated a moment. "The reason he called me in was to make me the head coach for the rest of the season."

Coach Zim smiled, reached over and shook his friend's hand. "Congratulations. You deserve it. You should have been the coach all along."

Rivard shook his head. "No, you should have been the coach all along."

Though his pulse had quickened at the thought of coaching again, he knew Craggy wouldn't let it happen. Still, for a few brief seconds, the smell of fresh cut grass, the feel of leaning onto the dugout stairs as he watched the game, the ping of an aluminum bat, the slap of a leather glove on a baseball, and the shouts from the crowd had all filled his mind as he contemplated the idea of being back in the dugout. Though he would deny it later, the thought filled him with an excitement he couldn't find anywhere else.

He wasn't too disappointed, though. It wasn't going to happen, and Paul Rivard was an excellent coach. He was genuinely happy for his old friend.

Tom Collins had taken to wearing his hair long enough to cover his swastika tattoos, but short enough to allow people to make them out. He liked the reactions his tattoos evoked – some positive, many negative, nearly all of them powerful. Collins strutted around the school hallways with his ever-present smirk and lurked in corners and under stairways before and after school, peddling his drugs.

Coach Zim knew what was going on – he'd have been an idiot not to – but was helpless to do anything about it. Touching a student was illegal. Searching a student for drugs was an invasion of his or her civil rights. Some teachers didn't care – Paul Rivard searched anyone he suspected of dealing drugs. A parent complained once, and even though little Joey had been caught with a large bag of pot and a bag of pills, Craggy called Rivard to his office and informed him that any searches of the students must be performed by the school resource officer. Rivard then informed Craggy that he'd fought in Vietnam for the freedom of America's citizens and even if the war turned out to be a crock of shit, he still believed in America and wasn't going to allow any punk selling drugs to fuck it up. And if he, Craggy, didn't believe in America, then he could kiss Rivard's ass.

That was the last time Craggy, or anyone, tried to stop Paul Rivard from performing searches. But the leniency didn't carry over to other teachers, and it certainly didn't include Coach Zim. Craggy would like nothing more than to have an excuse to suspend or fire Coach Zim, and so he did his best to ignore the cocky grins and winks from Collins when the teenager emerged with other druggies from an empty classroom or under a stairwell.

The day after Nutsack Horne was fired, Tom Collins passed Coach Zim's classroom on his way to first period. Scrawny arm slung around the shoulders of a plain-looking, purple-haired sophomore girl with tattoos on her forearms, Collins called out, "Hey Zimmerman, I heard they shitcanned Nutsack Horne and still didn't ask you to be head coach. They must really think a lot of you, huh?"

Coach Zim looked up from the picture a student was showing him on her iPad. "You know, Collins, I can still give you detention for swearing."

It was an empty threat and they both knew it. The last thing in the world that Coach Zim wanted to do was stay after school with Collins because he said the S-word.

"Guess I'll see you at the game after school. You'll be in the booth, cause nobody wants you on the field." He smirked. "And I'll be around, doing my thing. Earning a living."

Coach Zim turned his gaze down to the iPad, but couldn't help glancing up as Collins walked away. He wasn't in the habit of wishing ill on anyone, but he couldn't help hoping that Collins got hit in the head by a foul ball. He'd ask for forgiveness during his evening prayers, but for now he'd savor the thought.

Collins didn't get hit by a foul ball that afternoon. Instead, it was a Grim Disciple that hit Tom Collins. And though he hated the bikers almost as much as he hated Collins, Coach Zim still smiled when he heard the story.

Shortly after school let out, Collins arrived at the field. He'd skipped the last block to go home and replenish his stock of meth and coke and pot and heroin. Everything was prepackaged to sell, and he kept different drugs in different pockets of his pants and jacket. One thing he learned from his father was that a good drug dealer had to be organized. Extra supplies were kept in a hidden compartment under the back seat of his Chevy Blazer, which his father had fixed up from his junkyard and given to Tom for his sixteenth birthday.

He was just finishing up his first sale of the day – a couple of joints to three pimple-faced, long-haired eight graders under the bleacher stairs – when he heard the distant thunder of motorcycles. It grew louder, until he could feel the pounding in his chest as they pulled into the parking lot – six of them, a show of strength and power by the Grim Disciples. Led by Tyler Nass, they rolled in and backed their bikes up against the chain link fence on the first base side.

Collins was brash and cocky, but he wasn't stupid. He realized that openly selling drugs in their territory, or arguing about their vacated territory, would only make the Disciples angry. And he'd heard about what happened to people who made them angry. Six of them showing up today was a statement. Collins decided to step aside and allow them to be heard.

Still, that didn't mean he was going out of business. Only that he'd relocated. Instead of cruising the parking lot, food stand, and bleachers – networking and high visibility, staples of any successful sales business – he confined himself to the shade beneath the stairway, occasionally slipping in and out like a bottom feeder lurking in the shadows of an aquarium. Instead of being the aggressor, the shark, as was his natural tendency, he hung back until approached. Then the transaction was made out of sight beneath the stairs.

It wasn't until midway through the second inning that the Disciples noticed a lack of business coming their way. One of the smarter ones, Hawk, noticed several kids popping in and out from under the stairs and went over to investigate. Following a couple of girls in short shorts, Hawk ducked under the stairway and saw Tom Collins slip the girls a small baggy. One of the girls handed some money to Collins.

"What's going on here?"

Tiny squeaks escaped the girls as they jumped. Collins stepped back, stuffing the cash into his pocket. Seeing that the voice didn't belong to a cop, he relaxed. Then he noticed the denim vest. There was a Grim Disciples patch on the back, he was certain.

"Are you a cop?" one of the girls asked.

"Do I look like a cop, darlin?"

She smiled timidly. Her friend did the same. Hawk leered at them. They looked very young, with skinny legs and newly-formed hips and breasts. He liked them young. Most of the Disciples did.

"Why don't you come over and look at my motorcycle in a few minutes? Maybe we'll give you girls a ride."

One of the girls asked his name.

"Hawk," he replied.

The girls giggled. "Why do they call you Hawk?"

"Cause I can spot good pussy from a mile away." He leaned in toward the girls. Unsure of what to say, the girls moved around Hawk, giving him a wide berth, and hurried away. "Oh no, not you." Collins, who'd tried to follow the girls, winced as a large hand slapped his chest. "You and me are taking a walk."

Hawk grabbed Collins by the back of the neck and led him toward the other Disciples. Collins wanted to appear calm but felt himself shaking in the warm afternoon sun. He tried pulling away from Hawk, but the biker had a grip like a gorilla. He was led like a little boy to the motorcycles, where Hawk finally released his neck.

"Look who I found selling under the stairs."

From the seat of his motorcycle, Tyler Nass smiled. It wasn't a pleasant smile. "Collins? What the fuck. You know better than to sell here. This is our territory. Even when we ain't here, this is our territory."

"Well, I haven't seen you guys around for the past couple of weeks." Collins felt annoyed at how high his voice sounded. He coughed and rubbed the back of his neck. "I thought I'd keep things going until you got back. It's probably better for your business, really, because nobody left here to score somewhere else."

Tyler Nass continued to smile. Collins jammed his hands into his pockets to keep them from trembling.

"That's real thoughtful of you, kid. How much you make today?"

The question caught Collins off-guard. "Huh? Um, I don't know." He squeezed the thick wad of bills in his pocket. "About a hundred bucks, maybe."

"Empty your pockets."

"No." Collins felt himself being backed into a corner and grew angry. "Why the fuck should I?"

"Cause if you don't, Mac's gonna empty them for you."

Collins looked at Mac. Sitting on his motorcycle, Mac was taller than Collins – almost three hundred pounds of muscle and tattoos. Collins glanced at Tyler Nass, who was no longer smiling. Then he looked around. A small group of teenagers watched from a distance. Swearing under his breath, he emptied his front pockets, dropping everything on the ground at his feet.

Hawk moved forward and picked up a wad of bills. He thumbed through it quickly. "A hundred and eighty-five," he said to Nass, handing it over.

Tyler Nass pocketed the money. "Consider that rent payment for selling on our property. I see you here again, we won't be so understanding. Got it?"

Seething, Collins nodded. It took every ounce of willpower to not tell Tyler Nass to go fuck himself. Instead, he said, "My father's not going to be happy. That's his money. What are you going to do if he decides he doesn't want to supply you guys anymore?"

Nass laughed humorlessly. "You think your daddy's the only supplier we have? You should be asking yourself, what's your daddy going to do if we stop buying from him? Because without us he ain't gonna sell shit. And he's gonna blame you, Junior. So run along and play somewhere else, and keep your fucking mouth shut."

He'd get them back for this, Collins swore to himself. They'd regret ever embarrassing him in public. Not now, though. Another lesson from his father – revenge requires patience. This was a tough one – he wanted to light their fucking motorcycles on fire right here in the parking lot. But for now, he tucked his tail between his legs and turned to walk away.

"Hey, Junior," called Tyler Nass. "Pick your shit up off the ground. If there's one thing I can't stand, it's a litterbug."

Biting his lip until he tasted blood, Collins bent down to pick up what he'd dropped from his pocket – chapstick, a buck knife, a crumpled pack of cigarettes, a pack of gum.

When he reached for the chapstick Hawk kicked it, sending the plastic tube spinning across the parking lot.

Collins watched the tube roll away, then jumped to his feet. "Go pick it up, douchebag," he said, before he could catch himself.

In his experience with fighting, Collins rarely had to do anything except start it. His friends and tagalongs usually did the fighting for him, much like the field general who yells, "Attack!" and then stands back to watch the action. Also, Collins liked to make sure the odds were in his favor, usually five or six to one.

The odds were reversed on this day – six members of the Grim Disciples versus Tom Collins. But none of the other Disciples bothered to even stand up from their motorcycles – they let Hawk handle it. And even if Collins had his friends with him, it probably wouldn't have mattered because Hawk was among the best fighters in the club and would have wiped the parking lot with all of them.

As it was, Collins never saw the punch coming. It was a short hook, delivered by Hawk's non-dominant left hand because he was holding a cigarette in his right. For this, Collins was lucky – it dropped him to his knees but did not knock him out.

Hawk took a long drag from his cigarette while watching the teenager with the stupid head tattoos get to his feet. "Got something else to say to me?" he asked. Smoke curled from the corners of his mouth and drifted away.

Collins had nothing to say. Even if he had, his jaw hurt too badly to speak. He turned and walked away, hearing the rough laughter of the Grim Disciples and swearing that he'd get even with them. Not today, though, which pissed him off even more. He glared at everyone who looked his way, daring them to say anything. Somebody was going to pay for this. Today. He walked across the road to the parking lot to begin collecting.

From the announcer's box, Coach Zim watched the Warriors play a nearly flawless game. For the first time all year they didn't commit an error, and their base running was perfect. Though he'd coached several games while Nutsack Horne was injured, it was Paul Rivard's first official game as head coach and it seemed as though the team was showing him what they could really do. Coach Zim was proud of the players and proud of his old friend.

The crowd, however, was subdued, and it was clear why – without Nutsack Horne's antics on the field, the game had taken on its slow-paced traditional form. Coach Zim looked down from the box and saw a less-than-capacity house. Many of them had their phones out but appeared to be sending texts or looking at Facebook rather than excitedly holding them up, waiting for the moment when Nutsack shot some adrenaline into an otherwise boring game.

Even Charlie DeMar seemed somewhat passive, although Coach Zim soon found out that had nothing to do with the absence of Coach Horne. In the third inning, when the opposing pitcher got a warning from the umpire for hitting Brock Cooke in the leg with a fastball, Charlie only said, "At least the ball didn't hit him in the heart. There's no pain like a broken heart, my friends."

It didn't take a genius to figure out that Charlie's young old lady, Lacy, had broken up with him. He continued to slump over the microphone and report the game as though it were a funeral until the fifth inning, when he received a text. Coach Zim looked over when the phone dinged and saw the text – *miss u, can we talk later?* Charlie's face perked up like a house plant in sunlight. Suddenly he was talking faster, with his normal goofy excitement.

Coach Zim switched off his mike. "Seems like things have gotten better for you."

"Yeah, my old lady broke up with me. Said she needed a break. But I guess the break's over. She realizes now that it ain't easy living without Charming Charlie."

"Uh huh. How long did this break last?"

Charlie looked at his watch. "Two and a half hours."

Coach Zim nodded and turned his microphone back on. He hated high school romances.

The Warriors ended up winning the game by a score of 4-0. As soon as the final out was recorded, Lacy burst into the booth and rushed to Charlie. They stood in the center of the room, holding each other tightly, making up for their long time apart. They began making out, and the slurping sounds made Coach Zim wish he had a hose to turn on them. Instead, he took his half-full bottle of water and poured it over their heads. They never looked up. He left the booth without a word, hoping they didn't end up having sex in his chair.

He considered going down on the field to congratulate Paul Rivard on his first official victory as head coach, but doing so might take attention off the coach and players, where it belonged. Instead he walked with Luther across the parking lot, pretending not to hear the quiet taunts from the Grim Disciples, whose return he was not happy to see. On the sidewalk he asked Luther, as always, if he'd like a ride. As always, Luther said it was a good day for a walk. He crossed the street to the larger parking lot, whistling as he walked. When he reached his truck the whistling stopped, caught in his throat. A front tire was slashed.

Coach Zim stood in front of the tilted truck for a minute, staring at the sadly deflated tire. A swift stream of anger filled his veins. He looked around but saw nobody suspicious. He walked back to the field, looking for Tom Collins, but he was nowhere to be found. Several people smiled and said hello, but it was all he could do to nod. He went back to his truck, leaned on it, and took a few slow, deep breaths. It was a relaxation technique Angela had taught him. It was just a tire, after all. Nobody had been hurt. Although that might change when he found out who'd done it.

21

High on meth, Collins went into the bathroom, put the 1/4-inch guard on the clippers and shaved his head. He didn't like it completely smooth, but short enough that people could see the tats. Fuck hiding them. He was tired of it. Then he called a few friends – the subordinates to his General – and told them they were going out to fuck with people. Until he got revenge on the Grim Disciples, other people would have to pay. Anyone, he didn't care who. He'd already slashed another one of Zimmerman's tires, which made him feel better for about ten seconds.

They started at the Apple Brook McDonalds, where Collins roughed up a cashier while a couple of his flunkies walked behind the counter and stole a few cheeseburgers and sodas. Then it was on to 7-11, where they stood outside the door and harassed everyone coming in and out, going so far as to steal a bag of chips and soda from a ten-year-old kid, along with his change. They finally left when the thin, oily cashier came outside, armed with a baseball bat, and announced that he'd called the police. He hadn't, as he himself was on probation for smoking marijuana, but his bluff worked. After a load of threats, Collins and his group moved on.

After similar episodes throughout town, they ended up at Bruce's Market. Justin Dumont, a former juvenile delinquent himself, was known among the town's seedier youth as someone who would sell beer to anyone, regardless of age. Collins and his group entered the store loudly, wound on meth, and looked around. The building was over a hundred years old, with dim lighting and wide floorboards, warped and faded from a century of being walked on. The store was empty, save for a fortyish woman sitting behind the counter, reading a *People* magazine. There was a long braid starting above her ear and ending just above her breast. Men her age considered her pretty, but to the teens she was just an old woman.

Collins nodded to a couple of his underlings. Each grabbed a case of beer from the cooler. Leading them to the counter, he asked loudly, "Justin around?"

The woman looked up at Collins and his friends. She glanced down at the beer. A hint of a smile danced across her lips. "Justin got fired a few days ago," she said. "Apparently he was selling alcohol to minors."

The two teens holding the beer looked to Collins, unsure of what to do. He motioned for them to place the cases up on the counter. He then took a beaten leather wallet from his back pocket and pulled out a fifty dollar bill.

"Got any ID?" she asked, sounding bored.

Collins made a show of looking through his wallet. "I switch wallets sometimes. I must have left it in my other one."

"Uh huh. No ID, no sale. Sorry. Unless one of your friends has one? Or did they all forget them in their other wallets, too?"

Despite his buzz, Collins heard the sarcasm in her voice. Still, he tried to control his temper because he really wanted a beer.

"What's your name?" He flashed a fake-looking smile. She hesitated, then gave her name as Susan. "Listen Susan, if you sell us the beer, you can keep the change." He placed the fifty on the counter. "Just sell us one case, and you can keep the rest."

"Nope. That's how Justin got fired. I like my job. Thanks, though." To the confused-looking teenagers behind Collins, she said, "Could you boys please put these back in the cooler?"

Two of them reached for the cases. Collins slapped their hands away. "These ain't going back in the cooler, you fucking idiots! They're going with us." He leaned across the counter until his face was inches from Susan's. "Don't be stupid, bitch. Take the money."

Susan, who hadn't flinched, laughed and reached for the phone. "Okay, kids. Playtime's over. Time to call the police."

Collins slapped her in the face, hard. She staggered back, stunned. The phone dropped from her hand and onto the floor. Collins nodded, and the two who'd carried the beer from the cooler went behind the counter. Each grabbed an arm as she struggled to get away. Collins followed, taking his time. Without saying a word, he punched Susan in the stomach. She deflated like the tire he'd slashed earlier. Her knees buckled, and she would have fallen to the floor were it not for the teenagers holding her up.

Collins smiled as he watched her gasp for air. He pointed to the confederate flag on his scrawny arm. "You see this? You know what it means?"

"You're a Dukes of Hazard fan?" she wheezed.

He turned slowly, his face reddening. He jabbed a finger at the swastika over his ear. "How about this? Does this scare you?"

Still trying to catch her breath, Susan nevertheless stood up straight and proud. "What scares me is that they let any idiot get a tattoo. The fact that you are using your head as a canvas for racism evokes several emotions, but fear is not one of them."

She smiled and looked at the idiots holding her by the arms. They smiled, too, having no idea what the hell she'd just said. The rest of his friends on the other side of the counter, being just as stupid, smiled also. Collins glanced around. He felt his face growing hot. He didn't like being made fun of. He balled his right hand into a fist and swung as hard as he could, hitting Susan square on the jaw. There was a dull crack, her head sagged forward, and her body went limp. The two boys holding her looked at each other, frightened.

"Drop her and grab the beer," Collins ordered. He looked up at the surveillance camera in the corner. He had some experience with cameras, because his father's garage and back room where the drugs were produced were full of them. "Rip that camera down," he said to the subordinates on the other side of the counter.

Everyone snapped to action and Collins headed to the back room, where he knew there'd be a computer.

Coach Zim entered the teacher's lounge the next day at lunch. The first person he saw was Eileen Campbell, who looked up and smiled. Not wanting to get caught up in another conversation about her online dating life, he nodded to her and walked to the other side of the room, where Harold Iannucci sat alone at a table, grading a stack of papers while eating a tuna sandwich.

"Slow down, Harold." Coach Zim sat down heavily across the table. "If you can't take time to eat, you're working too hard."

Iannucci looked up and smiled. He slid the stack of papers to the side. Placing his red pen on top of the stack, he leaned forward and said in a low voice, "I just wanted to look busy so Campbell didn't talk to me. Last week she told me about a guy she met on an online dating site who asked if she'd read him poetry while he masturbates. She said she's considering it, because otherwise he seems pretty normal." He glanced over at her and frowned. "You know, she's pretty good-looking. Spacy, but cute. Why can't she find a guy in the real world, like at church or the grocery store or something? And more importantly, why can't she keep it to herself?"

Coach Zim chuckled. "How're the rides to and from school with Ackerson going?"

Iannucci smiled. "He's a good kid. Quiet, but nice. Polite. He's shown me a couple of his drawings. I don't know much about art, but I know that kid's got a lot of talent."

Coach, took a big bite of his ham sandwich. "He does."

"I've met his mom a couple of times. Nice lady." Iannucci's eyes widened. "Oh shit, she's looking over here. She probably wants to tell us both about her latest date. I'm outta here." He crammed the rest of his sandwich into his mouth, grabbed the stack of papers and stood up.

"Harold, sit your ass down," Coach Zim said, attempting to keep his voice down. Iannucci shook his head. "Jesus, don't leave me alone with her. What kind of friend are you?"

"The kind that can't listen to stories about poetry and masturbation after eating."

He hurried from the room, giving Eileen Campbell a curt nod on his way out. Coach Zim risked a glance over and saw Campbell sitting back down. She had a sad look on her face, like a girl with a secret and no one to tell it to. Suddenly she turned. Before he could look away their eyes met. Her face brightened and she popped back to her feet. Coach Zim closed his eyes for a moment and swore quietly.

But then, like a gift from God, Paul Rivard entered the room. Coach Zim started waving his arm like an impatient wife in a grocery store. Rivard nodded and sat down across from Coach Zim, unaware of Eileen Campbell's glare as she dropped back into her chair across the room.

"You excited to see me?" Rivard asked.

"Sorry. Trying to avoid talking to someone. Hey, congratulations on the game yesterday. You've got the team looking good."

Rivard nodded. "That's still your team. You're the reason we look good. I don't have anything to do with it."

"That's not true," said Coach Zim. He took a sip of milk. "If you believe it is, just think back to how they looked under Nutsack Horne."

Rivard smiled but didn't laugh. Coach Zim glanced at him as they ate in silence. Something seemed to be bothering his old friend. It wasn't like him to not complain about something. Finally, he asked what was wrong.

"Just something I heard this morning. You know about what happened at Bruce's Market?"

Coach Zim shook his head. He'd been too busy standing in the shaded trees, slapping away black flies and staking out the parking lot, to read about or hear any news that morning.

"I go there most mornings for my coffee. Green Mountain, my favorite. The old fella that owns it, Bruce Pratt, told me this morning that the woman who works evenings got beat up pretty bad last night. Knocked her out, broke a few bones in her face. Apparently she wouldn't sell a couple cases of beer to some punk minors and they didn't take it well."

"Wow," said Coach Zim. "Did they catch the person who did it?"

"Uh uh, not yet. Sounds like it was a group of them. They stole the surveillance camera and the computer from the back room, so there's no video. But get this." Rivard leaned forward. "She told the police that the one in charge had tattoos on his arm and his head."

"Let me guess. Swastikas and confederate flag?"

"Yup. Susan – that's her name – said he was real proud of the tattoos, shoved them in her face to give her a good look. In related news, you might've noticed Tom Collins is absent today. Busy hiding from the cops, I'll bet."

"Do you know this Susan?"

"No. I go the market in the morning because it's on my way to school. I rarely go there during the evening. She's middle-aged, pretty, from what Bruce says. Last name's Mallen. Or Mallet. Something like that. Bruce told me this morning and I already forgot. Price of getting old, I guess."

Coach Zim paused, the last bite of his sandwich hanging inches from his mouth. "Was it Malley? Susan Malley?"

Rivard nodded. "Yup, that's it. Susan Malley."

Coach Zim dropped his sandwich. He sat back and whistled softly. "Wow. Susan Malley. Paul, do you believe in karma, or cause and effect, or any of that bullshit?"

"Not much since Vietnam, no. I've seen young men, good boys, blown to pieces for absolutely no reason. Meanwhile, nothing bad ever happened to the rich old pricks who sent them there."

"Well, my friend, you are going to see that it does indeed exist. And very soon, I believe. Because Susan Malley is the girlfriend of Luther, our janitor."

Rivard considered this silently for a minute. "I didn't know he had a girlfriend," he finally said. "Course, I never asked."

"He does. Angela and I run into them once in a while. Nice girl. Pretty. They've been together a long time now." He paused for a moment. "I wonder if Luther knows yet that it was Collins who put his girlfriend in the hospital."

"When he does, my advice to Collins is to run. And to everyone else, stay the hell out of the way," Rivard said.

"Good advice," Coach Zim agreed. "But Collins isn't that smart."

The bell rang, ending lunch period. Coach Zim and Paul Rivard slowly got to their feet and left the room, discussing the baseball team while purposefully avoiding the hopeful gaze of Eileen Campbell.

22

Sparky snapped at one of the players on the bench, pulling Coach Zim out of his daydream. The Sea Dogs were in the middle of a nine-day home stand and he'd attended every game and practice that week. He sat at times in the dugout with Sparky, at other times behind home plate to get a better view. His job was important to the club and he was treated with respect, with most of the players and employees at the park calling him Mr. Zimmerman. He was due to travel to Boston to meet with Johnny Jones and the Red Sox general manager the following week. He finally had achieved his dream job.

Problem was, he was bored out of his mind. He couldn't focus on the Sea Dogs games because his mind kept drifting to Brandon Ackerson, or to the players on the Warriors team. He pictured Angela's smiling "I told you so" expression and regained focus, for about five minutes. It was hopeless.

When he got home that evening, he opened a beer and went to the office. He tried watching a video of the Pawtucket game but found himself daydreaming after five minutes. With a sigh, he looked up Johnny Jones's number and made the call.

The Warriors played three consecutive away games, winning two. The team was now in first place. With five games left, including that afternoon's home game, they appeared to be headed for the playoffs.

A light breeze blew as Coach Zim stepped out of his truck across the street from Duke Vincent field. The air was sweet with May flowers and leaves growing brighter each day. The grass on the field, tan and stiff only a month ago, now grew a soft emerald color. Days like this almost screamed baseball, and there was nowhere he'd rather be on such a day than a baseball field.

Coach Rivard and most of the team had beaten him to the field because he'd spent a little time hanging out with Brandon Ackerson after school. There was still no sign of Tom Collins, although everyone in the school – and the town – knew that he'd (allegedly) robbed a store and beaten the cashier, a middle aged woman, unconscious. Not everyone knew that the woman was Luther the janitor's girlfriend, but those who did wondered who would find Collins first, Luther or the police. For Collins, most agreed, this could mean the difference between life and death.

While pleased that Collins was no longer around, Coach Zim understood that his absence didn't guarantee Ackerson's safety. Collins was out there, somewhere – likely staying with one of his father's criminal friends – and probably desperate, especially if he'd found out whose girlfriend he'd assaulted. Even smart people do foolish things when desperate. Collins was smart but narcissistic, a dangerous combination. Coach Zim feared that he'd do something to Ackerson out of anger – Collins was the type to blame others for his mistakes. He might even kidnap him if given the chance, as a way of making some sort of deal with the police.

A couple of the boys who'd been with Collins that night, the two who'd carried the beer, had already been caught. Rather, they'd turned themselves in. Lacking the spine and conviction of their leader, the frightened teens had considered turning themselves in when the police started asking questions. Upon hearing that the woman they'd held while Collins punched her was the girlfriend of the school's very large, very intimidating, very black janitor, they'd freaked out and gone straight to the police station to admit everything and beg for police protection. The police laughed at them, then charged the youths and released them to the custody of their parents.

The other accomplices were nowhere to be found and assumed to be hiding with Collins. In actuality both had simply dropped out of school – since they'd rarely attended class anyway, few people noticed – and hitchhiked to Portland to stay with friends and lay low for a while.

Ackerson didn't seem to share Coach Zim's fear of what Collins might do, but Coach Zim believed he was just putting forth a brave front. Still, with Collins and his group no longer prowling the hallways, things had been a lot easier for Ackerson. This was evident by the way he smiled a bit more and had stopped scurrying from classroom to classroom. He'd won the statewide art contest, too, which seemed to give him a boost in confidence while making him more outgoing.

Coach Zim still insisted that Ackerson ride to and from school every day with Mr. Iannucci. Ackerson wasn't happy but he agreed. That afternoon they'd spent a few minutes after school looking through a fishing magazine. As a gift for winning the art contest, Coach Zim was buying Ackerson a fishing rod and letting him pick it out himself. After Brandon picked out the one he wanted they got online and ordered it, making plans to go fishing at Willow Pond on Memorial Day weekend.

Coach Zim walked to the field and leaned over the fence to wish Coach Rivard good luck. When he turned around he was surprised to see Luther walking toward the bleachers. He greeted him and walked with the janitor to his usual seat. By now most of the town knew what Tom Collins had done to his girlfriend. A few people looked at Luther as he passed, but they didn't look for long. Luther's aura wasn't exactly what would be referred to as inviting, and those who did stare did it from the corners of their eyes.

Coach Zim didn't ask Luther about Collins, either. It was none of his business, for one thing, and he really didn't want to make the janitor angry. He didn't think Luther would punch him, but he genuinely liked him and didn't want to rub salt in the wound.

After leaving Luther he made his way to the booth, greeting several people along the way. Thankfully the questions about when he was returning to coaching had been reduced; now he was asked by only about half the people he talked to. He smiled and chatted good-naturedly, even when he heard the deep rumble marking the arrival of the Grim Disciples. He didn't bother looking in the direction of the parking lot. It would only make him angry. Before reminding himself to wish ill on no man, Coach Zim hoped one of the bikers would ask Luther about Collins.

From the top of the stairs came the pungent smell of Axe cologne, meaning Charlie had already arrived. Making his way up to the booth, he grabbed a couple pieces of pizza and a coke from the side table and took his seat beside Charlie. Far from the awkwardness he'd felt during their first broadcast together, Coach Zim had grown comfortable in the booth and with Charlie. It wasn't coaching, but it was still baseball.

Just before the start of the game the crowd stirred, and even from the booth the murmuring was audible. Coach Zim leaned out the window to see almost everyone in the seats and half the players on the field looking toward the top of the bleacher stairs. At the foot of the home dugout, April Spring stood facing the bleachers and glaring. Hundreds of cell phones were held up and pointed in that direction.

Wondering what the hell was going on, Coach Zim looked over and saw Nutsack Horne and Victoria Purl, already growing plump with little baby Nutsack, making their way to a couple of empty seats. Horne, wearing his traditional white short shorts, seemed proud and held tight to his future bride's hand while smiling broadly. Victoria sat slowly, gingerly, but Horne did not join her. Instead, he acknowledged and waved to the crowd like a conquering hero. Facing the cameras, he went into a most muscular pose, holding it until his head appeared ready to burst. A few flashes went off but most people had their phones on video, hoping he'd do something they could send to ESPN.

Horne finally relaxed from his pose and took a deep breath. He gave the crowd another politician's smile and wave. The crowd groaned in disappointment when he sat down, but then the umpire yelled, "Play ball!" and their attention was diverted back to the field.

Coach Zim pulled his head back into the booth and noticed Charlie holding his cell phone out, aimed toward Horne. With a sigh, he pulled it back and sat down.

"That's the problem with celebrity, Charlie," Coach Zim said. "You have to keep doing something more and more outrageous to keep the public interested."

"I'm not worried," Charlie replied. "It's still early. I'm sure Nutsack will do something newsworthy by the end of the game."

Coach Zim didn't argue. Chances were good that Horne would do something stupid. And in modern day society, he knew, stupid was newsworthy.

The game was scoreless after four innings. This was surprising, considering how many fielding errors Apple Brook committed. Adam Nass, normally very sure-handed, committed two errors in one inning, both of which allowed runners to get on base. Luckily, Brock Cooke struck out the next two batters to get out of the inning.

While the Apple Brook fans seemed to forgive and forget Nass's uncharacteristic mistakes, his father did not. After the second error he yelled at Adam loud enough to be heard in the announcer's booth – "Hey Nass, maybe you should join the girls' softball team", and "Are you afraid of the ball, Nass? Maybe you need your girlfriend Krane to hold your hand!"

The loud taunting made the crowd uncomfortable, and they responded with almost total silence. The only noise heard, aside from the slap of the catcher's mitt and the umpire's sharp calls, was the deep laughter of the other five Grim Disciples every time Tyler Nass made a comment.

Charlie solved the problem temporarily by encouraging the crowd to make some noise in support of their Warriors. The fans clapped and hooted and cheered, temporarily drowning out Tyler Nass's taunts.

But in the middle of the fifth, as the Warriors jogged from the field after Cooke retired the side in order, Tyler Nass yelled, "Adam, get your ass over here! I want to check that glove for holes!"

Adam continued toward the dugout, staring straight ahead.

"I said get over here, boy! Before I climb over this fence and beat your ass. You're an embarrassment, boy. Who the fuck can't catch a ball?"

Nearing the dugout, Adam Nass, face flushed with anger, did something very out of character – he looked over at his father and gave him the finger. Tyler Nass reacted as expected – with rage. Shaking the chain link fence like a caged animal, he yelled at the top of his rough voice, "I'm coming after you, boy. You better have an apology ready or I'm gonna beat your ass. You hear me?"

Adam's teammates stared at his father for a moment, then went into the dugout to sit beside their captain. He smiled and tried to laugh it off, but it was obvious he was angry and scared. The crowd sat as silent and still as an early morning sunrise. The opposing players, warming up on the field, stopped throwing balls around to watch what was happening. The umpire, seemingly unsure of what to do, lifted his mask, stood next to the catcher and gazed over to the bikers.

Only Paul Rivard did anything. Dragging an aluminum bat at his side, he walked along the fence until he was opposite Tyler Nass. There he stopped and leaned on the bat. It was a familiar pose – it was how he stood just outside the dugout, relaxed, leaning, watching the action on the field during every game.

His posture was just as relaxed as it had been all game long, but his jaw was as tight as a strained rubber band. He quietly said, "Time for you boys to leave, Nass."

Tyler Nass leaned over the fence. There was alcohol on his breath. "I ain't in the mood, old man. My son disrespected me in front of my brothers and he's gonna be taught a lesson. So mind your own fucking business."

"These boys are my business. You aren't going to threaten any of them here again today, so get on your bikes and leave. I'm not going to tell you again."

"Oh really? You know, you keep acting like you're some badass soldier. But I got news for you – you're just some brittle-boned old fart. Now get out of my face and go take some Centrum before you really piss me off."

"I'm not going anywhere. I may be old, but at least I'm not some pussy who beats up kids and hangs out with a bunch of smelly dimwits in matching jackets like a cheerleading squad. Guys like you are only tough with people backing them up."

Tyler Nass's eyes narrowed, his nostrils flared. He took a wild swing at Rivard's head. Rivard stepped back slightly, just enough to watch Nass's fist whiff past his face. With a quick, smooth twist of his wrist the aluminum bat swung up in a short arc and smashed down on the top of Nass's head. It was a perfect hit, right on the sweet spot, ending in a dull thud. Coach Rivard pulled the bat back to his side as Nass went limp. Momentum carried his upper body over the fence, to the field side, while his lower body remained in the parking lot. He balanced for a few moments on the chain link fence, looking like a jacket thrown over the back of a chair, before falling forward onto the field. He landed on his hairy face, legs sticking up in the air due to his boots catching on the top of the fence.

The other Disciples pulled out knives and axe handles and moved in quickly. Rivard cocked the bat above his shoulder as though waiting for a fastball, the eagerness for battle visible on his face. As the bikers drew closer, Rivard saw movement from the corner of his eye. With a glance he saw the entire Warriors baseball team rushing over, bats in hand.

"You dipshits get out of here!" he yelled, trying to keep an eye on both his team and the approaching bikers. "Get back to the dugout now!"

"No way," said Adam Nass, the first one to reach Rivard. "A team sticks together, Coach Rivard. Besides, I've been waiting for years to take a crack at these assholes."

Rivard saw the look on Adam's face and gave a short nod. "Okay. But you boys stay behind me. I don't think I'm gonna need you, anyway. There's only five of them pansies left."

The closest Disciple, Hawk, leapt over the fence, knife in hand. Paul Rivard stepped forward, bat cocked, ready to welcome him to Duke Vincent Field.

Most of those in the bleachers had stood to watch the action. A few of the fans cheered when Coach Rivard cracked the biker in the skull with a baseball bat, but for the most part there was stunned disbelief at what the high school baseball game was turning into. A few friends and relatives, seeing the players grab bats and run over to join the fight, cried out in fear and worry and shouted for the boys to stop. As the players and bikers neared each other, every phone in the place was up and filming. Very quickly, the crowd grew noisy and restless with worry.

Realizing that something had to be done before someone got seriously hurt, Todd Horne thought quickly. This was a mistake, as sometimes even slow thought proved difficult for him. Beside him, Victoria held one hand protectively over her stomach while in the other a pink cell phone captured all the action along the first base line.

There was only one thing he could do to attract everyone's attention. He pushed his way to the front of the crowd and climbed on top of the Warrior's dugout. Tearing off his extra small shirt, Nutsack Horne went into the posing routine he planned to use in the Mr. Maine contest that fall. After he won that, he'd compete in the Mr. America contest, sign a few endorsement deals and make a living as a professional bodybuilder. As he moved smoothly into a side bicep pose, he imagined in his head the Survivor song, *Eye of the Tiger*. It was the song he planned to use with his routine at the Mr. Maine competition.

By the time he'd gracefully shifted to a front lat spread, Horne realized that very few people were paying attention to him. He began yelling – *"Come on. Come on!"* – until a few heads turned his way. Next was a front double bicep pose. Noticing a few more eyes on him, Horne decided to step back to give the crowd a better view. This may be the last time these scrawny small-town folks saw him before he was a famous professional bodybuilder, and he wanted to give them the best show possible.

Problem was, Horne had already backed up to the edge of the dugout. He went into the front double bicep and stepped back with his right foot. It slipped off the top of the dugout. Realizing too late what was happening, Horne hovered for a long moment, flapping his massive arms like a bird to regain his balance before plummeting to the hard ground below.

Many in the crowd, having recorded the spontaneous posing routine, rushed forward with their phones held aloft to record the end of the routine, which consisted of Todd Horne lying on his back, unconscious. One enormous arm was bent the wrong way, obviously broken.

He'd achieved his goal – almost everyone in the bleachers had turned their attention to him, completely distracted from the impending brawl between the bikers and players. Those who weren't paying attention to him were after he fell from the top of the dugout. Though he wasn't aware of it, by being unconscious he'd probably prevented a full-scale panic from seizing the crowd.

While nearly everyone in the bleachers excitedly aimed their phones, hoping Horne would regain consciousness, nobody made an attempt to actually help him except Victoria. She walked slowly down the stairs from the bleachers to the parking lot, one hand held protectively over her stomach. She entered the field through the fence gate –

within twenty feet of the full scale biker battle – and knelt down next to Horne.

Up close she could see that his arm was twisted at the elbow, causing his forearm and hand to face the wrong way. It looked like something a demented child would do to a doll. Her stomach turned, and before she could turn away she vomited on her unconscious fiancé. Hundreds of happy fans chose that moment as the grand finale and stopped filming. With smiles on their faces, they began sending the file all over the internet.

Bent over and hurling on her fiancé, Victoria did not see the entire opposing team sprint past her. Very few in the stands noticed, either. Victoria's sudden puking was a perfect ending, as though choreographed, and many of the fans would have applauded had they not been busy staring at their phones, checking to see how many hits their video had after ten seconds.

Had anyone bothered to look up, they would have seen the Grim Disciples take a beating like no other in the club's history. Hawk, the first one over the fence, hadn't even hit the ground when Paul Rivard's bat smashed him in the left knee, shattering his kneecap. Hawk's knife flew from his hand as he landed heavily and rolled around on the ground, writing in pain.

The four other Disciples made it over the fence and quickly surrounded Rivard. That was when the Warriors baseball team stepped forward. Adam Nass ran up behind Mac, the largest of the bikers, and swung. The bat hit Mac on the back of a massive tattooed arm. Instead of dropping him, the blow only seemed to make Mac angry. He turned and glared at Adam, who swung again. This time Mac caught the bat with his bare hand, ripped it from Adam's grip and tossed it to the side. Then Coach Rivard jumped onto Mac's back and got him in a hold that brought the enormous biker to his knees.

The other bikers were either ducking or catching bats with their hands, and it quickly became clear that they had a lot of experience fighting with weapons. Even Hawk had managed to enter the fray and hold his own on one leg.

Watching the Warriors battle the bikers, the opposing baseball team thought it would be fun to go over and kick some ass on the bikers. Over their coach's strenuous objections they grabbed bats and hurried over, full of teenage bravado.

Shortly afterward the bikers, battered and beaten by forty teenage athletes, crawled back over the fence and onto their motorcycles. Tyler Nass had by this time regained consciousness, though he had to be helped back onto his bike. The cheering of the victorious teenagers drowned out the roar of the retreating Harleys. Drowned out by all the commotion were the wailing sirens of approaching police cars and ambulances.

23

Paul Rivard sat in the small chair, back straight as a general's, staring at him. Garth Craggy coughed nervously. He tried reminding himself that he, Garth Craggy, school principal, was in charge of the situation, but the expression on the face of the old man sitting before him cast serious doubts on that. Craggy had heard the stories about how the old man had taken out half the Grim Disciples motorcycle club almost single handedly. The way Rivard looked at him now, Craggy wondered if he might be next.

"So, Paul, uh, as fine a job as you've done with the baseball team – you've certainly cleaned up my nephew's mess, ha ha – I'm sure you can see why you are being let go. Not from teaching – you are a fine teacher, very valuable to our school. No, no, no, certainly not. Don't worry about that." Craggy wiped cool sweat from his forehead. He wondered if Rivard could smell the tangy sweat soaking his armpits. "But this was a full-scale brawl that brought out the entire police force and two ambulances. Several boys were hurt, thankfully scratches and bruises that didn't require hospitalization. Not that anyone is blaming you, of course."

Rivard said nothing, only continued to stare.

"It was the superintendent's idea," Craggy added hastily. "I'd have kept you on. Like I said, you're doing a fine job with the team. Aside from the brawl, I mean."

After a few moments of silence, Rivard spoke. "Who's going to replace me?"

"Well, ah, there are only a few games left in the season, and we appear to be headed for the playoffs. Thanks to you." Craggy tried a smile, something he wasn't comfortable with under the best of circumstances, and quickly gave it up. "I'm going to ask Emilio Fernandez. The junior varsity season is over, and he's a very capable coach. And I'd like you to know, the change is only for this year. I'm sure, if you were interested, we'd love to have you back as coach next year."

"What about Coach Zim?"

"Hmmm? Ah, yes, well, at this time we don't feel that Jim Zimmerman is a good fit for the program. He's done wonderful things with the baseball program in previous years but we feel that his time may have passed."

"Stop saying we. It's you who doesn't like Jim and we all know it."

Craggy's face grew warm, but he controlled his temper out of a sense of decorum and a stronger sense of self-preservation. "That's not true, Paul. The decision was made collectively between the superintendent and I, as well as members of the school board."

"You're an asshole. And a liar." Paul Rivard stood up and finally released Craggy from his gaze. The principal felt a physical relief, as though a grip around his throat had been loosened. "I'm leaving. I have a class to teach."

Principal Craggy opened his mouth, reconsidered, and said nothing. There was a soft knock on the door and in stepped Vice Principal Simon. At the sight of Paul Rivard walking straight at him, Simon let out a small squeak, flattened himself against the wall and closed his eyes.

"You can relax, he's gone," Craggy said a minute later. "What do you need?"

"I heard you wanted me to be here for a meeting this morning."

"Yes. That meeting just happened. Judging by the way you almost pissed yourself at the sight of Paul Rivard, it's probably a good thing you weren't here."

"Sorry. Busy morning."

"I'm sure. Listen, I'd like you to go find Emilio Fernandez and tell him I need to see him as soon as possible. Can you do that without fucking it up?"

The vice principal nodded. "I'm on it," he said, backing out of the room.

"And Simon," Craggy called after him. "Close the door on the way out, will you?"

Word spread quickly about the school's new baseball coach. Never before in the history of Apple Brook High School baseball had there even been two coaches in a single year, never mind three. Fernandez had accepted the temporary job not because he wanted to, but because Craggy had threatened to fire him as coach of the junior varsity team if he didn't.

Emilio Fernandez had been an average high school baseball player and a below average college player in Florida, but he loved the game. When he moved to Maine with his wife –whom he'd met at the University of Florida – and began teaching at Apple Brook High, he'd jumped at the chance to coach JV baseball.

He was an average coach with no aspirations to move up the ladder. At the age of thirty-four he had five kids at home, ranging in age from one to nine. His wife didn't mind him coaching the JV team – the season was short and she knew he enjoyed coaching. But with five little ones there wasn't enough time for him to dedicate anywhere else.

And so, with the threat of having the one thing that got him out of the house for a few weeks a year taken away, he reluctantly agreed to coach the last few varsity games. Now he had to tell his wife.

Coach Zim leaned against his truck in the parking lot after school. Paul Rivard had parked his truck next to Coach Zim's and now sat inside, engine off. They were discussing the aftermath of the Duke Vincent Field Brawl, as the local paper called it.

"Nass's father is still in the hospital," Rivard said. "Cracked his skull, I guess. What a dumb shit. If he'd just left like I'd asked, none of this would have happened. Why do some assholes have to spend their lives making trouble?"

Coach Zim shrugged. "I can't think of a bigger asshole than Tyler Nass, except Tom Collins. Think you'll be charged with anything? Assault, maybe?"

"No." Rivard shook his head. "I already talked to Officer Dipshit. You may know him as Kyle Bertrand. You know that idiot was at the field the whole time? Says he was on the crapper when the fight started and he didn't see anything. But several of our guys saw him in the parking lot talking to a couple of teenage girls. They were swapping phone numbers when the fight started. Then he disappeared."

"Showed up again right when backup arrived, right?"

"Amazing how that happens. Anyway, Bertrand figures that Tyler Nass was the instigator and that I was only defending myself. Then he asked if I wanted to press charges against them." He gave a short laugh. "Them boys are facing enough charges – assault with a deadly weapon, to begin with. I don't want to be involved."

"Think the Disciples will come after you?"

"I don't think so," Rivard said. There was a dangerous gleam in his eye. "Not if they're smart."

"I heard Emilio is the new coach. That right?"

"Right. Three coaches in one year. I think Craggy's doing his Steinbrenner impression."

"Emilio will do fine. He's a good man. Coached most of these guys already in JV."

Just then Adam Nass and Devin Krane pulled up in Krane's beat-up Ford Focus. Judging by the sound of the pounding bass, the stereo was worth more than the car. The car skidded to a stop and the co-captains got out.

"Coach Rivard, we're really sorry to hear about what happened," Krane said, a dejected look on his face. "You're the reason we're in first place. We couldn't have done it without you." Then he turned to Coach Zim and smiled. "So are you coming back, Coach Zim? You're the best coach we've ever had. We need you." He glanced back at Rivard, smile fading as quickly as it had appeared. "But only because you are no longer with us, Coach Rivard."

"Krane, you ever think about getting into politics?" Rivard said, with a trace of a smile. "You're as full of crap as the rest of them." He started up his old truck, filling the air with a blue haze. Country music blared from the cab. "I'm not coming back, boys. Maybe next year, but only if this guy is in charge," he said, nodding toward Coach Zim. "For now, Coach Fernandez is in charge. He's a good man, and you boys have a good team. You should be fine."

Watching him pull away, Krane said, "It's really too bad that Coach Rivard got fired. It's not fair. He was only defending us. Nutsack gets a high school girl pregnant, and they get the same punishment."

"Not exactly," Coach Zim said. "Coach Rivard kept his job. And he'll be allowed to coach again next year, according to Principal Craggy."

Krane turned to him. "Speaking of coaching, how about it?"

"Don't start, guys." Coach Zim unlocked his truck door and got inside. "Principal Craggy named Coach

Fernandez as your head coach. He's a good coach. You'll do well. And I'll still be in the booth."

"The last four games are away," said Adam Nass.

"Well then, you'd better win them all," Coach Zim said, starting his truck. "So I'll be able to announce your home playoff games."

They watched him drive off. Krane said, "We only have to win one more game to be in the playoffs. We can win one game out of four, no problem."

"Yeah," Adam Nass agreed. "No problem."

News of yet another coaching change got around quickly, and soon the *Bring Back Coach Zim!* shirts were back in force. Coach Zim tried to ignore them as he prepared his students for final exams. Seniors were excused from final exams in his classroom, but all underclassmen were expected to take them. Because finals and counted as twenty-five percent of their final grades, Coach Zim did his best to ensure that every student was prepared. From the Constitution to the Industrial Age to the Age of Aquarius, they spent several days going over everything they'd learned that year about American history.

The last few weeks of school were always a difficult time. As the Maine weather got warmer the clothes got shorter and thinner, and it was like one giant mating season in the halls of the high school. The sight of skin, no matter how pasty white after months of being shielded by layers of flannel and cotton, was enough to drive the students into a sexual fervor. Giving history lessons on a sunny spring day was like trying to train sharks to square dance during a feeding frenzy.

And going hand in hand with the annual sweaty springtime teen sex frenzy was heartbreak.

Teenage girls, overly emotional on the best of days, risked becoming teary messes at this time of year. Coach Zim hated it because, for some reason, many these girls used his shoulder to cry on. He couldn't understand it – there were many other teachers, most with a far kinder manner than his. Why did they come to him? Angela said he had a way with women. Not on purpose, he thought. But Angela said they all think of him as a big teddy bear, maybe a little gruff on the outside but cuddly on the inside. This, he had to admit, was probably true. He'd heard a group of girls once describe him as sour patch candy, sour on the outside but sweet on the inside.

Most of his breaks between classes over the next several days, including lunch breaks, were spent attempting to comfort sobbing teenage girls. He sat and listened, not saying much of anything unless asked, and even then giving only the vaguest of replies. They usually didn't want advice, they just wanted someone to listen - a lesson he'd learned after several years of marriage. He kept several boxes of tissues in the bottom drawer of his desk for this time of year and handed them out by the fistful.

The first one to come to him this year was Iris Dore, the student he'd spoken to Mr. Beaudoin about a few weeks earlier. Iris's date to the prom, a boy with whom she'd been in love since way back in March, had broken up with her the day after the prom to go out with a sophomore who would put out. Iris had taken an abstinence pledge with her church group, she explained, which caused Coach Zim to shift uncomfortably in his chair. And this boy, who Coach Zim knew as a friend of Michael Barrow and therefore completely full of crap, had said that he believed waiting until they were married would make sex even more special. Trying very hard not to roll his eyes, Coach Zim nodded understandably and held out a box of tissues.

After letting it all out and having a good cry, Iris laughed hard as Coach Zim made a joke about her ex's new relationship and pointed out all that she had ahead in life. This he'd also learned over time – listen quietly, make a joke when the tears stopped (but never, never before) and show how much of life was still ahead.

After blowing her nose and wiping the tears from her face, Iris beamed and gave Coach Zim a hug. Hugging students was generally frowned upon because of the fear of accusations and lawsuits pervading America's schools, but Coach Zim didn't give a crap about that. He wasn't a hugger or a touchy-feely guy, but if an upset student needed a hug, he let them hug him. He was already facing a lawsuit from a student for doing the right thing and didn't feel bad about it. Almost never thought about it, in fact. So if someone was offended by his hugging a kid, too bad.

He'd seen and heard just about everything after almost thirty years of dealing with teenage angst, but it was still a surprise when April Spring pulled him aside one afternoon. He didn't particularly like April – he'd never cared for girls who held themselves above others just because of how they looked – and as far as he knew she'd never held him in particularly high regard.

She didn't cry and was very matter-of-fact when she told him that she was having guy trouble. As she described the problem – older guy breaks it off with her because he got someone else pregnant and now she never sees him – Coach Zim realized she was referring to Nutsack Horne. He'd suspected that she and Horne were messing around – had believed when the rumors started, as had most, that April was the student Horne had impregnated – but hearing confirmation of their sexual relationship was extremely awkward. Still, he listened.

April explained that she'd quit as manager of the baseball team because going to the field only reminded her of Horne. She'd been asked to the prom – of course she had, thought Coach Zim, she's gorgeous – but had turned everyone down because of her relationship with Horne. She wish she'd been the one to get pregnant by Todd Horne. True, he had too many mirrors in his house and liked flex before and after sex, but he'd really seemed to care about her. She went on until her voice quivered and tears formed in her eyes, though he noticed that her pretty face remained dry.

Finally, she wiped her eyes and stopped talking. Coach Zim wanted to tell her that she'd been taken advantage of by an older man who, although only a gym teacher, was in a position of power and should be arrested for what he'd done. And, he wanted to add, the idiot didn't know jack shit about baseball. But instead, he made a joke about all the boys she'd turned down for the prom and pointed out all that was ahead for her, including Penn State in the fall.

When she left, it was with a smile on her face. She gave Coach Zim a quick stiff hug before leaving, not one of the tight clingy grasps he usually received. He was glad she felt better and for some reason liked April a little more than he had before. His opinion of Nutsack Horne, though, fell to an even lower level, something he'd have previously thought impossible.

While it was mostly girls who sought him out there was the occasional guy, usually an athlete wanting to talk about girl problems. This year it was Brock Cooke, whose girlfriend broke up with him because she met an older college guy.

"And he's not even a baseball player," he said in disbelief.

Guys were much easier for Coach Zim to deal with. Most of them dealt with their emotional suffering not by crying, but instead becoming angry. Coach Zim understood anger – bang on a desk, punch a wall, swear at the top of your lungs. These actions made sense to him. His technique was much the same – listen, make a joke, paint an encouraging version of the future, and send the kid on his way. With a kid like Brock there were no tissues, the jokes were sometimes a little dirty, and instead of a hug there was an encouraging slap on the shoulder.

By the time Brock Cooke left his room the young man believed there were plenty of young women at the University of Maine waiting with lustful eagerness for his arrival. The entire conversation took ten minutes and not a tear had been shed. Coach Zim watched Cooke leave the room with a small grin and imagined this must be the way Dr. Phil often felt.

Unfortunately, Brock Cooke had waited until after he pitched against Portland High School to talk to Coach Zim. Cooke, who'd gone into the game with the lowest earned run average in the league, gave up eight runs in three innings on the way to a 10-4 thumping. He made calls on his cell phone to his ex between innings and hardly noticed the score.

He wasn't the only one playing poorly. Two days later, on the day before the start of Memorial Day weekend, the Warriors lost another game and sank into second place. With two games left, the team was in danger of missing the playoffs.

24

The following Tuesday the Warriors lost their third game in a row and their interim head coach, Emilio Fernandez, appeared to be on the verge of a nervous breakdown. Swollen dark circles had appeared under his eyes, and he visibly trembled. Though he'd known most of the players for years, he couldn't remember anybody's name or position. He arrived late for Tuesday's game, forgot to make out the lineup card, and spent most of the game sitting on the bench, texting. At one point players noticed tears running down his face.

The next morning, before school started, Emilio Fernandez was seen in the hallway near the school's front doors arguing quietly with his wife, Tasha. Four of their children climbed up and down them like ants on an anthill, in constant motion. The argument ended when Tasha marched into Principal Craggy's office carrying a child in each arm and announced that, as of that morning, her husband was no longer coaching the varsity baseball team. He would, however, be back to coach the junior varsity team the following year. If, for some reason, today's actions led him to losing his junior varsity coaching job, Tasha promised to rain a shit storm of biblical proportions down upon Craggy's head.

She left without another word, gathered up the other two kids from her husband, and walked out of the school. Emilio, unsure what to do, walked slowly to the principal's office, where Emma greeted him with a big smile.

"That was your wife?" she said.

Emilio nodded. "Yes, that was Tasha."

"I like her. A lot."

"Do you think I should go in there?" He nodded to the closed door with the *Principal Craggy* nameplate. "Or let him cool down?"

"Oh, head right in," Emma said cheerily. "I'll bet he's too stunned to be angry."

Emma was right. Principal Craggy wore the bewildered expression of someone who's just witnessed a tornado. He stared, wide-eyed and blinking, at Emilio standing in the center of his office as though he hadn't heard him enter.

"I'm guessing Tasha told you that I have to quit coaching the team," Emilio mumbled, head down. "Sorry about that. I wanted to tell you myself, but she gets impatient sometimes. It's just because of the kids at home. If they were a little older, you know, it wouldn't be a problem."

Craggy waved the explanation away. "Of course, perfectly understandable. So that was your wife, huh?"

"Yes." Fernandez grinned awkwardly. "She can be a little strong-headed sometimes."

"Well, sometimes that can be a good thing," mumbled Craggy. "I accept your resignation. And you can continue your coaching duties next spring with the junior varsity team."

"Thank you, Principal Craggy," he said, turning for the door. "And I really am sorry that I can't finish the season. You understand, right?"

Craggy nodded. Having a wife that scares the hell out of you? Yes, he certainly did understand. It wasn't going to get any better, he wanted to tell the young man. Run, run as though your life depends on it, before your face ends up looking like mine, before all the good times you could have had are long gone. But he knew Emilio Fernandez wouldn't run. He was a good man with five children. Craggy couldn't help but feel sorry for him.

He felt sorrier for himself, though, especially when his cell phone rang a minute later. It was his wife, of course. He pressed ignore. He'd had enough of crazy wives for one morning.

News got out quickly about Fernandez quitting, and by the next morning the school hallways were painted red with students wearing *Bring Back Coach Zim!* shirts. There were so many shirts, it was as though the previous shirts had babies. Even Brandon Ackerson wore one, though on the front of his a hilarious caricature of Coach Zim was drawn in black marker.

There were two days left before the final game. The entire season rested on this game – they were in the playoffs if they won but out if they lost – and the team had no coach. It made sense that the team would go with someone who'd been there before, the winningest coach in Maine high school baseball history. It seemed to be all that anyone was talking about in school – well, that and sex. Even Coach Zim allowed himself to feel excited about the possibility of coaching, but only for a moment. Because in reality, he knew that Craggy would never allow him to coach again.

Early that evening, as he and Angela (wearing her *Bring Back Coach Zim!* shirt) sat down to dinner, there was a knock on the door. Instead of getting up, Coach Zim took a large bite of a grilled chicken leg, hoping whoever was at the door would take the hint and leave. Another knock – louder this time – and Angela stood up. He shook his head and motioned for her to sit.

"I'll get it," he sighed, taking a swig from his beer. "Probably someone trying to sell religion or politics. I'm better at handling these people than you are."

"Slamming the door in their faces isn't what I'd call handling them well," she said, flashing a sweet smile.

He opened the door, chicken leg in hand and prepared for battle, but instead found Chief Walsh standing on his porch. He frowned, as most people do when the police show up at the door unexpectedly.

"Sorry to disturb you at dinnertime, Coach," he said, eyeing the chicken leg.

"Not a problem, Chief. What's up? Nothing bad, I hope."

"No, sir. I bring good news. It happens so infrequently these days that I like to deliver it myself." After eyeing the chicken again and rubbing his corpulent belly, he said, "I wanted to let you know that Tom Collins is in police custody."

"No kidding," said Coach Zim. "Well, that is good news. How did it happen?"

"Well, Coach, I can't really go into any details about that right now. Let's just say that it was due to long hours of diligent work by our dedicated officers."

"You received a tip, right?"

Chief Walsh appeared indignant. "I'm not at liberty to say anything about that. We'll be having a press conference tomorrow. I just thought you'd want to know right away."

"I'm just busting your butt, Chief," Coach Zim said with a grin. He took a bite of chicken. "Hey, you want to come in? I just grilled chicken legs and Angela made her world-famous potato salad."

"Come on in, Chief," Angela called from the kitchen. "There's plenty."

"I do like potato salad," Chief Walsh said. He leaned into the doorway and took a whiff. "But I'm on my way home for dinner and I'm already late. The wife made pea soup." He frowned. "I hate pea soup. You'd think after forty years she'd realize that."

"Hold on," Coach Zim said. He walked off and returned a minute later with two chicken legs and some potato salad in a small Tupperware container, along with a fork. "For the drive home."

Chief Walsh took the container with a big smile. "Thank you. You've saved me from starving tonight. Thank you, Angela," he called. "I'll return the container tomorrow."

"No rush," Coach said. "And thanks for the heads-up about Collins. I appreciate it."

He waved as the chief drove off, then returned to the table.

"They arrested Tom Collins?" Angela said. "That's good news, right?"

Coach Zim nodded, his mouth full with half a chicken leg. After swallowing, he said, "It's great news. I can't wait to hear how it happened."

There were two stories the following day regarding how Collins was finally found – the one told at the press conference, and the truth. Chief Walsh stood before a podium and announced to a crowd of five reporters that Tom Collins had been apprehended without a struggle by Officer Kyle Bertrand the previous morning. Collins was currently at Apple Brook hospital recovering from unspecified injuries and would be relocated to the county jail upon discharge.

Chief Walsh then answered a few questions. No, the injuries did not occur during the arrest. The suspect had been injured beforehand. Yes, the arrest had taken place in Apple Brook, putting to rest rumors that he'd fled the state. Yes, he agreed, the apprehension of such a dangerous suspect was a wonderful example of meticulous work by the entire department and Officer Bertrand in particular. No, at this time he was not at liberty to discuss any more details except to say that Collins had been arrested by Officer Bertrand and the town was once again safe.

They then posed for a few photos – Chief Walsh, straining valiantly to suck in his stomach, and Kyle Bertrand, wearing mirrored sunglasses under the fluorescent lights and a very serious expression on his pudgy round face. For Bertrand, this would be his first time on the front page of the *Apple Brook Journal.* He'd finally made the big time, and he wanted to look his best. This meant not smiling, thereby showing the town what a badass he was. Their picture would run at the top of the front page, beside the official version of the arrest of Tom Collins.

The truth was quite a different story, told to Coach Zim by Chief Walsh over a couple six packs of beer. He'd stopped over that evening to return the Tupperware, as promised. That he'd arrived at dinnertime may have been a coincidence, but Coach Zim thought not. Chief Walsh accepted the offer to join them for supper – grilled kabobs and leftover potato salad – without argument, saying the missus was meeting with her book club that evening.

They ate outside at a table on the back porch. The early evening was warm, with just enough of a breeze to keep the mosquitos and black flies away. From the surrounding neighborhood children laughed and screamed, dogs barked, and recently migrated birds sang the songs of spring. They ate slowly, drinking beer and talking and laughing.

After dinner, Angela left to see a movie with friends while the two men stayed on the back porch to drink and talk. After his third or fourth beer, Chief Walsh started to open up.

"Had the press conference today," he said. "You know, for the Collins arrest. My picture's gonna be on the front page of the Journal."

"So what's Collins in the hospital for? Did your guys rough him up a little too much during the arrest?"

"Oh, no, nothing like that. I really can't say what happened to him." Chief Walsh took a long swig of his beer. "Confidential information, you know. Important to the case."

"Oh, that's bullshit."

Chief Walsh tilted his head against the chair back and stared at the glowing pink horizon for a minute before answering. "You're right, it's bullshit. I was going to wait until tomorrow, make it more official, but I've got a couple of questions to ask you and I might as well ask while I'm here." He turned to look at Coach Zim, keeping his head relaxed against the chair back. "You have any idea of Luther Lemon's whereabouts a couple of nights ago?"

"Luther the janitor? That's his last name, Lemon? Luther Lemon. Huh." Finishing his beer, he went inside the house and returned with a bottle in each hand. "I have no idea where Luther was. I do know that he has been showing up for work every afternoon." He handed a cold bottle to Chief Walsh. "But I think most people would agree that it's best to give Luther his space, especially after what happened to his lady." A cold, frosty puff escaped from Coach Zim's bottle as he twisted off the cap. "He rough Collins up pretty good?"

"Somebody did. I've never seen anything like it." He laughed softly. "You won't believe how we found him."

Officer Kyle Bertrand had been working the graveyard shift – punishment for his lack of involvement in breaking up the Duke Vincent Field Brawl. Video had surfaced of Bertrand talking to a couple of teenage girls and entering their phone numbers in his cell phone while the sounds of the brawl could be clearly heard in the background. The video showed Bertrand finally look up, glance around nervously, and hurry away to the men's room. Luckily the video had been taken by a former cop and Chief Walsh had been able to contain it before it went viral.

It was standard procedure for the third-shift officer to park next to the Main Street Car Wash early in the shift and try to catch drunk drivers on their way home from the local bars. By two o'clock, though, there wasn't a car left on the road and things got pretty boring. Officer Bertrand did the same thing he'd done every night since starting the graveyard shift – looked at porn on his phone. After a while, he backed the car into a dark corner next to a storage shed behind the car wash. He then turned off the car and the radio, both against procedure, and began jerking off, also against procedure. He tried to make it last, because the shift was so long and boring, but three minutes later he was pulling out of the parking lot and headed to the station for a cup of coffee. He felt invigorated but slightly shamed. This would pass by the time he did it all over again in a couple hours.

Upon arriving at the police station, Bertrand got out of the car, washed his flashlight over himself to make sure he'd wiped up well, and headed inside through the front door. The only other place to get a coffee in Apple Brook at such a late hour was at the 7-11, but it was in a pretty rough area and so Bertrand tried to avoid it.

After filling his travel mug with coffee and ten packets of sugar, he spent a few minutes talking to Cheryl at the front desk. She was heavy and older but stirred an urge in him to look at more porn, so he said goodbye and hurried out the door.

While cutting across the grass to the parking lot he noticed something on the front yard of the police station. It looked like a sign of some sort. He pulled out his flashlight. It was a sign – KEEP OFF THE GRASS. The sign was nailed or stapled to a small stake which had been driven into the ground.

Destruction of police property, Officer Bertrand thought, gazing at the area where the stake penetrated the grass. He'd been trained in modern-day police procedure, where the goal was to pin as many nonsense charges as possible on a person and hope that one sticks. Bertrand was one of the best at this technique.

As he stood there, a sound came from his left, where a large maple tree shaded the walkway and entrance to the police station. Bertrand whipped the beam of his flashlight in the tree's direction and scanned the area. Then he heard it again – a moan, like the aching sound trees sometimes made on a cold winter's night. He approached the tree slowly, crouching low and drawing his firearm.

Then Bertrand saw it. A person – male, he determined, though it was difficult to tell at first with all the blood – hanging by his underwear from a tree branch, otherwise naked, bleeding profusely from head wounds.

Appearing to have an emergency on his hands, Bertrand shakily holstered his gun and approached the hanging body. There sure was a lot of blood, he thought. He backed away and considered what to do. Leaving it for someone arriving for first shift sounded like a good idea. But what if the underwear hanging victim died? There sure was a lot of blood. If he did report it, he might be a hero. Then again, it would mean an awful lot of paperwork.

He sipped his coffee, debating in his head. He decided to handle it himself. This was his chance to be a hero, and he was going to make the most of it. After taking a last sip of coffee, he drew his gun. He fired two rapid shots into the air – louder than expected in the still darkness, causing him to flinch and drop both his firearm and mug. He scrambled to pick up the gun, left the mug, and ran into the police station, yelling for help, leaving the victim hanging in the tree.

"The call went out that there was an assault at the police station," said Chief Walsh, shaking his head. He knew nothing about Bertrand's previous activities that night, only what happened after he discovered the victim hanging in the tree. "Half the force got out of bed and showed up, along with firetrucks and an ambulance."

"And it was Collins?" Coach Zim asked.

"Oh yes, it was Tom Collins. Hanging from the band of his tightie whities, unconscious and beat all to shit. You remember that line in the Jim Croce song, *Bad, Bad Leroy Brown*, where he says 'Leroy looked like a jigsaw puzzle with a couple of pieces gone'? That was Collins. Broken ribs, arm, jaw – it goes on. And that's not even the worst part." He paused to take a very large pull from his bottle. "There were areas of skin sliced off from his skull and his left arm."

"Tattoos," said Coach Zim. "Two swastikas and a confederate flag."

"That's right. I saw them. They were stapled to his forehead."

Neither man said anything for a while after that. They stared at the horizon, turned hot pink with the setting sun, and listened to the insects warming up for their evening chorus. Before long both men had finished their beer, and Coach Zim went inside to grab two more. After drinking about half of his new one, Coach Zim spoke.

"Any idea who might have done it?"

"We're looking into Luther Lemon, but so far he checks out." The Chief smiled grimly. "Looks like it may go unsolved."

"You questioned Luther?"

"I tried to. I stopped at the school this afternoon before coming over here. He was there, working. Didn't have much to say, other than he was glad to hear Collins was hurt. Then he told me he didn't know anything about the assault and told me to leave him alone. Then he mopped over my shoes." Chief Walsh shook his head. "Mister Lemon doesn't seem to have much respect for authority."

Coach Zim laughed. "Luther certainly marches to his own beat. And he's been a little grouchier than normal since his girlfriend was assaulted. So how long will Collins be in the hospital?"

"Kid's pretty messed up, has some internal injuries, too. Could be weeks, according to the doctors."

"All courtesy of the taxpayers of the State of Maine?"

"Well, yes. He is in police custody."

"How about his father? Is he suing the police for what happened to his son?"

Chief Walsh smiled and shook his head. Early the previous morning, as Tom Collins was being examined and patched up in the emergency room, the police department received an anonymous call regarding a meth lab behind Lester Collins's garage.

"We raided it, arrested Lester Collins on several charges. Looks like father and son may be spending a lot of time together behind bars."

"Was this information included in the press conference?"

"Well, uh, no." Chief Walsh shifted uncomfortably.

"Because you don't want it getting out how bad our town's drug problem has become, right?"

"Confidential information. Important to the case." Chief Walsh swallowed the last of his beer and stood up. "And I need to get home. If I'm not there when the old lady shows up, she'll have the state police looking for me."

After he left, Coach Zim went back outside to finish his beer. As the last remnants of daylight faded away, he found himself feeling sorry for Tom Collins. Then he remembered Brandon Ackerson lying unconscious and bleeding in the parking lot, beaten up by Ackerson and his crew for no good reason, and his sympathy vanished. Collins had gotten what was coming to him.

25

The hospital reeked of ammonia, medication and urine as Coach Zim walked the hallways early the next morning. He was going to be late for school – the bell was probably ringing at that very moment – but for some reason he felt compelled to see Collins. He had to make sure for himself.

The reason he was running late was because visiting hours didn't start until eight. The nurses all knew him and were ready to let him pass, but Coach Zim didn't want to get anybody into trouble and instead spent the time chatting and sipping coffee with a former student named Charlene, now working as a CNA. Charlene excitedly told Coach Zim that she was recently married and was expecting a baby in December. When he asked the name of the lucky guy, she appeared confused and explained that she was married to a woman. Coach Zim smiled, gave Charlene a hug, and congratulated her. He had no qualms against homosexuality, but gay marriage was difficult for him to understand and he sometimes wondered what was happening to the world. Still, Charlene seemed happy, and Coach Zim was happy for her.

He walked down the hallway, donut in one hand, coffee in the other, until he found room 228. The he paused. What would he say? Taking a bite of the donut, he bent down and peeked through the window in the door. The room was dark but he could see Collins asleep. His head was bandaged, and there were casts and gauze and bandages all over his body. Coach Zim gazed through the window for a few minutes, until his donut was finished. Satisfied with what he'd seen, he turned around and left.

He tried to hurry past Craggy's office, but Emma saw him and called his name.

"Principal Craggy would like to see you as soon as possible," she said when he approached. "He says it's urgent." Smiling broadly, she quietly said, "I think it's about the coaching job."

She reached out to call Principal Craggy, but Coach Zim shook his head. "Don't bother. I like to surprise him."

Principal Craggy looked up from his desk, startled, as his door burst open. Slamming the door closed behind him, Coach Zim strode into the office and took his favorite seat on the couch. By the time he'd gotten comfortable, Craggy's face was dark red, as though he were being strangled.

"You're late for school."

"Sorry, Principal Craggy. Please don't give me detention."

Craggy scowled. "I have a couple of things I'd like to discuss with you. First, I don't know if you've heard, but both Tom Collins and his father have been arrested."

"I've heard."

"I spoke to the superintendent this morning. Chances are good that the lawsuit they brought against us will be dropped. So your job should be safe." Craggy looked as though he's swallowed a bug while saying this.

"That's good news, but I wasn't worried. Hey, did you hear that Collins told the cops it was you that assaulted him?"

"What?" Craggy's eyes grew wide. "That's not true! Where did you hear this?" He picked the phone. "I'm calling Chief Walsh right now."

"Don't bother, Garth. I straightened it all out. I told the Chief that you said it was Luther who assaulted Collins. The police will be here later to arrest Luther and get a statement from you."

Craggy dropped the phone. "Why would you do such a thing? Luther, he's mean. Really mean. Have you heard about what he did to Collins? Cut off his tattoos, Chief Walsh told me. If he thinks I got him thrown in jail he'll kill me." He threw up his hands. "Do you hate me that much, Jim?"

Coach Zim smiled. "I'm just shittin you, Garth. Relax. Wow, you are really wound up today."

Craggy's face twisted, slowly running through the spectrum of emotions from fear to confusion to anger, and finally settling on rage. He looked so angry, Coach Zim wouldn't have been surprised to see steam blow out his ears.

"I'd better get to my class," Coach Zim said, slowly getting up. "I need to get them ready for finals. And you look like you might need a nip from that bottle you've got hidden in your desk."

"Sit down," Craggy snapped. He'd regained his composure. "I have something else I need to discuss with you." Coach Zim shrugged and sat back down. "As you know, Emilio Fernandez had to give up the varsity baseball coaching position." At the thought of Fernandez's wife he nearly shuddered, but restrained himself. "We need a new coach for the final game this afternoon. If we win, we're in the playoffs. If we lose, the season's over.

"And you want me to recommend someone, right?"

"No, Jim. I want you to return as coach."

Craggy tried his best to give a kind, welcoming smile, but his face more closely resembled that of a man about to receive a prostate exam. Coach Zim was surprised by the offer, and a few weeks earlier wouldn't have hesitated in saying yes. Now, he hesitated for only a moment before giving his answer.

"Nope."

Craggy's face, under a great deal of strain from the attempt to smile, appeared to collapse. "No? Maybe you didn't hear me. I'm offering you the head coaching position for the rest of the season."

"Oh, I heard you. The head coaching position that should have been mine to begin with. Was mine, until you took it away. Why the change of heart, Garth? Did you run out of coaches?"

"No, nothing like that." Through gritted teeth, Craggy said, "You're an excellent coach, Jim, and I've always wanted…" His eye began to twitch, and he clenched his fists. "Oh, fuck it! The superintendent ordered me to hire you. If I had my choice I'd have hired anyone else. Anyone! I'd have hired back my dumbfuck nephew with the broken arm and torn knee and pregnant teenage girlfriend before hiring you."

"Garth, you sure know how to butter a guy up. But the answer's still no."

"Jim, the team needs you."

Coach Zim laughed. "No, Garth, you need me. The superintendent must have given you a real ass chewing for you to do this."

That was one way to describe it. Superintendent Whitley had called the previous afternoon and lectured him for fifteen minutes about the baseball program, the Collins lawsuit, and everything else he could think of. At the conclusion of the lecture he ordered Craggy to rehire Coach Zim, informing him that, going forward, any coaching hires were to be first approved by the superintendent. He concluded the call by making it clear – very, very clear – that any deviation from these orders, any more slip-ups, would result in a new principal being assigned to Apple Brook High.

"It was a mutual decision," Craggy said.

"Is this position temporary?"

"That hasn't been decided as yet," Craggy lied. One of the superintendent's orders was to hire Coach Zim back as varsity coach, with a raise, and to sign any contract he wanted. So unless that prick Whitley croaked before next spring, Craggy was helpless. Even though Whitley was a tall, thin vegetarian and triathlete, Craggy held out hope that the fucker would keel over.

After thinking for a minute, Coach Zim said, "I kind of like working in the booth."

It surprised him to realize that this was the truth. He enjoyed the back and forth with Charlie DeMar, and working the home games in the booth gave him more time for other things, like fishing and staying after school to help students with their problems. Funny, but it took getting fired from coaching for him to realize (with Angela's help) that he was a teacher first and a coach second, not the other way around. And that he liked it that way.

On top of that, Johnny Jones had refused to accept his resignation. He'd talked Coach Zim into working for the Red Sox organization over the summer, starting at the end of the school year. If it didn't work out, no hard feelings, and it would be an experience he'd never forget. If, as Johnny hoped, it did work out, Coach Zim would be working for the Boston Red Sox, his dream job, and making a lot of money.

"Come on, Jim." Craggy was growing desperate. "The boys need you. If you don't coach them, they'll have to forfeit the last game and any chance of winning the championship."

"Oh, bullshit. If you had to, you could coach them. You couldn't do any worse than your idiot nephew."

Good point, thought Craggy. But if he didn't hire Coach Zim, he could probably kiss his job goodbye.

"I'm going to my class." Coach Zim raised his arms over his head and stretched. "Thanks for the offer, though."

"How about a raise?" said Craggy. "The superintendent has authorized a substantial raise."

Laughing, Coach Zim got up from the couch. "Sorry."

Watching him leave the office, Craggy called out, "The game's against Bedford High." Seeing Coach Zim stop, Craggy hurriedly continued, "If we win, we go to the playoffs. If Bedford wins, Max Dutch goes to the playoffs. Maybe wins another championship. He's getting pretty close to your state championship record, isn't he?"

Coach Zim slowly turned around. He looked thoughtful. "Max Dutch. I hate that guy. He's only got a couple championships, though."

"He may have one more at the end of this season. Without you, there's nobody who can beat him. In a few years he could have your record."

"Screw you. I'm not a naive student you can trick." He paused. "But still, Max Dutch. You remember that asshole back in school, Garth?"

Craggy nodded. He remembered Dutch as the most obnoxious teenager he'd ever seen, a kid who'd turned into one of the most obnoxious adults he'd ever seen. In high school, Dutch used to find out who the best player on the opposing team was going out with and then flirt with her between innings, right in front of everyone. He'd done it once to Craggy, before Jim Zimmerman took his spot as the Alpha player. And his girlfriend, the slut, had actually made out with Dutch after the game. Aside from Zimmerman, Craggy couldn't think of anyone he'd disliked more in high school than Max Dutch.

"Fine, I'll do it," Coach Zim said. "Records are meant to be broken, but not by that prick. But just for today, and the playoffs if we win. I'll have to think about next year."

"Excellent." Craggy folded his hands under his chin. "Excellent."

"Yeah, excellent." He glanced up at the clock over the door. "I've got a whole seven hours to prepare. Should be no problem, right?"

"You'll do fine, Jim. You've watched them all year and you've coached them before."

Coach Zim nodded and left Craggy's office. Emma raised her eyebrows, and Coach Zim nodded. She gave a little squeal and clapped her hands, bringing a smile to his face. Before going to class he walked outside the school and called Angela to let her know he'd be late for dinner.

At the beginning of his lunch period Coach Zim went to the art room. He pushed and jostled his way through a hallway full of kids wearing *Bring Back Coach Zim!* shirts and hats. Hats? He acknowledged the many shouts of congratulations and encouragement regarding the game that afternoon with curt nods. The high school information highway was obviously moving along just as quickly as ever.

As he'd hoped, Brandon Ackerson was in the art room. To Coach Zim's surprise, Ackerson wore one of the *Bring Back Coach Zim!* hats. He sat huddled over an old art magazine with a blue-haired boy wearing a retro Duran Duran t-shirt and pink skinny jeans. Coach Zim wondered if they were an item, quickly decided he really didn't want to know, and wiped the thought from his mind.

He pulled Ackerson aside and let him know that Collins had been arrested and was facing a multitude of charges, including assault, robbery, drug possession (meth and coke found in his clothes, which were piled under the tree he was hanging from), and destruction of police property (the band of his underwear had bent a tree branch). He was also charged in the police raid on his father's meth lab.

Though Ackerson tried to be cool and keep a straight face, he couldn't help but smile when hearing about Collins being hospitalized. It was a good smile, one he didn't show very often. Coach Zim hoped that would change now.

At the end of the school day, Coach Zim closed his classroom door and put on the windbreaker and Apple Brook baseball cap that Angela had dropped off for him that afternoon. He was nervous, more nervous than he had been about a baseball game in a long time. He closed his eyes for a moment and pictured the look on Max Dutch's face as he was handed another defeat. The thought calmed him, and he smiled.

Paul Rivard knocked on his door and the two talked for a few minutes, until it was time for him to leave. He asked Rivard to join the team in the dugout, but Rivard declined. "If you're coaching next year, I'll join you then," he said.

He walked down the hall, taller than everyone, nodding in acknowledgement of the words of encouragement from the few teachers and students who'd stayed after school. He left through the side door and walked across the grass, toward the parking lot and the waiting school bus. Behind the bus was a long line of cars, packed with fans following the team to Bedford. A chorus of bleating car horns filled the air. Coach Zim waved and gave a thumbs-up, resulting in more honking.

He stepped onto the bus. The roughhousing players sat down and grew silent. Coach Zim faced them for a moment, letting the tension grow. He asked, "Are we going to kick Bedford's ass?"

The players shouted "Yes!" and banged the backs of their seats with their leather gloves. Coach Zim nodded and sat in the front seat. When the bus started rolling, he smiled. He was back where he belonged.

I hope you enjoyed this book. Positive reviews really do help sell books, so please remember to leave a review on Amazon.com. I can be found at:

Facebook: @garyspraguewriter

Twitter: @gspraguester

Blog: garyspraguebooks.blogspot.com

Amazon Author Page: amazon.com/author/garysprague